Swipe Right
by
Jayson Swann

Front Matter

1: The Golden Cage

The desert sun beat down relentlessly, but in Las Vegas, the heat was merely another layer of illusion. Here, the air itself seemed to shimmer, not just with the mirage of distant mountains, but with the palpable energy of relentless ambition and whispered secrets. Las Vegas wasn't just a city; it was a stage, a dazzling, decadent spectacle built on the foundation of dreams sold and desires exploited. It was a place where fortunes were made and lost with the spin of a wheel, where the promise of a golden future glittered just beyond the next corner, and where the shadows held more power than the neon lights. This was the world Tasha Reed had chosen as her canvas, the glittering backdrop against which her empire would rise.

From the panoramic windows of her penthouse suite, high above the Strip, Tasha surveyed her domain. The city sprawled beneath her, a glittering tapestry woven with threads of light and ambition. The ceaseless hum of traffic, the distant wail of sirens, the muffled throb of bass from exclusive clubs – it all blended into a symphony of urban existence, a constant reminder of the churning machinery of wealth and desire that fueled this desert metropolis. Her own operation, the elite escort service known to its select clientele as 'Swipe Right,' was no mere business; it was a meticulously crafted ecosystem, a delicate balance of allure, discretion, and absolute control, all meticulously curated to serve the insatiable appetites of the city's most powerful men.

The penthouse itself was a testament to this carefully constructed reality. Sleek, minimalist, yet undeniably opulent, it exuded an aura of understated power. Floor-to-ceiling windows offered an unparalleled vista, transforming the city into a dynamic, ever-changing backdrop. Plush velvet furnishings, custom-designed art pieces, and the subtle gleam of polished chrome spoke of an immense fortune, earned and wielded with a precision that bordered on artistry. Every element was chosen, every detail scrutinized, to project an image of effortless success, a carefully manufactured façade designed to project power and attract those who wielded it. This was Tasha's sanctuary, her command center, and the symbolic heart of her meticulously constructed world.

'Swipe Right' wasn't just an app; it was the gilded key that unlocked the city's most exclusive doors. More than a platform for connecting clients with companions, it was a sophisticated mechanism for understanding and catering to the deepest, often unvoiced, desires of the city's elite. Tasha had built her empire on the principle of knowing her clients better than they knew themselves, anticipating their needs, and fulfilling them with a level of discretion that was as prized as the companionship itself. The app, with its sleek interface and seemingly innocuous purpose, was the perfect Trojan horse, a conduit for building relationships that went far beyond mere transactions. It was a system designed to gather intelligence, to understand the intricate networks of power that pulsed beneath the city's glittering surface.

The world Tasha inhabited was one of hushed conversations in dimly lit lounges, of champagne toasts in exclusive skyboxes, of clandestine meetings held in the opulent suites of world-class hotels. It was a realm where money was the ultimate arbiter, and where influence was a currency more valuable than gold. The women in Tasha's service were more than just beautiful faces; they were intelligent, adaptable, and possessed an innate understanding of the subtle dynamics of power and persuasion. They moved through this rarefied atmosphere with a practiced grace, navigating the complex social currents with a poise that belied the underlying precariousness of their existence. Each interaction, each carefully chosen word, each subtle gesture, was part of a larger, intricate dance, a performance orchestrated by Tasha herself.

The city's superficiality, its relentless pursuit of the next thrill, the next gamble, the next fleeting pleasure, was not something Tasha merely tolerated; it was the very air she breathed, the fertile ground upon which her empire flourished. The dazzling lights, the constant influx of wealth, the sheer audacity of its existence in the heart of a barren desert – it all spoke to a fundamental human desire for escape, for transcendence, for a taste of the extraordinary. Tasha understood this desire, not just as a businesswoman, but as a woman who had clawed her way to the top, who had learned to manipulate the system by offering precisely what others craved but could not obtain through conventional means. The superficiality was the lure, the glittering surface that drew in the moths, while the true operation pulsed beneath, hidden from casual view.

Her operation was a carefully constructed illusion, a testament to her own formidable intellect and her unwavering resolve. Tasha Reed was not a woman who left things to chance. Every girl was vetted, every client profile meticulously studied, every interaction logged and analyzed. The 'Swipe Right' app, while presenting a polished face to the world, was a sophisticated data-mining tool, a digital repository of the city's most intimate secrets. It was here, in the vast, intricate web of personal information, preferences, and vulnerabilities, that the true power of her enterprise lay dormant, a potent weapon waiting to be deployed. The city's opulence was the bait, the luxury the gilded cage, and Tasha Reed held the keys.

The inherent duality of Las Vegas, its ability to be both a place of boundless joy and profound despair, was a reflection of Tasha's own complex nature. She was a protector, fiercely loyal to the women under her wing, ensuring their safety and well-being with a vigilance that bordered on the obsessive. Yet, she was also a strategist, a tactician who understood that true power lay not just in protection, but in control. This dual nature, this blend of maternal instinct and ruthless pragmatism, was what made her so formidable, so unreadable, and so utterly captivating. She moved through the city's undercurrents like a phantom, her presence felt more than seen, her influence a silent, pervasive force.

The constant hum of money, the endless churn of transactions, was more than just background noise; it was the lifeblood of her operation. Tasha understood that wealth was a tool, a means to an end, and that in a city like Las Vegas, power was inextricably linked to financial leverage. Her clients were not merely men seeking companionship; they were titans of industry, political figures, and influential personalities, men who commanded vast resources and wielded significant power. To cater to them was to gain access to their world, to understand its intricacies, and to subtly influence its trajectory. The 'Swipe Right' app, in its own way, was a direct pipeline into the heart of this power structure, a conduit for information that could be used for purposes far beyond the immediate gratification of a client's desires.

The high-rise penthouses, the exclusive clubs, the private jets soaring overhead – these were not just symbols of wealth; they were manifestations of a deeper hunger, a desire for something more, something illicit, something forbidden. Tasha provided that something, expertly curated and delivered with an unparalleled level of sophistication. She was the architect of desire, the maestro of illusion, conducting a symphony of pleasure and power that resonated through the very foundations of the city. Her meticulously crafted operation was a reflection of her own mind – sharp, precise, and always a few steps ahead of everyone else.

The city itself served as a constant, silent partner in her enterprise. Las Vegas, with its manufactured reality and its intoxicating blend of fantasy and commerce, mirrored the very essence of Tasha's world. It was a place where identities were fluid, where fortunes could be made overnight, and where the line between reality and illusion was as blurred as the desert horizon. This constant flux, this inherent instability, was precisely what made it the perfect breeding ground for an operation like 'Swipe Right.' It was a city that thrived on deception, and Tasha Reed was its most brilliant exponent, a woman who had mastered the art of turning illusion into power, desire into dominance, and the seemingly innocent act of swiping right into the ultimate leverage.

The constant flow of new faces, the transient nature of its population, meant that secrets could be kept, reputations could be managed, and discretion was paramount. But even in a city built on ephemerality, the threads of connection, once woven, could become incredibly strong, and incredibly dangerous. Tasha understood this intrinsically. Her operation was a testament to the power of human connection, albeit one that was carefully managed and meticulously controlled. The allure of wealth and status was undeniable, but it was the human element – the desire for companionship, for intimacy, for validation – that truly fueled her empire. And Tasha, with her keen insight into the human psyche, had learned to harness that desire with an almost terrifying precision.

The sheer scale of ambition that defined Las Vegas was a force Tasha recognized and amplified. It was a city that dared to dream big, to build the impossible, and to chase the extraordinary. Tasha's own ambition was no less potent. She wasn't content with merely participating in the city's opulent game; she aimed to dominate it, to shape its very contours. Her operation, 'Swipe Right,' was her vehicle for achieving this, a sophisticated engine of influence designed to navigate the complex, often treacherous, currents of power and wealth that defined this unique desert metropolis. She was an artist, and the city was her canvas, ready to be splashed with the vibrant, and often dangerous, colors of her ambition.

The meticulous nature of Tasha's business extended to every facet of her operation, from the selection of her clientele to the training of her women. Each woman was not just an escort; she was an ambassador, a confidante, and a highly skilled negotiator, trained in the subtle art of conversation, emotional intelligence, and crisis management. They were taught to read people, to adapt to any situation, and to maintain an unshakeable composure, regardless of the circumstances. This dedication to excellence, this unwavering commitment to perfection, was what set 'Swipe Right' apart from any other service, elevating it from a mere escort agency to a sophisticated network of influence and power.

The inherent superficiality of the city was, for Tasha, a distinct advantage. It meant that most people were too preoccupied with the outward display of wealth and success to look too closely at the machinery beneath. They were blinded by the glitter, seduced by the promise of endless pleasure, and thus, blissfully unaware of the intricate web of control and influence that Tasha had so carefully woven around them. Her empire was built on this very blindness, on the assumption that the dazzling façade of Las Vegas was all there was to see. Tasha, however, knew better. She understood that true power lay in the shadows, in the unseen connections, and in the carefully guarded secrets.

The constant hum of activity, the ceaseless arrival and departure of planes, the endless stream of people drawn to the city's magnetic allure – it all served to reinforce the sense of isolation and anonymity that Tasha leveraged so effectively. In this sea of transient faces, her operation could thrive, shielded from the prying eyes of outsiders. The city's very nature, its transient population and its emphasis on superficial interaction, provided a natural buffer, a layer of obscurity that allowed Tasha to conduct her business with a remarkable degree of impunity. It was a city that welcomed reinvention, and Tasha had reinvented the very concept of discretion and influence.

The dazzling, deceptive world of 'Swipe Right' was a meticulously constructed reality, a sophisticated illusion designed to cater to the deepest desires of the city's elite. High-rise penthouses, exclusive clubs, and the constant hum of money set the stage for Tasha Reed's meticulously crafted operation. This initial glimpse established the city not just as a backdrop, but as a character in itself, reflecting the superficiality and hidden dangers that permeated every level of society. Las Vegas, with its glittering facade and its insatiable appetite for excess, was the perfect crucible for Tasha's ambition, a place where illusion was currency and control was the ultimate prize.

Tasha Reed was not a woman who was easily defined, nor one who sought such definition. She existed in the liminal spaces, the hushed corridors of power, the opulent suites where deals were struck and desires were traded. Her presence was less an announcement and more a subtle shift in the atmospheric pressure, a palpable aura of command that silenced idle chatter and commanded attention. She moved through her meticulously curated world with an unnerving stillness, a predatory grace that hinted at the coiled strength beneath the surface. Her eyes, the color of a storm-tossed sea, missed nothing, cataloging every flicker of an expression, every subtle shift in posture. They were eyes that had seen too much, learned too much, and now held the icy clarity of one who understood the true cost of everything.

She had built 'Swipe Right' not from a place of inherent privilege, but from a foundation of raw, unyielding will. The desert wind that whipped through Las Vegas, stripping away the superficial layers of sand and rock, was a metaphor for Tasha's own approach to life. She had shed the extraneous, the sentimental, the weakness, forging herself into a weapon honed by necessity and ambition. The city's inherent decadence, its relentless pursuit of pleasure and escape, was not just an environment for her; it was the very fuel that powered her ascent. She understood the primal drives that pulsed beneath the veneer of civility, the deep-seated loneliness that drove men to seek solace, validation, and dominion. And she had learned to capitalize on it, not with brute force, but with a scalpel-like precision that understood the intricate anatomy of desire.

Her penthouse, a sanctuary of glass and steel suspended high above the urban sprawl, was more than just a residence; it was a command center, a gilded cage from which she observed and manipulated the intricate dance of power and pleasure that defined her empire. From this vantage point, the city transformed into a living organism, its arteries pulsing with the flow of wealth and ambition, its hidden currents carrying whispers of secrets and clandestine rendezvous. She saw the players, the movers, the shakers, and she knew their vulnerabilities, their hidden cravings, their insatiable needs. This knowledge was her currency, her ultimate weapon, and she wielded it with the detached precision of a master strategist.

The women within her organization were not mere employees; they were assets, carefully cultivated and meticulously managed. Tasha saw them not as pawns in a game, but as intricate, complex individuals whose potential she had recognized and amplified. She offered them a path to financial independence, a degree of agency in a world that often sought to strip women of both. But this was not charity; it was a calculated investment. Each woman was a testament to Tasha's ability to identify and nurture talent, to mold raw potential into polished perfection. They were her eyes and ears on the ground, her ambassadors in the gilded salons and exclusive clubs where the real power resided. And Tasha, in turn, was their shield, their protector, their unwavering bulwark against the predatory nature of the world they inhabited.

This protectiveness, however, was not born of sentimentality. It was a strategic imperative. The loyalty of her women was paramount, their safety a non-negotiable prerequisite for the continued success of 'Swipe Right.' Any threat to them was a threat to her empire, and Tasha did not tolerate threats. Her responses were swift, decisive, and often brutal, though always conducted with an almost surgical discretion. She was a paradox: a woman who dealt in the commodification of intimacy, yet possessed an almost fierce, maternal protectiveness towards those under her charge. This duality was the source of her strength, the very essence of her formidable nature.

The 'Swipe Right' app, a marvel of discreet engineering, was the linchpin of her operation. It was a digital tapestry woven from the desires and insecurities of the city's elite, a sophisticated tool for data acquisition disguised as a luxury dating platform. Tasha poured over the analytics, the behavioral patterns, the subtle nuances of communication, gleaning insights that went far beyond the superficial. She understood that in a city built on illusion, the most valuable commodity was truth, meticulously extracted and expertly deployed. The app provided her with a constant stream of information, allowing her to anticipate trends, identify emerging power players, and subtly steer the course of events.

Her days were a meticulously orchestrated symphony of meetings, calls, and strategic planning. There were no wasted moments, no idle gestures. Every interaction, whether with a high-powered CEO or a newly recruited escort, was imbued with purpose. She was a master communicator, capable of conveying both immense warmth and chilling authority with equal ease. Her voice, a low, melodious instrument, could soothe anxieties or convey an unspoken threat with a mere inflection. She listened more than she spoke, her silence often more potent than any pronouncement. In that silence, she gathered intelligence, assessed intentions, and formulated her next move.

The glittering facade of Las Vegas, with its relentless pursuit of the next thrill, the next fleeting pleasure, was a world Tasha navigated with an almost uncanny intuition. She understood the human need for escape, for validation, for a taste of something forbidden. She provided that escape, that validation, that taste, but always on her terms, within her carefully constructed boundaries. She was not merely a facilitator of desires; she was an architect of experiences, orchestrating moments of exquisite pleasure and profound connection, all while maintaining an absolute, unyielding control.

She recalled her own early days, the desperate scramble for survival, the gnawing hunger for something more. Those memories were not a source of weakness, but of strength. They had forged her resilience, sharpened her focus, and instilled in her a profound understanding of the desperation that drove men to seek her services. She had learned to read the hunger in their eyes, the unspoken pleas hidden behind their bravado. And she had used that understanding to build an empire that defied the conventional boundaries of commerce and human connection.

The ethical considerations, the moral ambiguities of her profession, were not something Tasha dwelled upon. She operated in a realm where such distinctions blurred, where the pursuit of power and survival often dictated a different set of rules. Her focus was on results, on maintaining the integrity of her operation, and on protecting her people. She understood that in the cutthroat world of Las Vegas, sentimentality was a luxury she could not afford. Her decisions were guided by logic, by strategy, and by an unwavering commitment to the preservation and expansion of her empire.

Her meticulousness extended to every aspect of her life. Her wardrobe, while exuding understated elegance, was chosen for its practicality and its ability to convey an image of effortless authority. Her penthouse apartment, though a monument to luxury, was also a highly functional workspace, designed to facilitate her operations and maintain her privacy. Every detail was deliberate, every choice calculated to reinforce her image and her control.

Tasha Reed was more than just a businesswoman; she was a force of nature, a testament to the power of ambition and strategic intellect. She had carved out her own kingdom in the heart of the desert, a glittering empire built on the foundation of human desire and meticulously managed by an unwavering will. She was the architect of dreams, the purveyor of pleasure, and the silent ruler of a world that thrived in the shadows, a world she controlled with an absolute, unyielding grip. Her empire was a reflection of her own complex nature: formidable, alluring, and utterly unyielding. She was the queen of her own gilded cage, and the world beneath her penthouse shimmered in response to her silent command.

She believed that true power wasn't about brute force or overt displays of wealth, but about influence, about subtle manipulation, about understanding the unspoken currents that drove human behavior. Tasha had mastered this art. She understood that the desires of the elite were not always overt; often, they were buried deep, masked by layers of social conditioning and guarded by walls of self-preservation. Her skill lay in her ability to peel back those layers, to expose those hidden cravings, and to offer a tailored solution, delivered with an unparalleled level of discretion and sophistication. The 'Swipe Right' app was not just a tool for connecting people; it was a finely tuned instrument for deciphering the complex symphony of human need.

The constant influx of new clients, the transient nature of the city's visitors, provided a fertile ground for her operations. It meant that secrets could be kept, reputations could be managed, and discretion was not just a policy, but a necessity. However, Tasha also recognized the inherent danger in this transience. Connections made in such ephemeral circumstances could be volatile, prone to sudden rupture, or worse, to betrayal. This was why her vetting process was so rigorous, her background checks so exhaustive. She needed to know not just who her clients were, but who they were connected to, what their vulnerabilities were, and what potential threats they posed to her carefully constructed world.

She often found herself in the paradoxical position of fostering genuine connections, albeit within the carefully managed framework of her business. The women under her wing were not just employees; they were individuals with dreams, aspirations, and vulnerabilities of their own. Tasha's protectiveness stemmed from a deep understanding of their shared struggle, a recognition of the resilience it took to navigate the treacherous waters of their profession. She provided them with not just financial security, but with a sense of community, a network of support that shielded them from the harsher realities of their chosen path. This was not merely good business; it was a fundamental aspect of her philosophy.

The very superficiality of Las Vegas, the city's obsession with appearances and the illusion of success, was a distinct advantage for Tasha. Most of her clients were so absorbed in maintaining their own polished facades that they rarely looked beneath the surface, rarely questioned the seamless efficiency of her operation. They were blinded by the spectacle, seduced by the promise of unattainable pleasure, and thus, blissfully unaware of the intricate web of control and intelligence that Tasha had so meticulously woven around them. Her empire was built on this very blindness, on the assumption that the glittering surface of Las Vegas was all there was to see. Tasha, however, knew better. She understood that true power resided in the shadows, in the unseen connections, and in the carefully guarded secrets.

The constant hum of activity, the ceaseless arrival and departure of aircraft, the endless stream of people drawn to the city's magnetic allure – it all served to reinforce the sense of isolation and anonymity that Tasha leveraged so effectively. In this sea of transient faces, her operation could thrive, shielded from the prying eyes of outsiders. The city's very nature, its transient population and its emphasis on superficial interaction, provided a natural buffer, a layer of obscurity that allowed Tasha to conduct her business with a remarkable degree of impunity. It was a city that welcomed reinvention, and Tasha had reinvented the very concept of discretion and influence, transforming the transactional nature of desire into a sophisticated instrument of power.

The relentless pursuit of wealth and status that defined Las Vegas was a force that Tasha not only recognized but actively amplified. It was a city that dared to dream big, to build the impossible, and to chase the extraordinary. Tasha's own ambition was no less potent. She wasn't content with merely participating in the city's opulent game; she aimed to dominate it, to shape its very contours. Her operation, 'Swipe Right,' was her vehicle for achieving this, a sophisticated engine of influence designed to navigate the complex, often treacherous, currents of power and wealth that defined this unique desert metropolis. She was an artist, and Las Vegas was her canvas, ready to be splashed with the vibrant, and often dangerous, colors of her ambition.

The meticulous nature of Tasha's business extended to every facet of her operation, from the selection of her clientele to the training of her women. Each woman was not just an escort; she was an ambassador, a confidante, and a highly skilled negotiator, trained in the subtle art of conversation, emotional intelligence, and crisis management. They were taught to read people, to adapt to any situation, and to maintain an unshakeable composure, regardless of the circumstances. This dedication to excellence, this unwavering commitment to perfection, was what set 'Swipe Right' apart from any other service, elevating it from a mere escort agency to a sophisticated network of influence and power. It was this dedication that ensured her control, her dominance, and the continued prosperity of her meticulously crafted empire.

Malik Carter wasn't just a partner; he was a gravitational force, pulling Tasha's carefully constructed world into increasingly ambitious orbits. His charm was a finely honed weapon, capable of disarming the most hardened cynics and luring unsuspecting investors into his meticulously crafted schemes. To the outside world, he was the embodiment of Silicon Valley success, a visionary tech entrepreneur whose latest venture, 'Swipe Right,' promised to revolutionize social connections. But beneath the polished veneer of innovation and ambition, Malik harbored a predatory hunger, a relentless drive for expansion that saw 'Swipe Right' as far more than a high-end dating platform. For Malik, it was a data-mining goldmine, a sophisticated tool for social engineering, and a gateway to opportunities far more lucrative and far more dangerous than Tasha initially understood.

His vision for 'Swipe Right' extended far beyond the curated encounters and discreet arrangements that formed the bedrock of their operation. Malik saw the app as a conduit, a digital nervous system that could tap into the deepest desires and vulnerabilities of Las Vegas's elite. He envisioned it as a platform for information brokerage, for influencing public opinion, and for leveraging personal data for unprecedented profit. While Tasha had built her empire on understanding and satisfying human desire, Malik aimed to commodify it, to dissect it, and to weaponize it. This fundamental difference in perspective was the subtle, yet potent, undercurrent of tension that flowed between them, a simmering conflict that hinted at future betrayals and a brutal power struggle for control of their shared, illicit enterprise.

Malik's approach was diametrically opposed to Tasha's measured, strategic methodology. Where Tasha favored subtlety, precision, and an almost surgical dissection of her targets, Malik was a force of nature, impatient and driven by an insatiable desire for growth. He was the accelerant to Tasha's controlled burn, constantly pushing the boundaries, seeking new avenues for exploitation. He would pepper their conversations with audacious proposals, his eyes glinting with the thrill of risk and the promise of unparalleled reward. He spoke of infiltrating political circles, of influencing corporate decisions, of leveraging the curated intimacy of 'Swipe Right' to build a network of influence that transcended mere financial gain.

"Think bigger, Tasha," he'd urge, leaning forward across the polished mahogany of their private meeting room, the city lights glittering like scattered diamonds beyond the floor-to-ceiling windows. "We're not just connecting lonely billionaires with beautiful companions. We're building a proprietary database of the city's most powerful, most influential individuals. Their habits, their preferences, their secrets – we can leverage all of it. Imagine the possibilities, the... leverage." His voice, a smooth baritone, dripped with the seductive allure of forbidden knowledge and unchecked power.

Tasha, ever the pragmatist, would counter with a coolly delivered assessment of the risks, the potential fallout. She understood the delicate ecosystem they had cultivated, the intricate balance of discretion and pleasure that kept their operation thriving. Malik's audacious schemes, while undeniably lucrative in theory, carried a disproportionate amount of risk, threatening to expose the very foundations of their success. She saw the potential for catastrophic failure, for a swift and brutal backlash from the powerful individuals they catered to if their true intentions were ever revealed.

"Leverage comes with a cost, Malik," she would retort, her gaze steady, unwavering. "And the cost of exposure could be our entire operation. We build trust through discretion. Your 'bigger picture' involves tearing down that trust brick by brick."

But Malik was rarely deterred by caution. He viewed Tasha's meticulousness as a form of inhibition, a reluctance to embrace the full potential of their creation. He saw her protectiveness of her women as a sentimental attachment, a weakness that prevented her from fully capitalizing on every asset. His vision was a cold, calculated calculus of profit and power, where every interaction, every piece of data, was a potential commodity to be extracted and exploited.

"Sentimental attachments are a luxury we can't afford, Tasha," he'd say, his tone dismissive. "These women are valuable, yes, but their value is in their ability to gather intelligence, to open doors. We can't let emotional considerations cloud our judgment. We need to be ruthless. We need to be... comprehensive."

His ambition was a relentless tide, constantly eroding the carefully constructed seawalls of Tasha's caution. He was a master manipulator, adept at framing his increasingly audacious proposals as logical extensions of their current success, as necessary steps for their continued growth. He would highlight the immense profits generated by their existing model, then present his radical new strategies as the natural evolution, the inevitable next stage. He was a persuasive force, and Tasha, despite her own formidable intellect and strategic prowess, found herself increasingly challenged by his relentless drive and his willingness to disregard the very principles that had brought them so far.

One particular proposal, a plan to use 'Swipe Right' to influence a series of high-stakes corporate mergers by subtly feeding misinformation and leveraging the personal lives of key executives, sent a chill down Tasha's spine. It was a level of manipulation, of outright economic sabotage, that bordered on outright criminality, even by their already illicit standards.

"Malik, this is beyond anything we've ever considered," Tasha had said, her voice tight with apprehension. "We're talking about manipulating the stock market, about ruining careers. This isn't just about connecting people anymore; this is about destabilizing entire industries."

Malik had simply smiled, a predator's smile that held no warmth. "Destabilizing them to our advantage, Tasha. Think of the information we'd acquire. Think of the alliances we could forge. We'd become indispensable. We'd control the flow of capital, the direction of innovation. 'Swipe Right' wouldn't just be an app; it would be the command center of the global economy."

His vision was intoxicating, a siren song of ultimate power and wealth, and Tasha couldn't deny its allure, even as it repelled her. She saw the potential for immense profit, the ability to reshape the very landscape of power in Las Vegas and beyond.

But she also saw the precipice, the terrifying drop into a darkness from which there might be no return. Her own rise had been born from a need for survival, a pragmatic understanding of the transactional nature of desire. Malik's ambition, however, seemed to stem from a more primal, insatiable hunger, a need to dominate, to conquer, to leave his indelible mark on the world, no matter the cost.

The tension between them was a palpable thing, a coiled spring that grew tighter with each passing day. Tasha knew that Malik's relentless pursuit of expansion and profit would eventually lead them into territory that even she, with her unparalleled ability to navigate the morally ambiguous, would find difficult to traverse. He was a partner who saw the gilded cage they had built not as a sanctuary, but as a launchpad, and his sights were set on a world far more volatile, far more dangerous, than the discreet world of elite companionship. The question that gnawed at Tasha, the question that shadowed her every move, was not if Malik would push them too far, but when. And what would be left of them, of their empire, when he finally did? The shadow of Malik Carter, the shadow partner, was lengthening, and Tasha could feel its chill creeping into the heart of her meticulously crafted world. He was a force she had underestimated, a player whose ambition far outstripped her own careful calculations, and the future, once a landscape of controlled expansion, now felt like a treacherous terrain, riddled with the hidden traps of his insatiable desire for more.

The hum of the fluorescent lights in the precinct interrogation room was a familiar, grating soundtrack to Detective Lena Cross's life. It was a sound that burrowed deep, a constant reminder of the artificiality of justice, of the controlled chaos she navigated daily. Las Vegas. The name itself conjured images of glittering casinos, dazzling shows, and the relentless pursuit of fortune. But Lena knew a different Vegas, a city where the shadows held more sway than the spotlight, where desires were currency and secrets were the most valuable commodities. She was a hunter in this city of illusion, a bloodhound on the scent of a truth obscured by a thousand layers of deception.

Her current quarry was a phantom, a whisper in the city's opulent corridors. The initial tip had been vague, a hushed accusation dropped into a burner phone, hinting at something far more sinister than the usual sordid affairs that festered beneath the surface of the Strip's glamour. It spoke of manipulation, of leveraged influence, of a network that preyed on the very elite it purported to serve. The details were scarce, the evidence even scarcer, but something in the cryptic message had snagged Lena's attention, a persistent itch beneath her skin that refused to be ignored. It promised a complexity, a depth of depravity that resonated with the darker currents she felt pulsing through the city, currents that too many of her colleagues seemed content to ignore, blinded by the neon glare.

Lena wasn't a by-the-book detective. The book, in her experience, was often more of a suggestion than a definitive guide, especially in a city like Las Vegas. She'd learned to bend the rules, to operate in the liminal spaces where official protocols often dissolved into inconvenient red tape. Her methods were unorthodox, her contacts often unsavory, but her results were undeniable. She'd built a reputation for unearthing truths that others deemed untouchable, for finding the rot hidden beneath layers of polished chrome and curated smiles. This made her effective, but it also made her a target. The very systems that benefited from her silence were also the ones that scrutinized her actions, a constant tightrope walk between efficacy and damnation.

The case that had landed on her desk, or rather, had been discreetly slipped into her inbox by a source she trusted implicitly, spoke of a network that operated within the exclusive circles of Las Vegas society. It wasn't about illegal gambling or street-level narcotics. This was about something far more insidious: the subtle, almost imperceptible manipulation of power, wealth, and influence. The whispers spoke of an app, a high-end platform designed to connect the city's most affluent and powerful individuals with curated companionship. On the surface, it seemed innocuous, a digital concierge for the lonely titans of industry and entertainment. But the veiled accusations suggested it was a sophisticated tool for something far more profound, a mechanism for data extraction, social engineering, and the leveraging of personal vulnerabilities for gain.

Lena's instinct screamed that this was bigger than anything she'd tackled before. The players involved were likely untouchable, their lives meticulously shielded by layers of wealth and legal protection. To even attempt to penetrate their world required a delicate touch, a deep understanding of the unwritten rules that governed their existence. And that's where her own precarious position became a significant hurdle. Lena wasn't a free agent; she was entangled, a player in a game she was supposed to be policing. Her very presence in Las Vegas, her survival within its labyrinthine power structures, was predicated on a series of compromises, a carefully maintained equilibrium that could shatter with a single misstep.

The information regarding the app, codenamed 'Swipe Right' by her informant, was sparse but compelling. It detailed a system that not only facilitated introductions but also meticulously gathered data on its users – their preferences, their habits, their discreet indiscretions. The informant alleged that this information was being used for more than just client satisfaction; it was being leveraged, weaponized, in ways that could destabilize careers, influence corporate decisions, and even impact political outcomes. It painted a picture of a digital puppet master, pulling strings from the shadows, manipulating the city's most influential figures for profit and power.

Lena traced the initial whispers back to a man named Malik Carter. The name meant little to her initially, just another ghost in the machine. But as she dug deeper, peeling back the layers of carefully constructed public image, a more complex and unsettling portrait began to emerge. Carter was a tech visionary, a darling of the Silicon Valley elite, the charismatic face behind 'Swipe Right.' His public persona was one of innovation and disruption, a man who claimed to be simplifying connections in a disconnected world. Yet, the information Lena received suggested a far more predatory nature, a man who saw human desires not as something to be fulfilled, but as a resource to be exploited.

Her informant had mentioned a partner, a woman named Tasha, who was described as the operational architect, the one who understood the nuances of the elite clientele, the one who built the relationships and maintained the facade of discretion. Tasha was the silent force, the sculptor of the gilded cage that these powerful men inhabited, while Carter was the flamboyant showman, the one who preached the gospel of expansion and unchecked ambition. The dynamic between them was described as a volatile mix of shared vision and conflicting methodologies, a tension that Lena suspected was the breeding ground for the very exploitation she was investigating.

The problem was, Lena couldn't afford to be a purely objective observer. Her investigation into 'Swipe Right' was inextricably linked to her own survival. The compromises she had made to gain a foothold in Las Vegas, the alliances she had forged with individuals who occupied similar gray areas, meant that any significant disruption in the city's power dynamics could have dire repercussions for her. She operated in a constant state of calculated risk, her actions always balanced against the potential for exposure, for retribution. Exposing a network as deeply embedded as this one promised to be could very well bring the entire edifice of her own carefully constructed world crashing down.

She recalled a recent conversation with her superior, Captain Davies. Davies, a man who preferred the predictable certainty of solved cases and clean arrests, had warned her about the dangers of venturing too deep into the city's underbelly. "Cross," he'd said, his voice a low growl that always carried an undercurrent of impatience, "this is Las Vegas. It's built on illusions. You want to expose the tricks, fine. But don't get so caught up in the magic show that you forget the stage is rigged." His words echoed in her mind, a prescient warning about the precariousness of her position. Davies had a nose for trouble, and Lena knew he would be watching her, waiting for any sign that she was stepping too far out of line.

The personal stakes were also mounting. The informant, a ghost in the system with a history of providing invaluable intel, had alluded to a personal connection to the 'Swipe Right' operation, something that went beyond mere transactional information sharing. The details were cloaked in ambiguity, a deliberate obfuscation that hinted at a deep personal involvement, perhaps even a victimhood. Lena felt a growing obligation, a sense of responsibility for this shadowy figure who had placed their trust in her. This wasn't just about uncovering a criminal enterprise; it was about potentially saving someone, about rectifying a wrong that had been committed in the gilded cages of power.

She spent hours poring over the fragmented data. Encrypted messages, offshore accounts, shell corporations – the digital breadcrumbs were there, leading to a labyrinth of financial intrigue and hidden identities. Carter's company was a marvel of modern corporate structuring, designed to be as opaque as possible. He had built his empire on the principle that the less visible the gears, the more seamlessly the machine operated. And the machine, Lena was beginning to suspect, was designed for a specific kind of extraction, a harvesting of more than just financial data. It was about the harvesting of secrets, of vulnerabilities, of the very essence of human frailty.

The 'Swipe Right' app, according to the intel, was more than a matchmaking service. It was a data-mining operation of unprecedented scale and sophistication. Carter's vision, as described by her informant, was to create a comprehensive profile of the city's elite, a digital dossier that could be leveraged for immense influence. The discreet arrangements facilitated by the app were merely the gateway, the initial point of contact where trust could be established and information could be subtly extracted. Carter, it seemed, wasn't interested in simply connecting lonely billionaires with beautiful companions. He was building a proprietary database of the city's most powerful individuals, a repository of their habits, their preferences, their indiscretions

Lena leaned back in her chair, the worn leather groaning in protest. The weight of the information, the sheer audacity of Carter's alleged scheme, was almost overwhelming.

She understood the allure of power, the seductive whisper of control that came with knowing the secrets of the influential. But this was different. This was about weaponizing intimacy, about turning personal connections into instruments of manipulation. It was a form of social engineering that blurred the lines between consensual interaction and covert exploitation.

She thought of Tasha, the enigmatic partner. If Carter was the visionary, the architect of the grand plan, Tasha was the builder, the one who understood the intricate architecture of human desire and discretion. Her role was likely far more hands-on, more intimate, than Carter's detached, strategic oversight. This made Tasha a potentially crucial link, but also a more dangerous one. Someone who understood the nuances of the elite clientele so intimately could also be the most adept at exploiting them.

Lena's own life had been a series of calculated risks, a testament to her resilience and her ability to adapt. She had learned to navigate the treacherous currents of Las Vegas, to find allies in unexpected places, and to wield information as a weapon. But the more she delved into the 'Swipe Right' operation, the more she realized the extent to which she was compromised. Her involvement with certain individuals, the debts she owed, the favors she had called in – all of it made her vulnerable. If her investigation into Carter and his network were to come to light prematurely, it wouldn't just jeopardize the case; it could dismantle her entire existence in the city.

She pulled up a recent profile on Carter. The public image was impeccable: a Stanford graduate, a serial entrepreneur, a philanthropist. He spoke of democratizing access, of fostering genuine connections in an increasingly digital world. But Lena saw the carefully curated narrative, the glossy veneer that hid a more calculated, perhaps more sinister, agenda. His vision, as relayed by her informant, was not about fostering connection but about cultivating control. 'Swipe Right' was not just an app; it was a data-mining goldmine, a sophisticated tool for social engineering, and a gateway to opportunities far more lucrative and far more dangerous than Tasha initially understood.

Her informant had hinted at a darker purpose for 'Swipe Right,' beyond mere data collection. The app was allegedly being used as a conduit for information brokerage, for influencing public opinion, and for leveraging personal data for unprecedented profit. Carter's ambition extended far beyond the curated encounters and discreet arrangements that formed the bedrock of their operation. He envisioned it as a platform for building a network of influence that transcended mere financial gain, a tool to infiltrate political circles, to influence corporate decisions, and to leverage the curated intimacy of 'Swipe Right' to create a kingdom of power.

Lena's phone buzzed, a discreet vibration against her thigh. It was a coded message from her informant, a single word: "Danger." It was a stark reminder of the stakes involved, of the invisible forces at play. The shadows of Las Vegas were not merely atmospheric; they were populated by individuals who wielded immense power, and who would go to extreme lengths to protect their secrets.

The dilemma was stark. To continue the investigation meant pushing deeper into a world that threatened to engulf her. To back away meant allowing a potentially devastating operation to continue unchecked, and perhaps leaving her informant exposed. Lena was a detective, a seeker of truth, but she was also a survivor. And in Las Vegas, survival often meant making difficult choices, choices that skirted the edges of morality, choices that blurred the lines between right and wrong.

She thought of Carter's purported disdain for sentimentality, his view of the women who facilitated the 'Swipe Right' operation as assets to be utilized. "These women are valuable, yes," her informant had relayed, quoting Carter, "but their value is in their ability to gather intelligence, to open doors. We can't let emotional considerations cloud our judgment. We need to be ruthless. We need to be… comprehensive." The cold calculation in those words sent a shiver down Lena's spine. It was a stark contrast to Tasha's likely more nuanced approach, her presumed understanding of the human element, the very element Carter seemed so eager to discard.

The pressure was immense. Captain Davies was breathing down her neck, demanding tangible progress on cases that rarely yielded to conventional methods. The compromises Lena had made to operate effectively within the city's complex web of power meant that her every move was under scrutiny. Her own personal safety, her career, and the well-being of her informant all hung precariously in the balance. The 'Swipe Right' investigation wasn't just another case; it was a personal reckoning, a test of her resolve and her ability to navigate the treacherous moral landscape of Las Vegas.

She needed more information, concrete evidence that would stand up in court, or at least in the quiet backrooms where true justice was often dispensed. The initial intel was strong, but it was also circumstantial, whispered from the shadows by a source who remained deliberately anonymous. To bring down someone like Malik Carter, to dismantle a network as sophisticated as 'Swipe Right' promised to be, would require irrefutable proof, a smoking gun that could pierce through the layers of corporate camouflage and legal obfuscation.

Lena's mind raced, sifting through possibilities, evaluating risks. She couldn't afford to alert Carter directly. Any hint that she was investigating him could trigger a swift and brutal response. He was, after all, a man who operated in the shadows, a man who understood the power of information and the efficacy of a well-placed threat. Her own vulnerabilities, the very compromises that allowed her to operate, were also her greatest weaknesses.

The dilemma wasn't just about uncovering the truth; it was about surviving the pursuit of it. Lena knew that the gilded cage she was trying to expose was also a trap, a finely tuned mechanism designed to ensnare anyone who dared to look too closely. She was already operating in a morally gray zone, her hands not entirely clean. This made her investigation both more critical and more dangerous. If she was to succeed, she would have to outmaneuver not only Carter and his network but also the very systems that governed her own precarious existence. The challenge was immense, the path ahead fraught with peril, and the outcome, as always in Las Vegas, was anything but certain.

Jazmine Rios, or Jazzy as she preferred, stood on the precipice of a new life, a life meticulously crafted to erase the scars of her past. Las Vegas, a city synonymous with reinvention, offered a shimmering, almost deceptive, promise of a clean slate. Her escape from a life mired in poverty and the harsh realities of survival had been a calculated maneuver, a strategic retreat from the familiar desolation of her old world. She sought not just a change of scenery, but a fundamental alteration of her trajectory, a deliberate pivot away from the precipice of despair. The sterile, yet gleaming, lobby of the downtown boutique hotel she'd secured with her last few dollars felt like a fortress, a temporary bastion against the relentless tide of her history. She was a survivor, yes, but a survivor yearning for more than mere existence; she craved a life that sang, a life that sparkled, a life where the only limitations were those she set for herself.

Her early days in the city were a blur of earnest applications, of polite rejections that chipped away at her resolve, and of the gnawing anxiety that accompanied dwindling funds. She possessed a sharp intellect, honed by years of necessity and an innate resilience that had seen her through countless adversities. But intelligence and resilience, she was quickly learning, were not always enough to penetrate the gilded gates of opportunity in a city that worshipped wealth and influence above all else. She was adrift in a sea of neon and ambition, a small boat tossed by waves of opulence she could only observe from a distance. The polished facades of the casinos, the impossibly chic boutiques, the hushed tones of exclusive clubs – they all represented a world that felt impossibly out of reach, a mirage shimmering tantalizingly on the horizon.

It was during one of her many reconnaissance missions into the city's vibrant, yet often unforgiving, landscape that she first encountered Tasha. Not Tasha the architect of the 'Swipe Right' empire, not Tasha the shadowy figure whispered about in hushed tones by Lena Cross, but Tasha the patron of the arts, the woman who exuded an almost regal aura amidst the cacophony of the city. Jazzy had stumbled upon a small, exclusive art gallery nestled away from the main thoroughfares, a sanctuary of curated beauty. Tasha was there, a captivating presence, her attention drawn to a piece that resonated with a quiet intensity, much like Jazzy herself felt she could. There was a subtle exchange, a shared appreciation for the unspoken narrative within the artwork, and it was in that fleeting moment of connection that Tasha's perceptive gaze fell upon Jazzy.

Tasha's approach was disarmingly direct, yet infused with an innate grace. She didn't inquire about Jazzy's credentials or her background; instead, she spoke of potential, of the inherent value in a sharp mind and a discerning eye. She painted a picture of a world that, while undeniably opulent, also offered a unique platform for those with the intelligence and the drive to navigate its complexities. The conversation, initially about art, subtly shifted, weaving a tapestry of possibilities that spoke directly to Jazzy's deepest longings. Tasha spoke of mentorship, of opportunity, of a chance to learn and grow within a dynamic, fast-paced environment. It was an invitation, veiled in sophisticated language, to step out of the shadows and into a world of curated brilliance.

The offer was undeniably seductive. Tasha described a role that was far removed from the menial jobs Jazzy had been pursuing. It involved assisting with client relations, managing exclusive events, and offering a discerning perspective on aesthetics and experience. The compensation, Tasha hinted, was not merely monetary, but encompassed access to experiences, to knowledge, and to a network of influential individuals. It was a proposition that spoke to Jazzy's nascent ambition, a chance to utilize her sharp intellect and her inherent ability to read people and situations in a way that could elevate her beyond her current circumstances. The allure of luxury, of security, of a life lived without the constant threat of scarcity, was a powerful draw.

Jazzy, ever the pragmatist, harbored a healthy dose of skepticism. Her past had taught her to be wary of promises too good to be true. Yet, Tasha's demeanor, her effortless confidence, and the genuine interest she displayed in Jazzy's perspective, managed to disarm some of her inherent caution. There was a certain magnetism to Tasha, an aura of control and quiet power that Jazzy found both intimidating and compelling. She saw in Tasha not just a potential employer, but a glimpse into a world of influence and capability that she had only ever dreamed of. The idea of being mentored by such a woman, of learning the intricacies of navigating the high-stakes environment of Las Vegas from someone who clearly excelled at it, was an opportunity too significant to dismiss lightly.

During their initial meeting, Tasha had skillfully steered the conversation towards Jazzy's aspirations, subtly probing her strengths and her desires. She had a knack for asking questions that elicited more than just superficial answers, questions that seemed to uncover the hidden facets of Jazzy's personality and her potential. Jazzy found herself opening up, sharing her desire for autonomy, for a sense of purpose, and for the freedom to chart her own course. Tasha listened intently, her expression one of deep concentration, and then, with a subtle smile, she offered her proposition. It was a carefully crafted offer, designed to appeal to Jazzy's intelligence and her desire for self-improvement.

"We value discretion, intelligence, and a keen eye for detail, Jazmine," Tasha had said, her voice smooth as polished obsidian. "These are qualities I believe you possess in abundance. My work requires someone who understands the nuances of human interaction, someone who can anticipate needs and cultivate relationships. It's a world of curated experiences, of discerning clientele, and I believe you have the potential to thrive within it." The implicit promise was clear: join me, and you will learn to wield influence, to navigate the complex currents of power that define this city.

The initial stage of Jazzy's involvement was subtle, almost imperceptible. She began by assisting Tasha with smaller tasks – organizing schedules, vetting potential contacts, and offering her insights on various social engagements. These were not the clandestine operations Lena Cross was investigating, not yet. These were the outward-facing elements of Tasha's world, the meticulous construction of a facade that projected an image of refined sophistication and impeccable taste. Jazzy, with her sharp mind and her innate ability to blend into any environment, proved to be an invaluable asset. She absorbed information like a sponge, quickly understanding the unwritten rules of engagement, the subtle cues that dictated social hierarchies, and the delicate art of diplomacy required to navigate the city's elite circles.

The intoxicating allure of wealth and luxury began to weave its spell. Jazzy found herself attending events she could only have dreamed of before – exclusive parties where champagne flowed freely, art openings graced by the city's most influential figures, and private gatherings held in opulent residences that rivaled the grandest hotel suites. She was no longer an observer on the fringes; she was an integral part of the intricate machinery that powered Tasha's endeavors. The initial intention of finding safety and autonomy began to morph, subtly at first, then more decidedly, into a fascination with the power and influence that Tasha wielded.

The transition was not jarring, but rather a gradual immersion, like a slow, inexorable tide pulling her further from the shore. Tasha's world was a symphony of carefully orchestrated interactions, where every gesture, every word, carried weight and consequence. Jazzy learned to anticipate Tasha's needs, to understand the unspoken language of their professional relationship, and to project an image of competence and sophistication that mirrored Tasha's own. She was learning to be a chameleon, adapting her own persona to fit the requirements of the environment, a skill that served her well in her past but was now being honed to a razor's edge.

The financial remuneration was, as promised, significantly beyond anything Jazzy had previously earned. It wasn't just the salary, but the perquisites – the designer clothing provided for events, the access to exclusive venues, the opportunities to mingle with individuals who held sway in the city's economic and social spheres. These were tangible rewards, reinforcing the notion that she had indeed made a wise choice, that she was on an upward trajectory, moving towards the life of independence and influence she had envisioned. The tangible markers of success began to accumulate, creating a powerful sense of validation and accomplishment.

However, beneath the glittering surface, Jazzy began to sense a deeper current, a complex web of operations that extended beyond the curated events and discreet client interactions. Tasha, while outwardly projecting an image of refined elegance and unwavering control, was also a businesswoman of formidable acumen, and her endeavors, Jazzy suspected, were far more intricate than their outward presentation suggested. The conversations Jazzy overheard, the hushed phone calls Tasha took, the cryptic references to "arrangements" and "data points" – they all hinted at a larger, more clandestine enterprise.

The 'Swipe Right' app, the subject of Lena Cross's investigation, was not explicitly mentioned in Jazzy's initial brief, but the pervasive theme of facilitating connections, of understanding desires, and of leveraging influence was undeniably present in her daily work. She saw how Tasha meticulously gathered information about clients, not just their preferences for events or entertainment, but also their professional ambitions, their personal connections, and their perceived vulnerabilities. It was a process of observation and data accumulation that, in hindsight, bore a chilling resemblance to the very activities Lena was trying to uncover.

Jazzy's initial intention had been to find a safe harbor, a place of stability and autonomy. But the intoxicating allure of Tasha's empire, the sheer power and sophistication of the operation, began to pull her in with an irresistible force. She found herself not just assisting, but actively participating, her intelligence and adaptability making her an increasingly valuable asset to Tasha. The lines between her initial intentions and the unfolding reality of her involvement began to blur, and Jazzy, caught in the gravitational pull of wealth, influence, and the thrill of operating within a clandestine world, found herself embarking on a perilous journey into the heart of Tasha's carefully constructed empire. The gilded cage was slowly closing around her, and Jazzy, despite her inherent caution, was finding it increasingly difficult to resist its allure. She was, in essence, becoming a part of the machine she was initially meant to observe from a safe distance, her presence marking the first significant internal recruitment into the sophisticated mechanisms of the 'Swipe Right' operation, a testament to Tasha's ability to identify and cultivate talent that aligned with her vision, regardless of their initial aspirations.

2: Threads of Deception

The plush velvet of the designer suit felt alien against Jazzy's skin, a stark departure from the worn fabrics she was accustomed to. It was the first of many such ensembles Tasha had provided, each meticulously chosen to reflect a specific aesthetic, a particular level of affluence designed to project an image of effortless sophistication. The hotel suite, a sprawling expanse of marble and muted silk, was her new domain, a gilded cage that offered unparalleled comfort but also a palpable sense of being observed. Every surface gleamed, every amenity was at her disposal, yet a persistent hum of unease thrummed beneath the surface of this newfound luxury. Tasha, with her unnervingly perceptive gaze, had been meticulously assessing Jazzy since their first encounter, and this period of induction was a sophisticated form of trial by fire, a test of her adaptability, her discretion, and her willingness to embrace the intricate dance of Tasha's world.

Tasha's approach to integration was akin to a surgeon's, precise and deliberate. Jazzy's days were a carefully orchestrated series of lessons, not in traditional business practices, but in the unwritten laws of influence and discretion that governed Tasha's intricate network. The rules were simple, yet their implications were vast. Loyalty was paramount, silence an absolute virtue, and the ability to anticipate needs – both stated and unstated – a highly prized skill. Tasha herself acted as the primary instructor, her every interaction with Jazzy a subtle demonstration of the principles she sought to impart. She spoke in measured tones, her words laced with a quiet authority that demanded attention. Jazzy found herself constantly on alert, analyzing Tasha's subtle shifts in expression, the minute adjustments in her posture, deciphering the underlying currents of meaning in every seemingly innocuous conversation.

"You must understand, Jazmine," Tasha had said one afternoon, her voice a silken whisper as they surveyed the glittering cityscape from the suite's panoramic windows, "that perception is reality in this city. What people *believe* to be true often holds more sway than what actually *is*. Our role is to cultivate those perceptions, to shape them, to ensure they align with our objectives." Tasha's words hung in the air, heavy with implication. Jazzy nodded, absorbing the lesson, yet a flicker of apprehension tightened her chest. She was being trained to manipulate, to curate not just events and images, but the very fabric of perception. The initial allure of opportunity was slowly being overlaid with a growing awareness of the ethical tightrope she was beginning to walk.

The opulence was overwhelming, a constant barrage of sensory stimuli designed to immerse Jazzy completely. The designer clothing wasn't merely attire; it was a uniform, a symbol of belonging. The lavish accommodations were not just a perk; they were a testament to the success and influence of Tasha's enterprise. Yet, amidst this extravagance, Jazzy felt a growing dissonance. She was a guest in a world that felt increasingly like a meticulously constructed stage, and she was a player being carefully positioned for a role she was only beginning to comprehend. Tasha's constant observation was a palpable presence, a silent interrogation that probed the depths of Jazzy's resolve. Was she capable of shedding her past, of shedding parts of herself, to become the refined, discreet operative Tasha envisioned?

Tasha's evaluation of Jazzy was not confined to formal discussions. It was woven into the fabric of their daily interactions. Tasha would subtly introduce Jazzy to individuals of varying influence, observing how she navigated these encounters. Would she be intimidated? Would she overstep? Or would she instinctively grasp the nuances of social maneuvering, the delicate art of making connections that were both beneficial and discreet? Jazzy found herself relying on the survival instincts honed in her previous life, the ability to read a room, to gauge intentions, and to project a carefully constructed persona. However, the stakes were immeasurably higher now, the potential consequences far more severe than mere embarrassment or a missed opportunity.

One evening, Tasha orchestrated a small, intimate gathering at a private rooftop lounge, a venue known for its exclusivity and the caliber of its clientele. Jazzy was instructed to circulate, to engage in conversation, and to subtly gather information about the guests. The instruction was simple: "Learn who they are, what they want, and how they might be... useful." Jazzy felt a chill crawl down her spine. This wasn't about making pleasant conversation; it was about reconnaissance, about identifying potential assets and vulnerabilities within Tasha's network. She approached the task with a carefully cultivated blend of genuine curiosity and calculated detachment, mirroring Tasha's own poise.

She engaged a prominent real estate developer in a discussion about architectural trends, her mind simultaneously cataloging his nervous tic when discussing a particular deal and his offhand mention of a forthcoming venture that required significant, and discreet, financing. Later, she spoke with a well-known philanthropist, subtly steering the conversation towards his charitable foundation's funding challenges, noting his palpable relief when she casually mentioned Tasha's reputation for facilitating large donations, albeit with an implied expectation of reciprocal advantages. Each conversation was a puzzle piece, and Jazzy found herself surprisingly adept at piecing together the larger picture of influence, ambition, and hidden agendas that Tasha's world comprised.

Tasha observed these interactions from a distance, her expression unreadable. Later, back in the sterile opulence of the suite, she offered her assessment. "You have a natural inclination for observation, Jazmine," she stated, her tone devoid of overt praise, yet conveying a sense of approval. "You listen more than you speak, and when you do speak, your words are chosen with care. That is a rare and valuable quality." Tasha's feedback was always measured, never effusive, which paradoxically made it more impactful. It suggested a deeper, more critical evaluation was ongoing, that Jazzy was still very much on probation, her true mettle yet to be fully tested.

The financial aspect of her new life was as seductive as the lifestyle itself. The salary Tasha offered was astronomical compared to anything Jazzy had ever earned. Beyond that, there were the perquisites: the impeccably tailored clothing, access to exclusive events, and the subtle but constant reinforcement of her elevated status. These tangible rewards were designed to solidify her commitment, to bind her more tightly to Tasha's organization. They were also, Jazzy realized, a form of payment for something far more profound – her complicity, her loyalty, her willingness to operate within the shadowy confines of Tasha's ethical boundaries.

The contrast between the outward appearance of glamour and the underlying currents of manipulation was a constant source of internal conflict for Jazzy. She was being groomed to be a highly effective operative, a discreet facilitator within Tasha's intricate web of influence. The 'Swipe Right' app, she understood, was merely the visible tip of a much larger iceberg. Her role was to manage the unseen infrastructure, to cultivate the relationships, and to gather the intelligence that allowed Tasha's operations to flourish, often in ways that skirted the edges of legality and conventional morality.

Tasha's methods were insidious in their subtlety. She didn't issue overt commands; instead, she presented opportunities, framed as privileges. "I believe you'd be interested in attending the gala at the Bellagio tonight, Jazmine," she might say, her eyes holding Jazzy's. "It's an excellent opportunity to network with some of our key investors. Ensure you make a favorable impression." The expectation was implicit: Jazzy was not to attend as a guest, but as an agent, tasked with cultivating specific relationships, gathering intelligence, and subtly furthering Tasha's objectives. The lines between personal engagement and professional duty were meticulously blurred.

Jazzy found herself spending hours studying the profiles of individuals Tasha deemed important. She analyzed their public personas, their business dealings, their known associates, and any discernible vulnerabilities. This wasn't simple research; it was an act of dissecting lives, of identifying leverage points, of learning how to exploit desires and insecurities. The initial thrill of access and opportunity was slowly being replaced by a gnawing sense of unease. She was becoming a skilled architect of deception, her intellect and intuition now tools for manipulation.

Tasha's keen eye missed nothing. If Jazzy hesitated in a social interaction, if she failed to extract a crucial piece of information, Tasha would address it later, not with overt criticism, but with a subtle redirection, a re-framing of the objective. "Remember, Jazmine, our goal is not merely to be present, but to be *influential*," she would remind her, her voice smooth as polished glass. "Every interaction is an opportunity to solidify our position, to gather intelligence, to subtly guide outcomes." These private critiques were more potent than any public reprimand, designed to instill a sense of constant self-evaluation, a need to always perform at peak efficiency.

The opulence, while initially intoxicating, began to feel oppressive. The designer clothes felt like a costume, the lavish hotel suite a gilded cage. She was being systematically integrated into Tasha's world, her own identity slowly being subsumed by the demands of the organization. Tasha was not just an employer; she was a puppeteer, and Jazzy was a marionette, her strings being expertly manipulated. The true nature of the 'Swipe Right' empire, she was beginning to understand, was far more complex and far more dangerous than she could have ever imagined. It was a world built on secrets, on leverage, and on the careful cultivation of vulnerabilities, and Jazzy was rapidly becoming an indispensable part of its intricate, and morally ambiguous, machinery. Her susceptibility was being tested, not through overt pressure, but through the seductive allure of power, wealth, and belonging, a carefully calibrated strategy designed to ensure her complete assimilation into Tasha's vision. The labyrinth of deception was vast, and Jazzy had just taken her first, irreversible steps into its heart. She was learning to navigate the unspoken rules, the coded language, and the subtle power plays that defined this exclusive, and increasingly dangerous, ecosystem. The induction was not just about learning a job; it was about becoming part of a system, a system that demanded absolute discretion and an unwavering adherence to its complex, and often hidden, agenda.

The sheer scale of Tasha's operation was a revelation. 'Swipe Right' wasn't merely a platform for curated introductions; it was a sophisticated data-mining enterprise, a digital goldmine where personal lives were meticulously dissected, categorized, and leveraged. Jazzy, now immersed in the inner workings, began to see the app for what it truly was: a meticulously constructed facade, a honey trap designed to ensnare the powerful and the ambitious, extracting not just their desires, but their deepest secrets. Tasha's clients weren't simply seeking companionship or networking opportunities; they were unwittingly signing up to be observed, analyzed, and cataloged in a way that would make even the most seasoned intelligence agency blush.

The database, a sprawling, encrypted digital fortress, was the beating heart of Tasha's empire. It held the lifeblood of her influence, a compendium of power players meticulously charted for their every nuance. Jazzy found herself spending hours, then days, navigating its labyrinthine architecture. Each client profile was a dossier, a narrative woven from digital footprints, whispered confidences, and carefully observed behaviors. It was a chilling testament to the human desire for connection, twisted into a tool of unparalleled control. Here resided the titans of industry, their public faces carefully maintained, their private lives laid bare for Tasha's discerning gaze. There were the CEOs of multinational corporations, their strategic decisions documented, their financial vulnerabilities flagged. Beside them sat influential politicians, their voting records scrutinized, their extramarital affairs discreetly noted, their campaign finance loopholes meticulously identified. Even the artistic elite, the cultural arbiters of the city, found their creative processes, their patronage networks, and their personal peccadilloes archived.

The information wasn't simply collected; it was contextualized, analyzed, and cross-referenced. A client's preference for a particular vintage of wine might be linked to a business associate who owned the vineyard. A politician's stated stance on a controversial bill could be juxtaposed with private correspondence revealing a conflicting personal interest or a hidden debt. Jazzy saw how Tasha had built an intricate web of connections, not just between clients, but between their successes, their failures, their ambitions, and their deepest insecurities. This wasn't just information; it was ammunition.

One evening, while sifting through a particularly dense file, Jazzy stumbled upon a section labeled "Leverage Points." It was a chillingly clinical breakdown of each client's potential weaknesses, their soft underbellies exposed with brutal efficiency. For a prominent real estate magnate, the leverage point was a secret offshore account that facilitated tax evasion, a fact Jazzy had only learned through hushed rumors. For a rising political star, it was a clandestine affair with a rival's spouse, a dalliance that could shatter their meticulously crafted public image. Each entry was a potential dagger, waiting to be unsheathed.

Tasha, ever the conductor of this intricate symphony of data, would review these profiles with Jazzy, her insights as sharp as a scalpel. "Remember, Jazmine," she'd said, gesturing towards a particularly imposing photograph of a notoriously ruthless CEO, "he projects an image of absolute control, but his greatest fear is losing his public standing. A whisper about his company's declining market share, subtly amplified through the right channels, can be far more effective than any direct threat." It was a stark lesson in the power of suggestion, of exploiting perceived weaknesses to achieve desired outcomes.

The personal touches were often the most potent. The database didn't just record business dealings; it delved into the intimate details of people's lives. A client's phobia of heights might be noted, alongside their extensive travel itinerary, creating a subtle vulnerability for potential exploitation during a business trip. A deep-seated fear of public speaking could be cataloged, providing an opening for Tasha to subtly sabotage a client's upcoming presentation through misinformation or by orchestrating distractions. Jazzy realized with a growing sense of dread that Tasha wasn't just facilitating connections; she was building a comprehensive psychological profile of every individual who entered her orbit.

Malik's involvement, though initially presented as a partnership, began to cast a longer shadow. Jazzy observed the subtle shifts in Tasha's demeanor when discussing Malik's growing ambitions. Tasha was clearly intelligent, strategic, and possessed a formidable network, but Malik, Jazzy sensed, was a different breed of predator. His ambitions seemed less about curated influence and more about raw, unadulterated control. The database, Jazzy understood, was becoming his ultimate weapon, a reservoir of power he could tap into for purposes far removed from Tasha's calculated machinations.

There were instances where Malik's directives seemed to diverge from Tasha's carefully cultivated image of sophisticated discretion. Tasha might be focused on securing a favorable business deal for a client, while Malik would be interested in acquiring compromising information on a political opponent, regardless of the ethical implications or the potential collateral damage. Jazzy saw how Tasha, while undoubtedly ambitious, maintained a certain finesse, a strategic elegance in her dealings. Malik, on the other hand, was like a blunt instrument, his methods more direct, more forceful, and ultimately, more dangerous.

The database was the nexus where their differing objectives often clashed. Tasha would meticulously document a client's philanthropic efforts, aiming to build goodwill and long-term alliances. Malik, however, might see the same client's political donations as an opportunity to uncover quid pro quo arrangements or to identify vulnerabilities for blackmail. Jazzy found herself caught in the middle, privy to both Tasha's intricate strategies and Malik's increasingly aggressive agenda. The information she processed, the insights she gleaned, were no longer just tools for Tasha's curated network; they were becoming raw material for Malik's burgeoning power grab.

The sheer volume of data was staggering. Every communication, every interaction, every digital trace left by a client was captured and analyzed. Jazzy saw how Tasha's team, a faceless collection of analysts and researchers, worked tirelessly to maintain and expand this digital empire. They scrubbed public records, monitored social media, and utilized sophisticated algorithms to identify patterns and predict behavior. The result was a living, breathing organism of information, constantly evolving, constantly growing, and Tasha, with her unparalleled ability to interpret and deploy this data, was its undisputed sovereign.

The implications of this client list were profound. It wasn't just about knowing who was who; it was about understanding their motivations, their desires, their fears, and their connections. This intimate knowledge transformed Tasha from a simple facilitator into a master manipulator, capable of shaping events, influencing decisions, and ultimately, controlling outcomes. Jazzy began to grasp the true depth of Tasha's power, a power derived not from brute force or overt authority, but from the silent, insidious accumulation of knowledge.

The personal information, the seemingly innocuous details, were often the most valuable. A client's estranged relationship with a child could be subtly exploited to gain leverage over them. A past addiction, carefully concealed, could be brought to light at a strategically opportune moment. Jazzy saw how Tasha's operation had perfected the art of psychological warfare, using personal vulnerabilities as weapons in a high-stakes game of influence. The more Jazzy learned about the database, the more she understood the precarious position she occupied. She was not merely an employee; she was a guardian of secrets, a keeper of a trove of information that could make or break fortunes, careers, and even lives.

The ethical chasm widened with each passing day. Jazzy's initial fascination with the intricacies of Tasha's operation began to curdle into a deep-seated unease. She was privy to the dissection of human lives, the cataloging of weaknesses, and the subtle manipulation of desires. The 'Swipe Right' database was more than just a list of clients; it was a testament to the predatory nature of power, a chilling reminder that in Tasha's world, information was not just currency; it was control. And with Malik's growing influence, that control was becoming increasingly untethered, its ultimate destination shrouded in a dangerous ambiguity that promised to consume them all. The more she delved into the client list, the more she realized that she, too, was becoming a data point, her own vulnerabilities being assessed, her own loyalty being measured. The gilded cage was tightening its grip, and the true architects of her confinement were becoming terrifyingly clear. The intricate web spun by Tasha was designed to ensnare not just her clients, but anyone who dared to get too close to its heart. And Jazzy was now inextricably caught in its silken threads.

Malik's vision for the 'Swipe Right' data was a grotesque distortion of Tasha's meticulously cultivated enterprise. Where Tasha saw a sophisticated ecosystem of influence, a finely tuned instrument for shaping societal and corporate landscapes, Malik saw only raw, exploitable material. His ambition wasn't about wielding subtle power; it was about liquidating it, converting intimate knowledge into cold, hard cash and unrestrained leverage on the black market. Jazzy, observing the subtle shifts in Malik's directives and Tasha's increasingly strained responses, began to piece together the chilling scope of his true intentions. He wasn't interested in the long game of cultivating relationships or subtly nudging public opinion; he was a digital prospector, eager to strike gold by selling the most intimate secrets of the city's elite to the highest bidder, regardless of the consequences.

"He wants to weaponize everything," Tasha had confided in Jazzy, her voice a tight wire of frustration and concern, after a particularly tense meeting with Malik. "He's talking about auctioning off access to certain client profiles, creating bespoke disinformation campaigns for anyone willing to pay. It's... crude. And incredibly dangerous." Tasha, for all her own ethically dubious methods, operated with a certain degree of control, a strategic foresight that prioritized maintaining her own untouchability. Malik, however, seemed to relish the chaos his actions could unleash. His focus was on immediate profit, on turning the meticulously gathered data into a commodity that could be traded like illicit arms.

Jazzy had initially been drawn to Tasha's operation by the sheer audacity of it, the intellectual challenge of navigating such a complex system. But as Malik's influence grew, the ethical quandaries became impossible to ignore. She found herself cataloging not just the vulnerabilities of powerful figures, but the growing chasm between Tasha's calculated machinations and Malik's predatory greed. He envisioned 'Swipe Right' not as a discreet tool for power brokers, but as a vast, unregulated marketplace of secrets, where sensitive information – anything from a CEO's undisclosed offshore accounts to a politician's private indiscretions – would be bought and sold, creating a shadow economy of influence and blackmail.

Malik's approach was fundamentally different. While Tasha meticulously documented client preferences to facilitate introductions, Malik was already exploring ways to monetize those preferences on the dark web. He saw a client's stated interest in, say, rare art not as a personal passion, but as an entry point to understanding their financial capacity and potential for acquisition, information that could be sold to illicit art dealers or fence operations. A politician's voting record, which Tasha might analyze for strategic influence, Malik saw as a commodity to be traded to lobbyists or foreign entities seeking to manipulate policy. Jazzy's role, which had once felt like being privy to the inner workings of power, now felt like being an unwilling accomplice to its sale.

The internal friction between Tasha and Malik was palpable. Tasha's meticulously crafted image of sophisticated discretion was constantly at odds with Malik's increasingly aggressive and untidy methods. She tried to steer him towards a more controlled, strategic deployment of the data, emphasizing the long-term benefits of maintaining plausible deniability and safeguarding her own carefully constructed reputation. Malik, however, saw Tasha's caution as a weakness, an impediment to his own rapid ascent. He was impatient, his ambition a raw, untamed force that saw Tasha's ethical boundaries not as safeguards, but as obstacles to be bypassed.

"He doesn't understand that the real power lies in control, not in a fire sale," Tasha had explained to Jazzy, her frustration evident. "If we start openly peddling this information, we become just another data broker. We lose the mystique, the perceived exclusivity. We become predictable, and that's the fastest way to become irrelevant, or worse, targeted." Malik's vision was to turn the database into a commodity, something that could be traded, bought, and sold like any other good on the black market. Tasha, on the other hand, viewed the data as a lever, a tool to be used with surgical precision to exert influence and maintain her own position of power.

Jazzy was privy to the increasingly heated exchanges between them. Malik would dismiss Tasha's concerns with a wave of his hand, his eyes alight with the glint of acquisition. "Think of the capital, Tasha," he'd argue, his voice slick with persuasive charm. "We're sitting on a goldmine. Why limit ourselves? We can control markets, influence elections, bring down empires – all from the shadows, all anonymously. This isn't about subtle nudges; it's about seismic shifts." He saw the data as a weapon of mass disruption, a tool for wholesale societal engineering, and he was eager to unleash it.

The distinction was critical. Tasha's strategy was about creating and maintaining a sphere of influence. She leveraged the data to gain access, to build trust, and to subtly guide the actions of her clients, ensuring their continued reliance on her network and insights. Malik's agenda was more akin to a digital feudal lord, aiming to sell access to his vast informational fiefdom, granting licenses to exploit the data for various nefarious purposes. He envisioned creating tiers of access, premium packages for those who wanted to delve into specific sectors or target particular individuals, all while Tasha struggled to maintain a semblance of control over the information she had so painstakingly gathered.

The implications for Jazzy were deeply unsettling. She had become an integral part of Tasha's operation, privy to its deepest secrets. Now, she was witnessing the potential unraveling of that carefully constructed edifice, replaced by Malik's rapacious ambition. She found herself analyzing Malik's proposals with a growing sense of dread. He spoke of "data packets" for corporate espionage, "influence profiles" for political manipulation, and "compromise kits" for extortion. These were not the terms Tasha used. Tasha spoke of "strategic partnerships," "reputational management," and "discreet counsel." The language itself highlighted the fundamental divergence in their philosophies.

Malik's greed extended to every facet of the data. He wasn't just interested in the high-stakes profiles of CEOs and politicians; he saw potential in every byte. A client's online dating preferences could be sold to rival dating platforms for market analysis. A user's preferred streaming services could be used to target them with highly specific, potentially manipulative advertising. Even the metadata – the times of day a client was most active, their geographic locations, their device usage – was seen by Malik as valuable intel, ripe for exploitation by any number of shadowy actors. Tasha's vision of curated introductions and subtle influence was being overshadowed by Malik's desire for a complete data sell-off.

The pressure on Tasha was immense. Malik, with his aggressive tactics and seemingly boundless resources, was rapidly becoming the dominant force within their nascent partnership. He had a knack for leveraging existing relationships and making bold, often reckless, promises to potential buyers of the data. Tasha, while initially resistant, found herself increasingly pressured to accommodate his demands, fearing that any outright refusal would not only alienate him but also draw unwanted attention to the very existence of their vast data repository.

Jazzy observed Tasha's increasing weariness, the lines of stress deepening around her eyes. Tasha was a strategist, a player in a game of subtle power, and Malik was introducing a level of chaos and unpredictability that threatened to destabilize everything. She saw the database, once a testament to Tasha's genius, as a potential weapon that Malik intended to wield indiscriminately. He saw the data as a tool for disruption, a means to create chaos and profit from the ensuing fallout. Tasha, however, understood that true power came from controlled leverage, from maintaining a position of authority and influence, not from unleashing a data storm that could easily engulf its creators.

The conversations between Malik and Tasha, which Jazzy often overheard or was privy to through Tasha's hushed confidences, were increasingly strained. Malik would present elaborate spreadsheets detailing potential revenue streams from selling access to specific client segments, while Tasha would counter with projections of long-term influence and reputation management.

"Malik, selling targeted blackmail profiles to competing pharmaceutical companies will destroy our credibility," Tasha argued, her voice strained. "We'll be seen as mercenaries, and no one will trust us with anything sensitive again."

Malik scoffed, leaning back in his chair, a smug smile playing on his lips. "Credibility is a luxury, Tasha. Profit is a necessity. Besides, who are these 'trusting' clients? The ones already willing to pay for our services? They're not saints. They're players, just like us. And they'll pay handsomely for an edge, no matter how it's acquired." He saw the ethical considerations as mere roadblocks, impediments to maximizing profit.

Jazzy's own position became increasingly precarious. She was loyal to Tasha, respecting her strategic acumen and the almost artistic way she wielded information. But Malik's machinations were beginning to create a moral quagmire that even Tasha's carefully constructed ethical framework couldn't navigate. She began to see the vast database not just as a source of power, but as a ticking time bomb, its potential for destruction magnified by Malik's insatiable greed. He wasn't interested in building a network; he was interested in dismantling existing structures and rebuilding them in his own image, using the stolen secrets of the elite as his building blocks.

The data, for Malik, was a raw material to be refined and sold. For Tasha, it was a sophisticated tool for influence. This fundamental difference in perspective was the source of their escalating conflict, a conflict Jazzy was now intimately involved in. She found herself caught between Tasha's desire for controlled power and Malik's ambition for unrestrained financial gain, a dangerous middle ground where the true nature of their operation was being brutally redefined. Malik's vision was a descent into the digital underworld, a place where data was currency, and the highest bidder dictated the terms of engagement, regardless of the collateral damage. And as Tasha's control over her own creation began to slip, Jazzy feared they were all on the precipice of something far more dangerous than they could have imagined. The carefully curated world Tasha had built was fracturing under the weight of Malik's insatiable appetite for profit, threatening to unleash a torrent of chaos that would sweep them all away.

The sterile, beige walls of the precinct conference room did little to dampen the simmering unease that had settled over Detective Lena Cross. It was an occupational hazard, this constant dance on the precipice of the unknown, but lately, the music had been off-key, the rhythm jarring. Her assignment was simple, on paper: infiltrate the fringes of Tasha Petrova's opulent, shadowy world. But 'simple' was a word that had lost all meaning the moment she'd traded her badge for a fabricated identity, a carefully constructed facade designed to gain Tasha's – and by extension, Malik's – trust.

Lena's initial forays were tentative, like a diver testing the waters before plunging in. She'd adopted the persona of Anya Sharma, an ambitious young socialite with a penchant for expensive wine and even more expensive gossip, cultivating a presence at the exclusive charity galas and private auctions that served as Tasha's natural habitat. Each event was a minefield. A misplaced word, an overly familiar gesture, a flicker of recognition in her eyes – any of these could unravel the delicate tapestry of her disguise. Her handler, a grizzled veteran named Miller, had stressed the importance of patience, of allowing the target to become comfortable with her presence, of becoming a ghost in the machine, a whisper in the wind.

"Remember, Lena," Miller's voice had echoed in her earbud during her first few excursions, a low rumble of caution, "you're not just looking for evidence. You're looking for leverage. And sometimes, the deepest leverage isn't what they've done, but what they're afraid of being found out for." That advice gnawed at her, a constant reminder of the morally grey territory she was navigating. Was she any better than the criminals she was pursuing, using manipulation and deception to achieve her goals? The thought was a cold, unwelcome guest in the recesses of her mind.

Her first 'real' interaction with Tasha's inner circle occurred at a silent auction benefiting a local children's hospital, an event Tasha herself had sponsored. Lena, or Anya, as she was known, had positioned herself near the bar, nursing a glass of champagne, her eyes scanning the room with practiced casualness. Tasha, a vision in emerald silk, moved through the crowd with an aura of effortless command. Lena watched as Tasha engaged in hushed conversations, her laughter tinkling like distant chimes, her smile never quite reaching her eyes. There was a guardedness about her, a carefully maintained distance that intrigued Lena. Tasha wasn't just wealthy; she was a curator of influence, a puppeteer pulling strings with invisible threads.

It was during this event that Lena first encountered someone who would become a critical, albeit unwitting, pawn in her investigation: a man named Julian Vance. Vance was a well-connected art dealer, his reputation as robust as his collection of Renaissance sculptures. Tasha had a known interest in acquiring rare pieces, and Vance was a frequent guest at her private viewings. Lena saw an opportunity. She engineered a 'chance' encounter, feigning an amateurish interest in a particular abstract painting, using it as an opening to engage Vance in conversation.

"It's... striking, isn't it?" Lena had said, her voice light and a touch naive, gesturing towards the canvas. "I'm new to this scene, trying to understand what makes a piece truly valuable."

Vance, a man whose ego seemed to precede him, preened slightly. "Value, my dear Anya, is subjective, of course. But in this particular piece," he gestured with a flourish of his bejeweled hand, "you'll find a fascinating interplay of light and shadow, a subtle commentary on existential dread. It speaks to the soul, you see."

Lena played the part of the eager student, asking questions about provenance, about the artist's life, about the market for such works. As they spoke, she subtly steered the conversation towards Tasha, probing for any shared vulnerabilities or confidences Vance might have let slip. He spoke of Tasha with a mixture of admiration and subtle disdain, hinting at the ruthless pragmatism that lay beneath her polished exterior. "She's a formidable woman, Anya. Knows exactly what she wants, and rarely takes no for an answer. But then, who among us in this... circle... doesn't have their own particular brand of ambition?"

The conversation, while yielding little concrete evidence, was a crucial step. It confirmed Tasha's network, provided a potential avenue for future manipulation, and offered a glimpse into the subtle power dynamics at play. Lena meticulously cataloged every detail – Vance's nervous tic when discussing certain clients, the way his eyes flickered towards a particular security guard near Tasha, the almost imperceptible shift in his posture when Tasha herself passed by. These were the minutiae, the seemingly insignificant details, that could eventually paint the larger picture.

Her next move involved a more direct, yet still covert, approach. She learned, through careful monitoring of social media and discreet inquiries, that Tasha occasionally held informal 'strategy sessions' with a select few individuals at an exclusive, members-only lounge called 'The Obsidian Room.' Gaining access to such a place required more than just a fabricated invitation; it required a genuine, albeit manufactured, connection. Lena's investigation had unearthed a potential weakness in their security protocols – a vulnerability tied to their outsourced IT services, managed by a small, often overwhelmed firm that handled the digital needs of several high-profile establishments.

Lena, under the guise of Anya, sought out the firm's lead technician, a stressed-out coder named Kevin, who harbored a quiet resentment towards his more affluent clientele. She played on his ego, offering him a substantial sum of money – a portion of her 'discretionary fund' – to 'assist' her with a 'personal project' that involved 'accessing public databases' for 'research purposes.' The truth, of course, was far more sinister. She needed a temporary digital footprint, a ghost login that would allow her entry into the lounge's network, and potentially, a backdoor into Tasha's digital communications.

Kevin, blinded by the promised payday and flattered by the attention, readily agreed. He provided Lena with a burner phone and a set of encrypted credentials, warning her to be careful. "These places," he'd muttered, his fingers flying across a keyboard, "they guard their secrets like dragons guard gold. One wrong move, and you'll be toast."

Armed with this digital key, Lena secured a reservation at The Obsidian Room under a plausible alias, one connected to a minor but legitimate philanthropic foundation. The lounge itself was a study in understated luxury, all dark wood, plush velvet, and hushed conversations. The air thrummed with an almost palpable sense of exclusivity. Lena found a secluded booth, ordered a discreetly brewed herbal tea – her nerves already on edge – and began her observation.

Tasha was there, seated at a central table with a small group of individuals Lena recognized from various society pages and financial news outlets. Among them was a sharp-faced lawyer, known for brokering high-stakes corporate mergers, and a brooding, aristocratic man with a reputation for discreetly funding political campaigns. Their conversation was a low murmur, punctuated by bursts of laughter and the clinking of ice in glasses. Lena strained to catch snippets, her focus sharpened by adrenaline.

"The… situation… with the West Coast development is becoming untenable," the lawyer was saying, his voice a low growl. "Malik's approach is too… aggressive. It's drawing unwanted attention."

Tasha responded, her voice calm and measured. "Malik understands the need for decisive action. The market is volatile. We must be prepared to move swiftly."

Lena's heart quickened. This was it. The names, the operations, the internal friction she'd been tasked with uncovering. She subtly activated a miniature recording device concealed in her bracelet, hoping the ambient noise wouldn't drown out the crucial details. She watched as Tasha subtly controlled the flow of conversation, guiding it away from any potentially compromising topics, her every gesture deliberate and precise.

The presence of Malik was conspicuously absent from this particular gathering, a detail Lena logged. Was he deliberately excluded, or was his absence a testament to his own distinct sphere of influence, one that operated parallel to Tasha's curated world? The initial briefing had painted a picture of a volatile partnership, Tasha the strategist and Malik the enforcer, or perhaps, the shark. The more Lena saw, the more she understood the delicate balance they maintained, a balance Malik's aggressive nature seemed poised to shatter.

As the evening wore on, Lena managed another 'accidental' encounter, this time with the lawyer, a man named Sterling. She used the pretext of seeking advice on a potential investment, a thinly veiled attempt to gauge his own allegiances and his perception of Tasha's operation. Sterling, a man clearly accustomed to wielding power, was guarded but not entirely dismissive.

"Tasha Petrova is… unique," he said, swirling the amber liquid in his glass. "She has a remarkable ability to connect disparate elements, to create order from chaos. However," he paused, his eyes meeting Lena's with a flicker of something unreadable, "there are those who believe her methods, and the company she keeps, tread a very fine line indeed."

"The company she keeps?" Lena prompted, feigning innocent curiosity. "You mean Mr. Malik?"

Sterling offered a tight smile. "Mr. Malik operates on a different frequency, Ms. Sharma. Where Tasha builds, he… excavates. And sometimes, what he excavates is best left buried."

The veiled warning sent a shiver down Lena's spine. It confirmed that Malik was indeed the volatile element, the force pushing Tasha's operation into more dangerous waters. The 'Swipe Right' data, as it was known internally, was the source of their power, but also their greatest vulnerability. Malik's plan to monetize it on the black market, as Tasha had confessed to Jazzy, was a terrifying prospect, a potential explosion waiting to happen. Lena's mission wasn't just to expose Tasha; it was to understand the full extent of Malik's involvement and to prevent the catastrophic fallout that his unchecked ambition could unleash.

Her undercover role was proving to be more than just a logistical challenge; it was an ethical tightrope walk. The more she delved into Tasha's world, the more she encountered individuals who, while operating in morally questionable spheres, weren't necessarily outright criminals. Tasha herself, despite her dealings, seemed to possess a code, a certain finesse that Malik demonstrably lacked. Lena found herself questioning the simplistic black-and-white narrative the precinct had presented. Was Tasha a victim of Malik's rapaciousness, or a willing accomplice in a far grander scheme? The lines were blurring, and Lena had to tread even more carefully, lest she become so entangled in the deception that she lost sight of her own objective. Her own moral compass, honed by years on the force, felt increasingly disoriented in this labyrinth of half-truths and calculated omissions. She was playing a dangerous game, and the stakes were rising with every carefully chosen word, every feigned smile, every shared confidence. The shadow play had begun, and Lena found herself not just observing it, but actively participating, hoping to emerge from the darkness with the truth, untainted.

The air in Tasha Petrova's penthouse apartment was thick with the cloying scent of expensive perfume and the fainter, yet more pervasive, aroma of freshly cut lilies. For Jazzy, who had only a few weeks prior been navigating the grimy, predictable streets of her old neighborhood, it was an olfactory assault of pure, unadulterated luxury. She traced the rim of her crystal wine glass, the chilled condensation a stark contrast to the warmth that had begun to bloom within her, a slow, insidious unfurling of desire.

The life Tasha offered was a siren's song, a melody of glittering promises whispered directly into the ears of the discontented, and Jazzy found herself utterly, irrevocably captivated.

Initially, the thrill had been laced with a potent cocktail of fear and adrenaline. The clandestine meetings, the hushed conversations about illicit transactions, the sheer audacity of Tasha's operations – it had all felt like a dangerous game, a high-stakes gamble with her freedom as the ante. But Tasha, with her effortless charm and uncanny ability to make everyone feel seen, had woven a different narrative for Jazzy. She'd presented not a life of crime, but one of opportunity, of shrewd business acumen, of breaking free from the suffocating constraints of societal expectations. And Jazzy, with her sharp mind and a deep-seated yearning for something more than the suffocating mediocrity she'd always known, had readily bought into it.

She'd watched Tasha navigate the intricate dance of power with a grace that was both terrifying and intoxicating. The way Tasha commanded a room with a single glance, the respect – or perhaps more accurately, the *fear* – she elicited from even the most hardened individuals, it was a form of power Jazzy had only ever dreamt of wielding. Her own small apartment, a testament to her limited means and even more limited prospects, seemed to shrink in her memory, replaced by the vast, sweeping panoramas of the city visible from Tasha's floor-to-ceiling windows. The drab anonymity of her past life was being systematically erased, replaced by a vibrant, intoxicating new identity.

The financial independence Tasha had dangled before her was a powerful lure. No longer was Jazzy scrabbling for every dollar, pinching pennies, and sacrificing every small pleasure. Now, there were designer handbags, clothes that seemed to float on air, and the freedom to indulge in the spontaneous whims of a burgeoning appetite for the finer things. Tasha had secured her a small, but tastefully decorated, apartment in a prestigious building, a symbol of her growing importance within their clandestine circle. It was a gilded cage, perhaps, but it was undeniably beautiful.

"You look pensive, darling," Tasha's voice, a silken caress, cut through Jazzy's reverie. She was perched on the edge of a plush velvet chaise, a glass of champagne held loosely in her hand, her eyes, sharp and assessing, fixed on Jazzy.

Jazzy forced a smile, trying to mask the knot of conflicting emotions churning within her. "Just… admiring the view, Tasha. It's still so… surreal."

Tasha chuckled, a low, throaty sound. "Surreal is good, Jazzy. It means you're living, truly living. Not just existing." She gestured with her glass. "And you're doing so well. You've adapted beautifully. I'm proud of you."

The praise, so readily given, felt like a balm to Jazzy's soul. It was the validation she had craved for so long, the recognition that she was more than just another face in the crowd. She was becoming someone. Someone important. And the thought was both exhilarating and deeply unsettling.

The truth was, the initial fear had long since evaporated, replaced by a comfortable familiarity, then a burgeoning sense of entitlement. The danger, once a sharp, ever-present threat, had become a dull hum in the background, a necessary component of the exhilarating lifestyle. She'd started by assisting Tasha with basic administrative tasks, sorting through coded messages, and making discreet deliveries. But Tasha, recognizing Jazzy's intelligence and her growing loyalty, had begun to involve her in more significant aspects of their enterprise.

There was the incident with the offshore account, the one that needed to be meticulously untangled and restructured to deflect any prying eyes. Tasha had presented it as a complex puzzle, a test of Jazzy's financial acumen. Jazzy had spent three sleepless nights poring over spreadsheets, her mind a whirlwind of numbers and cryptic alphanumeric sequences, but she'd succeeded. The satisfaction of solving it, of seeing Tasha's genuine appreciation, had been more potent than any drug.

Then there were the introductions. Tasha had a knack for weaving Jazzy into her elite social circles, presenting her as a bright, ambitious protégée with a keen eye for emerging trends. Jazzy found herself attending exclusive parties, meeting influential people, and speaking with a confidence she never knew she possessed. She learned to navigate conversations with ease, to flatter when necessary, to subtly glean information without appearing overtly curious. Each successful interaction was another brick laid in the foundation of her new identity, solidifying her place within this glamorous, dangerous world.

However, beneath the veneer of opulence and the intoxicating rush of power, a subtle shift had occurred within Jazzy. The initial moral quandary – the nagging voice that whispered about the illegality and the inherent risks of their operation – had begun to fade, replaced by a pragmatic acceptance. She saw the people Tasha dealt with not as criminals, but as shrewd entrepreneurs, albeit ones operating outside the conventional boundaries. They were resourceful, daring, and undeniably successful. And in Jazzy's mind, success was the ultimate arbiter of morality.

She found herself envying Tasha's seemingly unshakeable conviction, her ability to operate with such ruthless efficiency. Tasha never seemed to doubt herself, never wavered in her pursuit of her goals. She was a force of nature, and Jazzy, increasingly, wanted to be a part of that force. The desire to be more than just a pawn, more than just a trusted assistant, began to take root. She wanted to understand the intricacies of the business, to contribute in a more substantial way, to truly become indispensable.

Her conversations with Tasha had become less about fetching coffee and more about strategizing. Jazzy found herself offering insights, questioning certain approaches, and even proposing alternative solutions. Tasha, to her credit, listened. She didn't dismiss Jazzy's ideas, but instead, dissected them, offered her own perspective, and sometimes, even incorporated them. This intellectual engagement, this feeling of being a valued contributor, was intoxicating. It was a far cry from the condescending pity or outright dismissal she had often faced in her previous life.

The allure of this new life wasn't just about the material possessions or the superficial glamour. It was about the sense of belonging, the feeling of being part of something significant, something that operated beyond the mundane realities of everyday life. She was no longer just Jazzy, the girl from the wrong side of the tracks. She was Jazzy, Tasha Petrova's confidante, her trusted ally, a woman of growing influence in her own right.

This perceived security, however, was a fragile illusion, a carefully constructed façade designed to mask the precariousness of their entire operation. The empire Tasha had built was a house of cards, precariously balanced, susceptible to the slightest gust of wind. And Jazzy, blinded by the dazzling allure of the life Tasha had provided, was becoming increasingly oblivious to the structural weaknesses. The attention she craved, the financial independence, the sense of belonging – these were the gilded bars of a cage that was slowly, imperceptibly, closing around her.

She had started to anticipate Tasha's needs, to learn the unspoken language of their clandestine world. She knew which coded phrases signified urgency, which gestures indicated danger, and which individuals were to be trusted implicitly. This immersion, this deepening understanding, felt like empowerment. It felt like evolution. But it also meant a growing detachment from her old life, from the values she had once held dear. Her friendships from her previous life had withered, unable to compete with the magnetic pull of Tasha's orbit. Her family, unaware of the true nature of her involvement, saw only her newfound success, their pride a sharp, almost painful contrast to the growing deception she harbored.

One evening, as they were reviewing a new shipment of high-end counterfeit goods destined for a discerning clientele, Jazzy voiced a concern that had been bothering her. "Tasha," she began, choosing her words carefully, "are we sure about this buyer? The details seem a little... loose. What if it's a sting operation?"

Tasha looked up from the ledger, her expression unreadable for a moment. Then, a slow smile spread across her lips. "You're thinking like a businessman now, Jazzy. That's good. But you need to learn to trust the process. And you need to trust *me*." She reached across the polished mahogany desk and placed a hand on Jazzy's, her touch surprisingly warm. "We've done our due diligence. This buyer is vetted. And even if, by some slim chance, there were complications, we have contingency plans for everything."

Jazzy felt a jolt of reassurance, mingled with a twinge of unease. Tasha's confidence was infectious, her reassurance almost absolute. Yet, the word "complications" hung in the air, a subtle reminder of the inherent risks. But then Tasha began to outline their next venture, a daring plan to infiltrate a rival organization, and Jazzy's anxieties were once again swept away by the sheer audacity and excitement of it all. The allure of the chase, the thrill of the strategic maneuver, the promise of even greater rewards – it was a powerful intoxicant.

She found herself adapting her mannerisms, her speech patterns, even her way of thinking, to mirror Tasha's. She adopted Tasha's quiet confidence, her analytical approach to problem-solving, and her pragmatic, almost detached, view of morality. The lines between Jazzy and Anya – the persona Lena Cross had created – were beginning to blur in Jazzy's own mind. She was no longer playing a role; she was becoming it. And the deeper she delved, the more secure she felt, mistaking the increasing complexity of her deception for genuine strength. The gilded cage, with its luxurious furnishings and seemingly endless comforts, was becoming her reality, and the thought of breaking free, of returning to her former life, was becoming increasingly alien, increasingly terrifying. The siren's song had become a lullaby, lulling her into a dangerous, blissful slumber.

3: The Price of Loyalty

The city lights, usually a dazzling panorama from Tasha's penthouse, seemed to hold a different kind of allure tonight. Jazzy, caught in the ambient glow, found herself replaying a recent conversation with Tasha. It wasn't about illicit deals or clandestine meetings; it was about Anya, a girl Tasha had taken under her wing not long ago. Anya, barely eighteen, was raw, her innocence a stark contrast to the hardened cynicism Jazzy herself was beginning to cultivate. Tasha had noticed Anya's vulnerability, the way her eyes flinched at the harsh realities of their world, and had taken swift, decisive action.

"She's too young for this, Jazzy," Tasha had said, her voice devoid of its usual businesslike sharpness, replaced by something softer, more protective. They were in Tasha's private study, the scent of aged leather and faint jasmine filling the air. "The clients… some of them, they see desperation, not a person. And Anya… she's radiating desperation like a beacon."

Jazzy had nodded, remembering Anya's trembling hands as she'd recounted a particularly unsettling encounter with a regular client, a man whose polite requests masked a predatory undertone. Jazzy had felt a flicker of her old self then, a pang of empathy for the girl's fear. But Tasha's reaction was different; it was a hardening, a resolve that Jazzy was only just beginning to understand.

"I've already made arrangements," Tasha continued, turning to face Jazzy fully. Her dark eyes, usually so calculating, held a glint of fierce determination. "Anya won't be seeing that particular client again. Ever." She paused, letting the weight of her words settle. "And I've assigned Elena to her. Elena's experienced, she knows how to handle these situations, how to de-escalate, how to shield."

Elena. Jazzy knew Elena by reputation. A quiet, no-nonsense woman who had been with Tasha for years, Elena was one of the few Tasha trusted implicitly, not just for her discretion, but for her unwavering loyalty and her ability to anticipate trouble before it even materialized. Elena was a protector, a silent guardian in a world that often devoured the unprotected.

"Elena will be her shadow," Tasha elaborated, her tone leaving no room for argument. "She'll be there for every booking, every interaction. If Anya so much as gets a bad vibe, Elena will intervene. No questions asked. She'll handle the client, smooth things over, make sure Anya is safe."

Jazzy felt a strange mix of relief and... something else. Envy, perhaps? Tasha's protective instincts, while admirable, were also a stark reminder of the precariousness of their own positions. While Tasha was actively shielding Anya, what about the rest of them? Jazzy, in particular, was navigating increasingly complex operations, venturing into territory that felt more volatile than the simple transactional exchanges of the early days.

"And what about... the other risks?" Jazzy ventured, thinking of the escalating pressure from rival factions, the whispers of investigations, the constant undercurrent of danger that seemed to be tightening its grip around their operation.

Tasha's gaze softened, a rare moment of vulnerability crossing her features. "That's where you come in, Jazzy." She rose from her chair and walked towards the expansive window, looking out at the glittering cityscape. "You're sharp. You see things I might miss. You're learning the business, and you're learning it fast. I need you to be my eyes and ears, not just in the deals, but for the people too."

She turned back, her expression serious. "If you see anything that feels off, anything that makes you uncomfortable, about a client, about a situation, about another girl... you tell me. Immediately. Don't try to handle it yourself. Don't try to be a hero. Just report it." Tasha walked back to her desk, picking up a small, intricately carved wooden bird. "Think of it like this, Jazzy: Anya has Elena. The rest of us... we have each other. And we have me. But I can't be everywhere at once. I need you to be my early warning system."

The weight of Tasha's words settled heavily on Jazzy. It was a responsibility, a trust, that felt both flattering and terrifying. It was a tacit acknowledgment that Jazzy was no longer just an apprentice, but a vital part of the inner circle, a stakeholder in their collective survival.

This wasn't just about managing assets or executing transactions; it was about safeguarding lives within their particular ecosystem. Tasha, despite her ruthlessness in business, possessed a fiercely protective streak for the women who served her. It wasn't a sentimental, overbearing protection, but a pragmatic, almost territorial one. She saw them not as disposable commodities, but as assets that needed to be maintained, secured, and, when necessary, defended.

Jazzy recalled another instance, a few weeks prior, when a high-profile client, known for his volatile temper and entitled demands, had become overly aggressive with one of the newer girls, a timid woman named Chloe. Chloe had been visibly shaken, her composure fracturing under his unwanted advances. Jazzy had been present, observing the scene unfold with a growing sense of unease. Before Jazzy could even decide how to intervene, Tasha had glided into the room, her presence commanding immediate attention.

"Mr. Sterling," Tasha had said, her voice smooth as silk, yet with an undercurrent of steel that brooked no defiance. "I believe our agreement was for a professional service, not... personal commentary. Chloe is one of my most valued associates, and I expect her to be treated with the utmost respect." Her eyes, dark and unwavering, had met Sterling's, pinning him in place. "Perhaps if you're finding it difficult to maintain your decorum, it would be best if we concluded our arrangement for the evening."

Sterling, a man accustomed to dictating terms, had been taken aback. He stammered an apology, his bluster deflating under Tasha's steely gaze. Tasha hadn't needed to raise her voice or resort to threats. Her quiet authority, her unwavering control, was enough. She had then turned to Chloe, offering a brief, reassuring nod before escorting Sterling out herself, ensuring he left the premises without further incident.

Later that evening, Tasha had found Chloe in her dressing room, still trembling. Instead of reprimanding her for attracting the client's ire, Tasha had simply sat beside her, placing a comforting hand on her shoulder. "It's not your fault, my dear," she had said, her voice low and soothing. "Some men are simply... unpleasant. But you are not to blame. You did nothing wrong." She had then pulled out a small, velvet pouch. "This is for you. A little something to remind you of your worth. And remember, if anyone ever makes you feel uncomfortable again, you come to me, or to Jazzy, or to Elena. We are your shield."

The pouch contained a delicate diamond bracelet, its sparkle a stark contrast to Chloe's tear-streaked face. It was a gesture of immense generosity, a tangible reassurance that their safety and well-being were Tasha's priority. It wasn't just about business for Tasha; it was about building a loyalty that ran deeper than mere financial transaction. She understood that in their world, where vulnerability was often exploited, creating a safe haven, however fragile, was paramount.

Jazzy herself had experienced Tasha's protective instincts firsthand. Shortly after joining, she had been tasked with delivering a package to a dimly lit bar in a less reputable part of the city. The instructions had been clear: be discreet, be quick, and under no circumstances engage with anyone outside the transaction. As Jazzy made her way through the crowded, noisy bar, a burly man blocked her path, his intentions clearly unwelcome. Jazzy's heart had hammered against her ribs; she was completely out of her depth. Before she could even formulate a response, Tasha's voice, a calm, resonant tone that cut through the cacophony, had boomed from across the room.

"Jazzy, darling, a moment!" Tasha had called out, her eyes locking with Jazzy's. She had then turned to the man who was accosting Jazzy, her expression unreadable. "Excuse me, sir," Tasha had said, her voice polite but firm, "you're in my way. My associate and I have business to attend to." The man, recognizing Tasha's authority and the implicit threat in her words, had immediately stepped aside, mumbling an apology.

Tasha had then approached Jazzy, her gaze sweeping over her, assessing. "Are you alright?" she had asked, her tone laced with concern. "You look a little pale. Perhaps this particular delivery was too much for your first solo run." She had then taken the package from Jazzy, a subtle assertion of control. "Let me handle this. You wait for me outside. And Jazzy," she had added, her eyes holding Jazzy's, "if you ever feel unsafe, even for a second, you walk away. You come straight to me. That's an order. Your safety is non-negotiable."

This wasn't just about managing risk for the business; it was about managing risk for the individuals within it. Tasha cultivated loyalty not through fear alone, but through a careful balance of power and protection. She was a strategist, a negotiator, a manipulator, yes, but she was also, in her own complex way, a guardian. She understood that the loyalty of her associates was directly proportional to their belief that she would protect them when the wolves came calling.

The incidents with Anya, Chloe, and even Jazzy herself weren't isolated acts of kindness. They were calculated displays of leadership, designed to reinforce the unspoken contract between Tasha and the women she employed. By demonstrating her willingness to shield them from the worst excesses of their clientele and the inherent dangers of their profession, Tasha solidified her position as more than just a boss; she became a figure of maternalistic authority, a powerful matriarch in a world that often treated women as disposable.

This maternal instinct wasn't about coddling or weakness. It was a strategic imperative. A protected asset was a reliable asset. A loyal associate was an asset that wouldn't betray her when the heat was on. Tasha understood that fostering an environment where her associates felt valued and, crucially, *safe*, was essential for the long-term stability of her empire. It was about creating a family, albeit a dysfunctional and morally compromised one, bound by mutual interest and Tasha's unwavering, and often fierce, protection. Jazzy was beginning to understand that the price of loyalty, for Tasha, was not just adherence to her rules, but the assurance of her unwavering shield. And in this dangerous, glittering world, that shield was the most valuable commodity of all. It was the promise that even when the predators circled, there was one person who would fight to keep them at bay. This understanding deepened Jazzy's own commitment, not just to Tasha, but to the precarious safety Tasha provided for all of them. It was a dangerous game, but for the first time, Jazzy felt a sense of belonging, a feeling that she wasn't entirely alone against the encroaching darkness. Tasha's protection was a silent, powerful force, a testament to her complex, formidable leadership, and Jazzy found herself increasingly reliant on its reassuring, albeit dangerous, embrace.

Malik's ambition wasn't merely a personal quest for wealth; it was a hunger that gnawed at the very foundations of their carefully constructed world. His latest foray into acquisitions wasn't about acquiring new territories for Tasha, but for himself, carving out personal fiefdoms within their shared enterprise. He began by discreetly acquiring underperforming clubs and lounges on the city's periphery, places where the clientele was rougher, the deals shadier, and the oversight minimal. These weren't the gilded establishments Tasha favored, the ones that projected an image of sophisticated indulgence. Malik was delving into the city's underbelly, a place Tasha had meticulously avoided for years, deeming it too volatile, too unpredictable, and most importantly, too lacking in the discerning clientele that funded their more refined operations.

His justification, when questioned by Tasha through intermediaries, was always couched in terms of "diversification" and "reaching new markets." But Tasha, with her keen eye for deception, saw the naked self-interest behind his pronouncements. These were not strategic moves that benefited the collective; they were calculated gambits to build his own independent power base, leveraging resources that rightfully belonged to their shared venture. He was a cancer, subtly metastasizing, and Tasha felt the insidious spread of his influence with a growing sense of dread.

The new faces Malik began to introduce were a testament to his escalating recklessness. These weren't the polished, discreet professionals Tasha vetted with painstaking care. They were men with eyes that glinted with a predatory hunger, their smiles too wide, their laughter too coarse. One, a bulking brute named Silas, with a scarred face and a perpetual scowl, seemed to relish intimidation. He spoke in clipped, guttural sentences, his presence alone radiating a palpable sense of threat. Malik had brought him in to "manage security" at one of his newly acquired establishments, but Tasha recognized the type instantly: a hired thug, brought in to enforce Malik's will through fear, not diplomacy.

Another addition was a wiry, twitchy individual named Vinnie, whose fingers were perpetually stained with ink, suggesting a history of forged documents and illicit paperwork. Vinnie moved with a nervous energy, his eyes darting around constantly, as if expecting trouble at every turn. Malik described him as a "financial consultant," but Tasha's instincts screamed otherwise. Vinnie reeked of desperation and the kind of illicit dealings that attracted the wrong kind of attention, the kind that brought down law enforcement like a swarm of locusts. He was the sort of man who dealt in whispers and shadows, a purveyor of untraceable transactions, and his presence was an open invitation to scrutiny.

The ripple effects of Malik's actions were swift and undeniable. Jazzy, tasked with overseeing a new, more discreet courier service Tasha was developing – a service designed to handle sensitive information and high-value items without attracting undue attention – found herself increasingly entangled in the fallout. Malik, seeing this as another opportunity for expansion, had begun rerouting some of his less savory transactions through Jazzy's network. He'd used his newfound influence to subtly pressure her, implying that cooperation was expected, that her loyalty to Tasha should extend to facilitating his personal ventures.

One particular incident stood out with chilling clarity. Jazzy had been assigned a delivery to a private party hosted by a notoriously corrupt politician, a man known for his insatiable appetites and his connections to organized crime. The package was innocuous, a seemingly ordinary encrypted data drive. However, the instructions were explicit: the delivery had to be made directly into the hands of the politician's personal aide, a man whose reputation for cruelty preceded him. As Jazzy approached the heavily guarded estate, she noticed Silas and two of his associates loitering near the entrance, their presence an overt show of force, an unspoken message that this was Malik's territory now.

When Jazzy presented the package, the aide, a man with cold, reptilian eyes, demanded to see its contents. Jazzy refused, adhering to Tasha's strict protocols regarding package integrity. A tense standoff ensued, the aide's hand inching towards a concealed weapon. It was then that Silas stepped forward, a menacing grin splitting his scarred face. "Malik sent us," he growled, his voice a low rumble of menace. "He says you're part of the family. And family looks after family." He nudged Jazzy forward, his rough hand gripping her arm. "Now, you let us see what you've got, or things get messy. Malik's orders."

Jazzy felt a surge of pure terror, a primal instinct screaming at her to flee. This wasn't the calculated risk Tasha usually managed; this was brute force, an intimidation tactic designed to assert Malik's control, not just over her, but over Tasha's operation. The aide, mollified by Silas's presence and Malik's apparent endorsement, reluctantly accepted the drive. But the encounter left Jazzy deeply shaken. Malik was no longer content to work within Tasha's framework; he was actively undermining it, using her operatives as pawns in his own escalating game.

Tasha, upon hearing of the incident from a distraught Jazzy, was incensed. The intrusion into her courier service, the blatant disregard for her established protocols, and the use of her personnel for Malik's dubious dealings were acts of outright defiance. The introduction of Silas and Vinnie into their network, men Tasha would never have sanctioned, was an insult to her authority. She confronted Malik directly, a rare occurrence that spoke volumes of her displeasure.

Their meeting took place in Tasha's private study, the air thick with unspoken animosity. The ornate room, usually a sanctuary of calm deliberation, felt charged with tension. Malik, sprawled carelessly on an antique chaise lounge, exuded an air of smug defiance.

"Silas and Vinnie are… necessary assets, Tasha," Malik began, his tone dismissive of her concerns. "They handle the… less delicate aspects of expansion. You can't expect to grow without getting your hands a little dirty."

Tasha's gaze, usually a calm, assessing blue, was now a glacial Arctic ice. "My hands have always been clean, Malik, and so have yours, by my design. Your 'expansion' is a reckless pursuit that jeopardizes everything we've built. You're bringing a level of violence and unpredictability into our operations that I will not tolerate."

"Tolerance isn't going to keep us on top, Tasha," Malik retorted, a smirk playing on his lips. "Ruthlessness is. And I'm willing to be ruthless. These new ventures, they're mine. I'm simply utilizing the resources we have available."

"Resources that are meant for *our* collective success, Malik, not for your personal empire-building," Tasha countered, her voice dangerously low. "You're crossing a line. You're bringing in men who represent a threat not only to our operations, but to the safety of the women who work for us. Anya, Jazzy, the others – they are under my protection. And your associates are a direct threat to that protection."

Malik laughed, a harsh, grating sound. "Protection? Tasha, you're running a business, not a charity. These girls understand the risks. If they can't handle a little… roughhousing, perhaps they're not cut out for this world."

The casual cruelty in his words struck Tasha like a physical blow. It was a stark betrayal of the protective ethos she had so carefully cultivated. Her reputation, her entire operation, was built on a foundation of trust and the assurance of safety for those under her wing. Malik's disregard for this was not just a business disagreement; it was a fundamental philosophical clash.

"Get out, Malik," Tasha said, her voice barely a whisper, but carrying an authority that brooked no argument. "You have until the end of the week to divest yourself of any interests that encroach on my operations. And Silas, Vinnie, and anyone else you've brought into my sphere of influence are to be removed. If you fail to comply, I will ensure you have no sphere of influence left."

Malik's eyes narrowed, his casual demeanor replaced by a flicker of genuine anger. He rose from the chaise lounge, straightening his impeccably tailored suit. "You think you can dictate terms to me, Tasha? I've been a part of this from the beginning. I've taken risks you wouldn't dream of."

"And you've become greedy and careless," Tasha stated, her gaze unwavering. "Your ambition has blinded you to the consequences. You're no longer an asset, Malik. You're a liability. And I don't keep liabilities."

Malik sneered, a venomous glint in his eyes. "We'll see about that, Tasha. We'll see who's the liability." He turned and walked towards the door, his exit as aggressive as his presence. The silence he left behind was deafening, punctuated only by the distant hum of the city, a city Tasha now feared Malik's escalating recklessness was slowly but surely corrupting from the inside out. The delicate balance of their partnership was irrevocably fractured, and Tasha knew, with a chilling certainty, that Malik's escalation was just the beginning of a far more dangerous game. The price of loyalty, she realized, was no longer just about her own unwavering commitment; it was about defending her people from the very partners she had once trusted. And that, she suspected, would come at a far steeper cost than she had ever anticipated. The whispers of Malik's expansion were no longer just whispers; they were the prelude to a storm, and Tasha found herself bracing for the inevitable tempest. The introduction of Silas and Vinnie was more than just a personnel change; it was a declaration of war, a brutal and explicit statement of Malik's intent to seize control, regardless of the collateral damage. Tasha understood that Malik's ambition wasn't confined to acquiring assets; it was about dismantling her carefully crafted order and rebuilding it in his own image, an image that prioritized brute force and unchecked greed over the nuanced strategies and protective measures she had so meticulously implemented. The mere presence of Silas at Jazzy's delivery was a blatant violation of Tasha's territorial integrity, a forceful assertion that Malik was no longer content to operate within the established boundaries. He was actively seeking to erode them, to infiltrate and corrupt every facet of her operation, starting with the very couriers Tasha relied on for discreet and secure transactions. The data drive Jazzy was carrying, while seemingly innocuous, represented a critical piece of intelligence, and Malik's intervention, his veiled threats through Silas, was an attempt to gain leverage, to insert himself into Tasha's most sensitive operations. The fact that Jazzy, one of Tasha's most trusted operatives, was subjected to such intimidation was an unforgivable transgression. It wasn't just about the package; it was about the message Malik was sending, a message that Tasha's control was weakening, and his own was ascendant.

The introduction of Vinnie, with his shadowy reputation and evident connections to illicit financial dealings, further amplified Tasha's concerns. Vinnie represented a different, yet equally dangerous, facet of Malik's expansion: the infiltration of their network by individuals who operated outside the realm of legitimate finance and attracted the unwelcome scrutiny of law enforcement. Tasha's business, while operating in a morally gray area, had always strived for a degree of discretion and compartmentalization that kept the more aggressive elements of the underworld at bay. Vinnie's presence threatened to shatter that delicate insulation, to draw unwanted attention to their operations like a moth to a flame. Malik's insistence on classifying Vinnie as a "financial consultant" was a transparent attempt to legitimize a clear liability, and Tasha saw through the charade with immediate clarity. She understood that Vinnie's expertise lay not in strategic financial planning, but in the obfuscation of funds, the laundering of illicit gains, and the creation of complex financial webs that could easily ensnare anyone caught within them. The risk of detection, of attracting the attention of federal agencies or rival organizations that preyed on such vulnerabilities, was astronomically high. Malik's willingness to embrace such a risk, to bring Vinnie into their fold, demonstrated a profound lack of foresight and a disturbing disregard for the long-term stability of their enterprise. Tasha's confrontation with Malik was not merely a business dispute; it was a battle for the soul of their organization. His casual dismissal of the women under her care, his assertion that their vulnerability was a weakness rather than a concern to be addressed, revealed a chasm in their fundamental values. Tasha viewed the protection of her associates as paramount, a non-negotiable aspect of her leadership. Malik, on the other hand, saw them as disposable assets, easily replaceable cogs in his relentless pursuit of profit. This fundamental difference in perspective made their partnership increasingly untenable. Malik's ambition was no longer about shared growth; it was about dominance, about supplanting Tasha and reshaping their operation in his own image, an image characterized by recklessness and a callous disregard for human welfare. The ultimatum Tasha issued was not born of anger, but of necessity. She recognized that Malik's current trajectory posed an existential threat to everything she had built. His continued presence, his unchecked expansion, would inevitably lead to their downfall, either through direct confrontation with rivals, exposure by law enforcement, or the erosion of loyalty from within her own ranks. The introduction of Silas and Vinnie was the final straw, the tangible evidence of Malik's defiance and his intention to operate independently, using Tasha's resources for his own gain. The expulsion of these individuals, and a complete divestment of Malik's encroaching interests, was Tasha's attempt to salvage what remained of their enterprise, to reassert her authority and protect her people from the corrosive influence of Malik's ambition. However, Malik's defiant retort, his assertion that he too had been a foundational element and had taken risks, indicated that he would not capitly concede. The threat that he would actively work to undermine Tasha, to demonstrate her own perceived weakness, was a chilling omen. Tasha understood that the days of subtle maneuvering were over. Malik's escalation had forced her hand, transforming a business partnership into a direct, and potentially violent, conflict. The price of loyalty, once a concept she believed she understood within the confines of their shared ambition, had transformed into a much more dangerous and personal battle for survival. The question of who was truly the liability now hung heavy in the air, a harbinger of the inevitable confrontation that lay ahead. The city lights outside Tasha's window, once a symbol of opportunity and allure, now seemed to cast long, ominous shadows, mirroring the darkness that Malik's actions had injected into their world.

The sterile scent of the precinct, usually a comfort in its predictable order, now felt like a suffocating shroud for Detective Maya Cross. Each fluorescent hum, each muffled shout from down the hall, served as a stark reminder of her precarious position. Her investigation into the encroaching influence of Malik, and by extension, the deep-seated corruption Tasha's empire was beginning to attract, was no longer a detached pursuit of justice; it was a personal crusade, fraught with the kind of moral compromises she'd sworn to avoid. The synopsis hinted at a entanglement, a personal connection that had her walking a tightrope over an abyss of her own making.

Her informant, a jittery low-level bookie named Frankie "Fingers" Malone, fidgeted across the grimy diner table, his eyes darting around the sparse lunchtime crowd as if anticipating an ambush. Frankie's usual bravado was laced with a new, palpable fear. "They're watching, Maya," he whispered, his voice raspy from disuse and anxiety. "Malik's boys. Silas, that... animal. They're everywhere now. Not just the clubs anymore. They're sniffing around the docks, the warehouses... places that ain't got nothin' to do with Tasha's fancy nightlife."

Maya nodded, her jaw tight. She'd heard similar whispers from other sources, fragmented reports of Malik's newfound reach extending into areas previously considered neutral territory, even for Tasha's more overt operations. This wasn't diversification; it was an aggressive land grab, and Silas, the hulking enforcer Malik had brought in, was the blunt instrument of this expansion. "What kind of 'sniffing around,' Frankie? What are they looking for?"

Frankie picked at a loose thread on his stained jacket. "Information, mostly. Shipping manifests. Delivery schedules. Anything that looks... important. Like they're trying to map out how everything moves. And they ain't asking nicely. Heard one of Vinnie's guys roughed up a dockworker last week, just for looking suspicious. Vinnie's the money man, right? The one with the shifty eyes and the fast fingers?"

The mention of Vinnie sent a prickle of unease down Maya's spine. Vinnie, the purported "financial consultant," was Tasha's blind spot, the one Malik had successfully injected into their operations with minimal resistance from Tasha herself, at least initially. If Vinnie was now directing muscle to gather intelligence on logistical movements, it meant Malik was meticulously dissecting Tasha's operational infrastructure, not just acquiring peripheral assets. This was about intelligence gathering, about identifying vulnerabilities, and Maya suspected Malik's ultimate goal was far more insidious than mere financial enrichment. He was positioning himself to seize control, and Vinnie's role in this was to provide the financial scaffolding for such a takeover, likely through illicit means.

"They're looking for weak points, Frankie," Maya said, her gaze never leaving Frankie's. "For ways to disrupt things. Or worse, to control them. Have you seen Silas yourself?"

"Not up close," Frankie admitted, swallowing hard. "Just seen him from a distance. Big. Scarred. Looks like he eats nails for breakfast. And he's always got a couple of those street thugs with him. The kind who don't ask questions, just do. Malik's really outgrown his leash, hasn't he?"

The question hung in the air, heavy with unspoken implications. Frankie, like many others caught in the periphery of Tasha's sprawling network, was becoming increasingly aware of the shifting power dynamics. Malik's ambition had undoubtedly fractured the carefully maintained equilibrium. Maya knew that the closer she got to Malik's new operations, the greater the risk. Her own compromised position, her unconventional methods to infiltrate this world, meant that any slip-up, any misstep, could have catastrophic consequences.

Later that day, Maya found herself navigating the labyrinthine corridors of the city's financial district, a stark contrast to the grimy diner. Her objective: Vinnie's supposed "office," a nondescript suite of rooms in a building that exuded an air of discreet wealth, the kind that often masked less savory activities. Her clearance was limited, her access heavily scrutinized. She was operating under the guise of a financial auditor, a role that allowed her to ask questions without immediately raising red flags, but one that also required a delicate dance, a constant performance of plausible deniability.

The receptionist, a woman with an unnervingly placid expression and eyes that seemed to miss nothing, greeted Maya with a polite, yet distant, smile. "May I help you?"

"Detective Maya Cross, City PD. I'm here to see Mr. Vinnie Moretti regarding a routine inquiry into some recent... transactional irregularities," Maya stated, her voice calm and measured, betraying none of the tension coiling in her gut.

The receptionist's smile didn't falter, but her fingers hovered over her keyboard, a subtle shift in her posture betraying a flicker of concern. "Mr. Moretti is currently in a meeting. May I take a message, or perhaps schedule an appointment for you?"

"I believe this requires immediate attention," Maya pressed, her tone hardening slightly. "It pertains to financial activity that could have broader implications." She let the ambiguity of her statement hang in the air, a subtle threat wrapped in bureaucratic jargon.

The receptionist's gaze flickered to a small, discreet camera above Maya's head before returning to her screen. "One moment, please." She tapped a few keys, then spoke into a small microphone. A few terse words, a name, and Maya knew her presence had been registered, her identity verified. The clock was ticking. The more attention she drew, the more vulnerable she became.

A few minutes later, a man emerged from a frosted glass door, his movements sharp and jerky. Vinnie. He was exactly as Frankie had described: wiry, with a nervous energy that seemed to vibrate off him. His fingers, indeed stained with a faint, inky residue, tapped incessantly against his thigh as he approached. His eyes, a muddy brown, darted between Maya and the receptionist, a constant assessment of his surroundings.

"Detective Cross, is it?" Vinnie's voice was thin, reedy, and carried a hint of an accent Maya couldn't quite place, but it was the nervous energy that was most striking. He exuded an aura of someone perpetually on the verge of being caught. "What can I do for you? I assure you, my financial dealings are impeccably… clean." The last word was spoken with a slight upward inflection, as if seeking confirmation rather than offering it.

"I'm looking into some transactions that have crossed our desk, Mr. Moretti," Maya began, stepping into the corridor and signaling with a subtle tilt of her head that they should speak away from the receptionist's earshot. "Specifically, those involving certain… peripheral businesses that have recently changed hands. Businesses with ties to your client, Mr. Malik."

Vinnie's eyes narrowed, a flicker of something akin to panic darting behind their shifty surface. "Malik? I handle a variety of clients. I'm a financial consultant. My work is confidential." He glanced back towards the receptionist, a silent plea for discretion.

"Confidentiality is important," Maya agreed, her voice dropping to a conspiratorial whisper. "But so is legality. We've received information that suggests some of these recent acquisitions may have been financed through… less than conventional means. Means that could attract the attention of regulatory bodies. And perhaps, other less savory elements who might be interested in exploiting such vulnerabilities." She watched his reaction closely. The mention of "other less savory elements" was a deliberate gambit, designed to play on his inherent paranoia and his likely knowledge of the darker underbelly of illicit finance.

Vinnie's Adam's apple bobbed. He licked his thin lips. "I… I don't know what you're talking about. My clients' business is their business." He started to turn away, his twitchy energy escalating.

"Mr. Moretti," Maya said, her voice cutting through his attempt to disengage. "I'm not here to audit your clients' private lives. I'm here about the paperwork. The channels through which the funds flowed. There are certain… anomalies. Transfers that appear to have been routed through shell corporations with no discernible assets. And more concerningly, a recent influx of untraceable capital into accounts that were previously dormant. This kind of activity, especially if linked to organized crime, is a serious concern for us." She was fabricating details, weaving a narrative of an investigation that was already well underway, hoping to spook him into revealing something crucial.

Vinnie visibly paled. His fingers stilled their incessant tapping, replaced by a frantic fiddling with the cuff of his shirt. "Shell corporations? Untraceable capital? I... I can't discuss client accounts, Detective. That's illegal."

"Is it illegal to ensure your clients are operating within the bounds of the law, Mr. Moretti?" Maya countered, stepping closer. The air between them crackled with unspoken tension. She could feel his fear, a potent, almost tangible thing. It was the smell of desperation, and it was her most valuable tool. "Because if Mr. Malik is involved in anything that puts his – and by extension, your – operations at risk, I'd hate for you to be caught in the crossfire. Especially when your name is on the dotted line, facilitating these... irregularities."

He flinched at the mention of his name being "on the dotted line." It was a confirmation, however subtle, that he was deeply enmeshed in whatever Malik was orchestrating. "I... I need to speak with Mr. Malik," Vinnie stammered, his eyes wide with a newfound alarm. "He'll... he'll want to know about this."

"I'm sure he will," Maya said, a small, grim smile touching her lips. "But first, I need to understand your role in all this. Who's been moving the money, Mr. Moretti? And where is it going?"

The pressure was building, not just from her superiors who were implicitly aware of her investigation, but from the very nature of her entanglement. The synopsis hinted at something more personal, a connection that made this investigation far more than just a professional duty. It was a vulnerability, a potential leverage point that could be used against her, and she knew it. This personal stake made every decision, every interaction, exponentially more dangerous. She was not just risking her career; she was risking something far more profound, something she was determined to protect, even if it meant blurring the lines of her own carefully constructed morality.

Her next move was a calculated risk. Tasha, despite her growing unease with Malik's actions, remained a powerful force, and Maya knew that Tasha's cooperation, however reluctant, would be invaluable. But approaching Tasha directly was a diplomatic minefield. Tasha operated on a different plane, her world one of calculated risks and carefully guarded secrets, a world Maya had only ever glimpsed from the outside.

Maya arranged a meeting through a series of discreet channels, a clandestine encounter in a neutral, public space – a quiet art gallery on a rainy Tuesday afternoon. The hushed atmosphere, the abstract splashes of color on the walls, provided a thin veneer of normalcy for what was essentially a high-stakes negotiation. Tasha arrived precisely on time, her presence commanding, her composure unruffled by the downpour outside. She moved with an elegance that belied the ruthless nature of her business, her sharp eyes scanning the room before settling on Maya.

"Detective Cross," Tasha acknowledged, her voice a low, melodious contralto. There was no warmth in her tone, only a cool assessment. "You requested this meeting."

"Ms. Thorne," Maya replied, stepping forward. "Thank you for agreeing to meet. I believe we have a mutual interest in… understanding recent developments within your organization."

Tasha's gaze flickered, a subtle tightening around her eyes. "I'm not certain I understand your meaning."

"Malik," Maya stated plainly, cutting through the pretense. "His recent acquisitions. The new personnel he's brought on board. Silas, Vinnie. These are not your usual associates, Ms. Thorne. They represent a significant deviation from your established protocols. A deviation that's drawing a considerable amount of unwanted attention."

A beat of silence stretched between them, thick with unspoken tension. Tasha's composure remained, but Maya detected a subtle shift, a flicker of something that could be concern, or perhaps just annoyance. "Malik operates independently within certain parameters," Tasha replied, her voice carefully neutral. "His ventures are his own, though I expect them to adhere to our overarching principles of discretion."

"His ventures are starting to bleed into yours, Ms. Thorne," Maya pressed, her voice firm. "I have sources indicating that his new operations are impacting your courier services. That his associates are attempting to leverage your infrastructure. And the individuals he's brought in… they operate with a level of brutality that is antithetical to everything you've built." Maya decided to introduce the personal element, the aspect hinted at in the synopsis, carefully. "And I'm also aware that these individuals, particularly Silas, have a reputation for… enforcing loyalty through intimidation.

Intimidation that could extend to anyone associated with you, directly or indirectly. Anyone who might be considered... close."

The veiled accusation hung in the air. Tasha's eyes narrowed, and for the first time, Maya saw a flash of something raw, something personal, beneath the polished veneer. The mention of Silas, of intimidation, seemed to strike a nerve. Was there someone Tasha was protecting? Someone whose vulnerability was being exploited by Malik's brute force? The synopsis's hint of entanglement began to make a chilling kind of sense.

"My associates are my responsibility, Detective," Tasha said, her voice dropping to a dangerous whisper. "And their safety is my absolute priority. If Malik's actions pose a threat to them, then he has crossed a line."

"He has," Maya confirmed. "And that's why I'm here. I need your cooperation, Ms. Thorne. I need to know what Malik is truly planning. What Vinnie is facilitating. And I need to understand the nature of his 'expansion' before it escalates into something far more destructive." Maya held Tasha's gaze, her own a mixture of professional urgency and a nascent, unspoken plea. "There are people under your protection, Ms. Thorne, who are increasingly vulnerable due to Malik's reckless ambition. And I'm not just talking about business assets."

Tasha's jaw tightened almost imperceptibly. "Vulnerability is a part of this world, Detective. But the exploitation of it... that is a different matter entirely." She paused, her gaze drifting towards a large abstract painting of a tempestuous sea. "Malik has always been... ambitious. Perhaps more so than I realized. His recent activities have indeed raised concerns."

"Concerns that go beyond financial risk?" Maya probed, sensing a crack in Tasha's carefully constructed facade.

Tasha turned back to Maya, her expression unreadable. "There are... personal considerations, Detective. Matters that are not directly business-related. Silas's presence, his methods... they are a concern. He's a blunt instrument, and Malik wields him with an alarming lack of foresight."

"Is there someone specific he's targeting?" Maya asked, pushing gently. "Someone you're trying to protect?"

Tasha's lips thinned. "My concern is for all those who work under my protection. However," she conceded, her voice barely audible, "certain individuals are... more exposed than others. Jazzy, for instance. She's been placed in a particularly difficult position by Malik's recent directives."

The mention of Jazzy, the courier whose near-miss with Silas had first alerted Tasha to the severity of Malik's transgression, was significant. It confirmed that Malik's actions were not merely abstract business maneuvers but had direct, tangible consequences for Tasha's people. And if Tasha was personally invested in Jazzy's safety, then Malik's exploitation of her network was a direct assault on Tasha's most deeply held loyalties. This was the entanglement. This was the nexus of their conflict, and Maya was determined to use it.

"Jazzy is a key operative, Ms. Thorne. Her safety is paramount, and if Malik is using her as a pawn, or putting her at risk, that's a line that cannot be tolerated," Maya stated, her voice firm. "I need to know everything you know about Malik's plans, about the funds Vinnie is managing, and about any specific threats you perceive to your people. If we are to counter him effectively, we need to work together, however distasteful that may be."

Tasha considered her for a long moment, her gaze sharp and appraising. "Cooperation is a dangerous game, Detective. Especially when the players involved are as... unpredictable as Malik. But you are correct. His actions are becoming increasingly disruptive, and his methods... are unacceptable." She took a slow breath. "I will provide you with what information I can. But you must understand, Detective, my primary concern is the well-being of my people. If your investigation puts them in further danger, our fragile alliance will shatter."

The agreement, tentative as it was, felt like a small victory, but one that was overshadowed by the growing weight of the personal risks involved. Maya knew that her own compromised position, the implied entanglement that the synopsis alluded to, was a double-edged sword. It gave her an edge, an understanding of the stakes that went beyond the merely professional, but it also made her susceptible to the very tactics Malik employed. She was playing a dangerous game, navigating the treacherous underbelly of a world where loyalty was a commodity, and betrayal was often the price of ambition. And as she left the gallery, the rain still falling, Maya felt a chilling certainty: the price of loyalty, for everyone involved, was about to become exceptionally high. She had to tread carefully, not only for the sake of justice, but for reasons that were becoming increasingly, and alarmingly, personal. The lines she was willing to cross were no longer drawn in the sand; they were being etched in stone by the actions of men like Malik, and the protective instincts of women like Tasha. The investigation had evolved, and Maya was no longer just a detective; she was a participant in a drama far more complex and dangerous than she had ever anticipated. The whisper of an entanglement was now a roar in her ears, a constant reminder of the personal stakes that amplified every risk, every decision, every dangerous step she took into the heart of this unfolding conspiracy.

The opulent velvet of the chaise lounge offered no solace. Jazzy, nestled amidst the plush cushions in what was supposed to be Tasha's private sanctuary – a gilded cage of comfort and curated luxury – felt a tremor of something far colder than the expensive silk of her gown. The earlier hushed urgency in Tasha's voice, the almost imperceptible tightening around her eyes when Silas's name had been mentioned, had been a chilling prelude. It was the subtle discord in the symphony of Tasha's usual, impeccably controlled demeanor that truly unsettled Jazzy. Tasha, a woman who navigated the dangerous currents of her empire with the grace of a seasoned captain, had shown a rare crack in her armor. And that crack had widened considerably when Jazzy's own name had been spoken, linked to Malik's disturbing directives.

Jazzy had always seen her role as a courier, a facilitator of transactions, a discreet presence moving through the periphery of Tasha's world. She was the whisper in the ear, the discreet package delivered, the one who navigated the shadows without attracting undue attention. The danger was a known entity, an occupational hazard, a calculated risk she had accepted when she'd first entered Tasha's orbit. But she had perceived it as a controlled danger, a manageable risk overseen by Tasha's formidable intelligence and unwavering authority. It was a danger she believed was carefully compartmentalized, kept at arm's length from her own life, her own small corner of autonomy.

But the recent shift in Malik's behavior, the unsettling expansion into territories that felt less about business and more about... something else, something harder and more predatory, had begun to erode that perception. The brief, chilling encounter with Silas, the sheer physicality of his threat, had been a stark warning. It had been a glimpse behind the curtain, a revelation of the brute force Malik was willing to wield. And Tasha's admission that Jazzy had been "placed in a particularly difficult position" by Malik's directives confirmed Jazzy's burgeoning unease. She wasn't just a courier; she was a pawn, her movements dictated by forces beyond her control, forces that were increasingly violent and unpredictable.

The catalyst for Jazzy's stark awakening wasn't a grand, dramatic explosion, but a quiet, chilling descent into chaos that unfolded within the gilded walls of one of Tasha's more exclusive establishments. It happened during a night that had promised the usual blend of hushed transactions and superficial revelry. A high-stakes client, a man whose name whispered through the city's elite circles like a poisoned breath, had requested Jazzy's personal attention. He was a regular, someone who appreciated her discretion, her ability to anticipate his needs before he even voiced them. He was also, Jazzy knew, a man teetering on the precipice of a dangerous addiction, a secret he kept tightly guarded behind a mask of calculated charm.

Tonight, however, the mask had slipped. The client, a Mr. Sterling, a man known for his meticulous appearance and his even more meticulous dealings, had been unusually agitated. His eyes, usually sharp and calculating, held a feverish glint. His hands, accustomed to the delicate handling of rare vintages and illicit substances, trembled as he reached for the meticulously arranged vials Jazzy had presented. There was a desperation in his movements, a frantic energy that made Jazzy's professional instincts prickle with alarm. She had been trained to recognize the signs, to understand the subtle cues that indicated a client was pushing too hard, venturing too far into the abyss.

"Just a little more, Jazzy," he'd rasped, his voice strained. "I need to... level out. The pressure... it's immense." He gestured vaguely, his eyes unfocused, already lost in the haze of what was to come.

Jazzy hesitated. Tasha's directives were clear: facilitate, discreetly satisfy. But Tasha's directives also included a line, a boundary of acceptable risk. She had never been asked to directly administer, never been placed in the position of an enabler for something this extreme. Her role was to deliver, not to preside over the ensuing devastation.

"Mr. Sterling," she began, her voice pitched low and steady, an attempt to project a calm she didn't feel. "Perhaps this is enough for tonight. We can arrange for your... transport. Ensure you get home safely."

His laugh was a harsh, dry sound, devoid of humor. "Home? Home is for the weak, Jazzy. I need to stay sharp. Malik's men are... they're everywhere. Always watching. Always waiting for a misstep." He fumbled with a vial, his fingers clumsy. "You understand, don't you? You're in this too. You know the stakes."

The mention of Malik, of his men, sent a shiver down Jazzy's spine. It was the first time a client had explicitly linked the oppressive vigilance she'd been hearing about to their own personal struggles. It was a grim confirmation that Malik's reach was not confined to corporate maneuvering and logistical disruptions; it was bleeding into the personal lives of Tasha's clientele, injecting a new layer of fear and paranoia into the carefully constructed facade of exclusivity.

Before Jazzy could respond, before she could even formulate a response that might de-escalate the situation, Sterling's hand slipped. The small glass vial clattered onto the polished mahogany table, spilling its contents in a dark, viscous pool. His eyes widened, a flicker of terror finally breaking through the drug-induced haze. He gasped, a guttural, choked sound, and then slumped forward, his body hitting the table with a sickening thud.

The silence that followed was deafening, broken only by the faint, tinny strains of music from the other room. Jazzy stared, frozen, the carefully curated calm of the establishment shattering around her. This was not a discreet transaction. This was not a controlled risk. This was an overdose. A man's life, quite possibly extinguished, under her watch, in a place under Tasha's dominion. The weight of her complicity, however passive, descended upon her with crushing force.

Panic, cold and sharp, began to claw at her throat. She looked around the opulent room, the silk drapes, the expensive artwork, the carefully placed lighting – all designed to create an illusion of sophisticated control. But the illusion was shattered. The façade had crumbled, revealing the grim reality that lay beneath. Tasha's empire, which had always seemed like a gilded cage offering a certain kind of protection, was also a place where lives could be so casually, so brutally, extinguished.

Her first instinct was to call for help, to alert security, to follow protocol. But the memory of Silas, of his menacing presence and the implicit threat he represented, stayed her hand. She knew that an incident like this, especially with Malik's men already sniffing around, would be an invitation for an even deeper investigation, an interrogation of Tasha's operations, and by extension, of her own role within them. And she knew, with chilling certainty, that Malik's "men" would not be interested in discreetly resolving a personal tragedy. They would be interested in leverage, in exploiting a vulnerability, in ensuring that Tasha, and everyone associated with her, understood the true cost of any perceived misstep.

Jazzy's mind raced, a frantic scramble for a way out, for a way to contain the damage. She thought of Tasha, of the conversation she'd had with Detective Cross. Tasha, who had spoken of "personal considerations," of protecting her people. Jazzy had always been a discreet asset, valuable for her efficiency and her quiet compliance. But now, she was a liability. An inconvenient truth that could unravel the carefully constructed narrative of Tasha's control.

She felt a surge of something akin to anger, a simmering resentment that had been building since her encounter with Silas. She had been loyal, meticulous, discreet. She had followed Tasha's rules, operated within the carefully defined boundaries of her role. And yet, here she was, facing the devastating consequences of a world that was spiraling out of Tasha's control, a world where Malik's influence was becoming a palpable, suffocating force.

She carefully examined Sterling. His chest was still, his face ashen. There was no doubt. He was gone. She couldn't save him. But she could, perhaps, save herself. She could try to shield Tasha from further scrutiny. She could try to preserve the illusion of order, even as the foundations of that order were crumbling beneath her feet.

With trembling hands, Jazzy began to subtly alter the scene. She carefully gathered the spilled vials, wiping away the dark residue with a silk handkerchief. She placed Sterling's body in a more natural, less incriminating position. Her movements were precise, almost automatic, the result of countless hours of training in discretion and damage control. But with each calculated action, a profound disillusionment settled within her. This was not just about managing transactions anymore. This was about managing consequences, about covering up the uglier truths that lay beneath the surface.

As she worked, a single, chilling thought echoed in her mind, a direct consequence of Detective Cross's words to Tasha: "Jazzy... she's been placed in a particularly difficult position by Malik's recent directives." It was the confirmation that her current predicament was not an accident, but a consequence of larger, more sinister machinations. Malik, it seemed, was not just expanding his reach; he was actively targeting Tasha's operatives, using them as pawns, as leverage, as potential casualties in his bid for control.

The image of Silas's scarred face, his predatory grin, flashed in her mind. She remembered the casual way he had dismissed her, the utter lack of concern for her well-being. He was the blunt instrument, as Tasha had said, wielded with a terrifying disregard for collateral damage. And Jazzy was now undeniably collateral damage, a victim of the escalating power struggle between Malik and Tasha.

She had entered Tasha's world seeking a sense of belonging, a purpose, perhaps even a certain degree of empowerment. She had admired Tasha's strength, her control, her ability to navigate a world dominated by men with such unwavering poise. But now, looking at the still form of Mr. Sterling, contemplating the implications of Malik's encroaching ruthlessness, Jazzy saw the empire in a different light. It was not just a sanctuary; it was a battlefield. And she, the discreet courier, was caught squarely in the crossfire.

The seeds of doubt, once a faint tremor, had blossomed into a full-blown crisis of faith. Her loyalty, once an unquestioning allegiance to Tasha's vision, was beginning to waver. The illusion of safety had been shattered, replaced by the stark, terrifying reality of her own vulnerability. She was no longer just a player in Tasha's game; she was a pawn being moved, manipulated, and ultimately, discarded by forces far more dangerous and unpredictable than she had ever imagined. The quiet understanding she thought she had with Tasha, the unspoken pact of loyalty and protection, felt like a cruel deception. She was alone, adrift in a sea of consequence, with no clear path forward and the chilling certainty that the price of her loyalty, and her proximity to Tasha's empire, was escalating with every passing moment. The question was no longer whether Tasha could protect her, but whether Tasha herself was even truly in control. And that, Jazzy realized with a sinking heart, was the most terrifying realization of all. The gilded cage had revealed its bars, and the glittering facade had cracked, exposing the brutal, unforgiving reality beneath.

The air in Tasha's private study, usually a sanctuary of calm deliberation, now hummed with a nervous energy that Jazzy found increasingly difficult to ignore. The polished mahogany desk, a symbol of Tasha's authority, seemed to gleam with a cold, accusatory light. Jazzy had retreated here after the Sterling incident, the stench of fear and a potent cocktail of chemical and human despair clinging to her like a second skin. She had performed her role with chilling efficiency, meticulously cleaning the scene, erasing any trace of the catastrophic event, her hands moving with the practiced grace of someone long accustomed to managing the fallout of Tasha's operations. But the internal aftermath was far more chaotic. The carefully constructed edifice of her professional detachment had crumbled, revealing the raw, terrified woman beneath.

Tasha had been... distant. Not angry, not overtly disappointed, but a subtle shift in her gaze, a new wariness in her tone when she'd briefly acknowledged Jazzy's return, had spoken volumes. It was the look of a strategist re-evaluating her assets, a queen measuring the damage to her kingdom and the loyalty of her subjects. Jazzy felt less like a valued operative and more like a potentially compromised piece on a chessboard, a piece that Malik's aggressive moves had now placed directly in the path of impending destruction. The memory of Sterling's final, desperate moments, the sheer helplessness of his demise, replayed endlessly in her mind, a stark indictment of the world she inhabited. It wasn't just about delivering packages or facilitating discreet exchanges anymore; it was about the lives that were irrevocably altered, or extinguished, by the very mechanisms she helped to operate.

The whispers had started long before Sterling's tragic end, subtle currents of discontent rippling through the usually placid waters of Tasha's inner circle. Now, however, those whispers had a new urgency, a sharper edge of fear. Jazzy caught snippets of hushed conversations, furtive glances exchanged when Tasha was out of sight. Silas, his scarred face a constant, chilling reminder of Malik's brute force, was becoming an increasingly visible presence. He moved through Tasha's established territories not as an outsider, but as a conqueror, his entourage a tangible manifestation of Malik's growing dominance. The respect, even admiration, that had once been Tasha's to command, seemed to be fraying at the edges, replaced by a grudging deference to Malik's increasingly overt displays of power.

One evening, during a clandestine meeting held in the dimly lit back room of a discreet jazz club – a neutral territory Jazzy had painstakingly secured – the unease became palpable. Tasha's lieutenants, individuals Jazzy had always considered the bedrock of her loyalty, were present. There was Marcus, Tasha's head of security, a man whose stoic demeanor was usually as unshakeable as granite. But tonight, his jaw was set, his eyes darting towards the entrance with an unnerving frequency. Across from him sat Elena, Tasha's chief legal counsel, her sharp intellect usually her most formidable weapon. Now, however, her usual confident posture was marred by a subtle tension in her shoulders, a nervous habit of twisting a delicate silver ring on her finger. And then there was Julian, Tasha's financial advisor, a man whose meticulous nature usually extended to his own carefully cultivated image. Tonight, his usually immaculate suit seemed slightly rumpled, his usual unflappable calm replaced by a restless fidgeting.

Tasha, as always, was the epitome of composed authority, her voice a silken thread that usually wove them all into a tapestry of unwavering loyalty. But even she seemed to sense the shift, the subtle fracturing of their collective resolve. She spoke of increased pressure from Malik's 'associates,' of logistical challenges that seemed almost orchestrated to cripple their operations. She spoke of a need for greater discretion, for tighter operational security. But her words, usually a beacon of reassurance, now felt like pronouncements from a distant shore, her grip on their reality loosening with every passing day.

"Malik is making moves," Tasha stated, her gaze sweeping across their faces, seeking to gauge their reactions, to shore up their wavering allegiance. "He's exploiting every vulnerability. We need to remain vigilant. Our operations must continue without interruption."

Marcus, his voice a low rumble, finally broke the tense silence. "Vigilant is one thing, Tasha. But Silas and his men... they're not just observing anymore. They're actively interfering. I've had operatives roughed up, equipment 'confiscated.' It's not just business; it's intimidation." His knuckles were white where he gripped the edge of the table. "This isn't the game we agreed to play."

Elena, her voice a strained whisper, chimed in. "From a legal standpoint, Tasha, the pressure is also mounting. Malik's people are asking questions. Questions that... skirt the edges of our established protocols. They're looking for leverage, and if they find any... the fallout could be catastrophic." She met Tasha's eyes, a silent plea for understanding, for a recognition of the dangerous precipice they were teetering on.

Julian, his voice barely audible, added, "The financial repercussions of these disruptions... they're becoming significant. We're losing revenue. And frankly, Tasha, some of the... demands being made by Malik's associates are becoming untenable. They're not just asking for preferential treatment; they're dictating terms. Terms that are... risky."

Jazzy listened, her own anxieties echoing the growing dissent around the table. She saw it in their eyes: the dawning realization that Tasha's carefully constructed empire was no longer an impenetrable fortress, but a vulnerable entity, its defenses compromised by an increasingly ruthless adversary. The unspoken question hung heavy in the air: was Tasha still capable of protecting them? Or were they all, Jazzy included, becoming liabilities in a war they were no longer equipped to win?

The Sterling incident had been a brutal awakening for Jazzy, a stark illustration of the escalating brutality that Malik represented. It had stripped away the comfortable illusion of control, replacing it with the chilling reality of chaos. She had always believed in Tasha's vision, in the order and efficacy she brought to a chaotic world. But now, that belief was being tested by the very forces Tasha claimed to be managing. The question of loyalty wasn't just a theoretical concept anymore; it was a matter of survival. And as Jazzy observed the thinly veiled fear in the eyes of Tasha's most trusted lieutenants, she began to understand that survival might require looking beyond Tasha's immediate circle, seeking alliances with those who, like her, felt the ground shifting beneath their feet.

Malik's influence was like a creeping vine, slowly but surely constricting Tasha's territory. His methods were crude, yet undeniably effective. He wasn't interested in the subtle nuances of Tasha's meticulously crafted network; he dealt in blunt force, in coercion, in the calculated application of fear. Jazzy had seen it firsthand with Silas, and now she saw its corrosive effect on Tasha's own people. Marcus's frustration was a clear indicator of the pressure he was under, the impossible choices he was being forced to make between Tasha's directives and the escalating aggression he was facing on the ground. Elena's legal concerns were not just about professional ethics; they were about the very real threat of legal repercussions that could dismantle everything Tasha had built. And Julian's financial anxieties stemmed from a very tangible reality: Malik's interventions were not just disruptive; they were designed to destabilize and ultimately, to seize control.

The evening devolved into a strained discussion of damage control, of contingency plans that felt increasingly desperate. Tasha, while projecting an image of unwavering resolve, couldn't entirely mask the strain. There were moments when her voice faltered, when a flicker of doubt crossed her face before she quickly regained her composure. It was a subtle crack in her formidable armor, a vulnerability that didn't escape Jazzy's notice. And in those fleeting moments, Jazzy felt a peculiar kinship with Tasha, a shared burden of navigating an increasingly perilous landscape.

However, the true shift for Jazzy wasn't just in witnessing Tasha's struggle, but in the tentative connections she began to forge with others who shared her growing disillusionment. It started subtly, with shared glances of understanding between Jazzy and Marcus after Tasha had issued a particularly risky directive. It evolved into brief, almost imperceptible nods of acknowledgment from Elena when Malik's tactics were discussed in hushed tones. These were not overt acts of defiance, but quiet affirmations of a shared unease, a silent acknowledgment of the precariousness of their positions.

One afternoon, while Tasha was engaged in a protracted, tense negotiation with an external entity – a situation that required Jazzy's discreet information gathering – Jazzy found herself alone with Marcus in a less frequented corridor of one of their secure facilities. The air was thick with the scent of ozone from the nearby server rooms, and the low hum of machinery provided a backdrop to their conversation.

"He's crossing lines, Jazzy," Marcus stated, his voice low and gravelly, devoid of its usual professional polish. He wasn't asking a question; he was making a statement of fact, a raw expression of his growing frustration. He gestured vaguely with his chin towards the direction of Malik's increased presence. "Silas and his crew... they're not just pushing boundaries; they're erasing them. I can't protect my people effectively when we're constantly looking over our shoulders, anticipating the next... disruption."

Jazzy felt a surge of adrenaline, a recognition of her own burgeoning fears mirrored in Marcus's words. "I understand," she replied softly, her voice barely above a whisper. "Sterling... it was bad, Marcus. Truly bad. And it felt... like a warning."

Marcus's gaze, usually direct and unwavering, now held a haunted quality. "A warning for all of us. Tasha... she's a brilliant strategist, but I'm starting to wonder if she's underestimated the sheer ruthlessness of Malik. He's not playing by any rules we recognize." He ran a hand over his face, the gesture one of utter exhaustion. "I've served Tasha for years. My loyalty is absolute. But I also have people who depend on me. And I can't, in good conscience, continue to put them in harm's way without a clear strategy for their protection."

This was it. The first concrete step beyond mere observation. Jazzy felt a strange mix of fear and exhilaration. She was reaching out, not to Tasha, but to someone else within the organization who was experiencing the same disquiet. "What if," Jazzy began, choosing her words carefully, "what if there are others who feel the same? Others who are... looking for a way through this without becoming casualties?"

Marcus's eyes narrowed, a flicker of suspicion crossing his face, quickly followed by a grudging understanding. He knew Jazzy's role, her proximity to Tasha's most sensitive operations. He also knew she was not prone to rash decisions or emotional outbursts. "You're talking about more than just observation, aren't you?" he asked, his tone measured.

"I'm talking about survival, Marcus," Jazzy replied, her voice steady, projecting a confidence she didn't entirely feel. "And survival might mean looking for allies, even within our own... structure. Malik's influence is growing, and it feels like Tasha is being forced to react, rather than dictate. If we can't rely on Tasha to shield us, then perhaps we need to find our own shield."

Their conversation was cut short by the distant sound of footsteps approaching, forcing them to retreat into their respective roles. But the seed had been planted. Jazzy knew she wasn't alone in her apprehension. The growing sense of disquiet was a shared burden, a common thread weaving through the organization. She started to pay closer attention to the subtle cues from Elena and Julian as well. Elena, during a brief encounter in the archives, had alluded to "complex legal entanglements" that were "increasingly difficult to navigate" due to external pressures, her veiled words hinting at Malik's legal maneuvering. Julian, in a seemingly casual conversation about market fluctuations, had expressed concerns about "unforeseen volatility" and "speculative acquisitions" that were impacting their financial stability – a clear indication of Malik's economic tactics.

Jazzy understood that a direct confrontation with Tasha, or an open declaration of dissent, would be professional suicide. Her strategy had to be far more nuanced, far more insidious. It was about building a network of quiet dissent, of shared understanding, of individuals who, like her, were beginning to question Tasha's ability to navigate the encroaching storm and were therefore seeking alternative paths to security. She wasn't betraying Tasha, not yet. She was simply acknowledging a harsh reality: Tasha's leadership, once an unassailable pillar, was showing signs of strain under Malik's relentless pressure.

The price of loyalty was becoming clear, and for Jazzy, that price was a terrifying degree of vulnerability. The Sterling incident had cemented her understanding of the risks involved, not just to her career, but to her very life. It had stripped away any lingering naivete she might have held about the true nature of Tasha's empire. It was a world of calculated risks, yes, but those calculations were being thrown into disarray by Malik's brutal pragmatism. And as Jazzy continued to operate within Tasha's organization, she began to realize that her most valuable asset might not be her discretion or her efficiency, but her growing ability to read the subtle shifts in loyalty, to identify those who, like her, were beginning to wonder if Tasha's reign was coming to an end, and if Malik's brutal ascent was the inevitable, terrifying future. She was no longer just a pawn; she was becoming a player, maneuvering in the shadows, forging tentative alliances in a desperate bid for self-preservation. The game had changed, and Jazzy was determined to survive it, even if it meant playing a new, dangerous hand of her own.

4: The Data Breach

The hum of the servers in the secure data hub was usually a comforting lullaby to Jazzy, a testament to the intricate, invisible architecture that underpinned Tasha's operations. Tonight, however, that familiar thrum felt discordant, a frantic pulse mirroring her own rising anxiety. Tasha's data management system, a labyrinth of encrypted networks and meticulously curated client profiles, was supposed to be the unbreachable bedrock of their entire enterprise. It was where identities were meticulously crafted, vulnerabilities cataloged, and leverage points meticulously mapped. It was the digital arsenal from which Tasha commanded her influence. Yet, Silas's recent incursions, his unnervingly precise disruptions, hinted at a breach far more fundamental than mere physical intimidation. The whispers among the tech team, usually stoic and reserved, had become more frequent, laced with a hushed urgency that Jazzy found impossible to ignore. They spoke of anomalies, of phantom access attempts, of data streams that seemed to flicker and distort when Tasha's back was turned. These weren't the brute-force attacks Malik was known for; this was something far more insidious, something that suggested an intimate knowledge of the system's inner workings.

Tasha had always prided herself on the sophistication of her digital infrastructure, a sentiment echoed by Julian in his hushed discussions of proprietary algorithms and advanced cybersecurity protocols. He had often described the system as a fortress, its defenses layered with multiple firewalls, biometric scanners, and constant AI monitoring. But even the most sophisticated fortress had its unseen weaknesses, its forgotten service tunnels, its blind spots. Jazzy had always operated on the periphery of this digital realm, her expertise lying in the human element, in extracting information from flesh and blood rather than silicon and code. Yet, she understood enough to recognize that a compromise in Tasha's data core would be catastrophic. It wouldn't be a localized skirmish; it would be an existential threat, unraveling the very fabric of their operations and exposing every carefully guarded secret. The Sterling incident, with its brutal display of Malik's escalating aggression, had already proven how quickly Tasha's carefully controlled environment could descend into chaos. A data breach would amplify that chaos a thousandfold, turning Tasha's most potent weapon into her most devastating liability.

She recalled a conversation she'd had with Anya, Tasha's lead systems analyst, a few weeks prior. Anya, a woman of quiet brilliance and meticulous attention to detail, had been discussing a routine system update. "It's like a living organism, Jazzy," Anya had explained, her eyes alight with a mixture of pride and apprehension. "We feed it, we monitor it, we patch it. But sometimes… sometimes you find a tiny inconsistency, a single misplaced line of code that, if exploited, could cascade into something… unmanageable. We've implemented every known safeguard, of course. But there's always that theoretical vulnerability, that one infinitesimally small crack in the armor." Anya had then gone on to describe a peculiar subroutine, buried deep within the system's legacy code – a relic from an earlier iteration that had never been fully decommissioned. It was designed, she'd explained, for a now-obsolete diagnostic function, intended to allow for a direct, low-level interface with the core database in emergency situations. It was theoretically locked down, inaccessible without multiple layers of authentication, yet Anya admitted a lingering unease about its very existence. "It's a ghost in the machine, Jazzy," she'd murmured, a shiver tracing its way down her spine. "A backdoor we hope no one ever discovers, or knows how to open."

The implications of Anya's seemingly innocuous technical detail began to crystallize in Jazzy's mind. If Silas, or someone acting on Malik's behalf, possessed an intimate understanding of Tasha's system, they might have discovered this forgotten backdoor. It wouldn't require brute force; it would demand precision, knowledge, and a deep dive into the system's foundational architecture. This wasn't about cracking passwords; it was about exploiting a pre-existing flaw, a vulnerability that Tasha's own engineers had inadvertently left behind. The thought sent a fresh wave of dread through her. Tasha's strength lay in her information, her ability to anticipate and manipulate. If that information was compromised, if her clients' identities and secrets were laid bare, her empire would crumble not with a bang, but with a chilling, silent implosion.

The potential consequences were staggering. Tasha's client list was a who's who of influential figures, individuals who valued discretion above all else. Exposure of their involvement in Tasha's discreet operations would not only ruin their reputations but could also trigger a cascade of legal and political ramifications that would invariably trace back to Tasha. Moreover, the intimate details of Tasha's own operations – her supply chains, her extraction protocols, her network of contacts – would be in the hands of her most dangerous adversary. Malik, with his crude but effective methods, would be able to dismantle Tasha's carefully constructed network piece by piece, turning her own assets against her. The notion of a digital Achilles' heel, a single point of failure that could bring down the entire edifice, was a terrifying prospect. It explained Silas's subtle but persistent presence, not as a physical threat, but as a silent probe, testing the defenses from within.

Jazzy began to connect the dots, the seemingly disparate pieces of information falling into place with a sickening clarity. The subtle shift in Tasha's demeanor, the increased paranoia evident in Marcus's tight-lipped reassurances, Elena's veiled legal concerns about "unforeseen data exposure" – it all pointed towards a growing awareness within Tasha's inner circle that their digital fortress was not as impenetrable as they had believed. The Sterling incident, while seemingly a physical entanglement, could have been a calculated distraction, a smokescreen for a more profound intrusion happening in the digital shadows. While Jazzy had been meticulously cleaning the physical scene, a silent, invisible war was likely being waged within Tasha's data core.

She remembered Marcus mentioning a brief but intense period of system instability a few weeks prior, attributed to a "minor hardware malfunction" by the IT department. At the time, it had seemed like a temporary glitch, a fleeting disruption. But now, in light of Anya's unsettling revelation about the legacy subroutine, Jazzy wondered if that "malfunction" was in fact the initial probing, the stealthy exploration of that forgotten backdoor. If Malik's operatives had managed to gain even limited access to the diagnostic interface, they could have mapped out the system's architecture, identified critical data repositories, and perhaps even planted dormant malware designed to activate at a later, more opportune moment.

The vulnerability wasn't necessarily a gaping hole, but a meticulously disguised seam, a hairline fracture that, with the right pressure, could widen into an unmanageable chasm. This was the kind of threat that preyed on Jazzy's deepest fears. She operated in a world of tangible consequences, of visible threats and concrete actions. The idea of an invisible enemy, operating in the ethereal realm of data, capable of unraveling everything with a few keystrokes, was a new and deeply unsettling dimension to the danger she faced. It meant that the meticulously crafted identities, the fabricated backgrounds, the carefully curated intel that Tasha leveraged, could all be exposed, rendering her network ineffective and her operatives vulnerable.

Jazzy decided to approach Anya directly, a risky move given the sensitive nature of her inquiry. She found Anya hunched over her console in the hushed, sterile environment of the data center, the glow of multiple monitors reflecting in her glasses. "Anya," Jazzy began, her voice low, "about that diagnostic subroutine you mentioned... the legacy one."

Anya looked up, her brow furrowed, a flicker of apprehension in her eyes. "Yes? What about it?"

"Has anyone… else accessed it? Or tried to?" Jazzy pressed, choosing her words carefully.

Anya's gaze sharpened, and she instinctively glanced around the empty data center before turning back to Jazzy, her voice a near whisper. "Why do you ask? It's been flagged as inert, permanently offline after the last security audit. Only I have the… conceptual knowledge of its existence, and even then, accessing it would require a direct physical connection and a specific override sequence that's been… modified for increased security." She paused, a troubled expression settling on her face. "Though… there was that brief period of instability a few weeks ago. The logs were… scrubbed, supposedly due to corruption. But the anomaly report… it did indicate an unscheduled, high-privilege access attempt during that window. It was dismissed as a system glitch, a false positive from the network monitoring. But…" Anya trailed off, her unease palpable.

"But it wasn't a glitch, was it?" Jazzy finished for her. "It was Silas, or someone like him, finding that ghost in the machine. They didn't brute force their way in; they used a key that was already there, hidden in plain sight."

Anya's face drained of color. "That's… impossible. The security protocols…"

"Protocols can be circumvented, Anya, especially if the exploit is built into the system itself," Jazzy said, the chilling logic of it settling upon her. "If they know about that subroutine, they know how to access the core database. They can see everything Tasha has, everyone she's worked with."

The implications were chilling. If Malik's network had gained access to Tasha's client database, they wouldn't just have names; they would have the intimate details that Tasha cultivated: personal habits, financial vulnerabilities, hidden allegiances, and deeply buried secrets. This wasn't just about financial data; it was about blackmail, about leverage, about turning Tasha's carefully constructed network of influence into a weapon against her. Imagine the chaos if client X's involvement in a sensitive operation was leaked to their political rivals, or if client Y's discreet financial dealings were exposed to the public. The fallout would be immediate and devastating, not only for the clients but for Tasha herself, whose reputation for absolute discretion would be shattered.

Jazzy felt a cold dread seep into her bones. The Sterling incident, the increased presence of Silas, the growing unease among Tasha's lieutenants – it all coalesced into a single, terrifying narrative. Malik wasn't just trying to dismantle Tasha's operations through brute force; he was systematically targeting her intelligence network, her most vital asset. By exposing her data, he could cripple her ability to operate, to anticipate, to control. He could unravel years of meticulous work with a single, devastating digital strike. This was a vulnerability that went beyond technical defenses; it was a fundamental flaw in the very design of Tasha's operational security, a weakness born from a forgotten piece of code that now threatened to expose everyone. The vulnerability wasn't just in the system; it was in the inherent human tendency to overlook the past, to assume that what was once secured remains eternally so. Anya's legacy subroutine, a relic of a bygone era of Tasha's operations, had become the linchpin for a new and terrifying threat, a threat that could destabilize Tasha's empire and plunge everyone involved into a level of danger they had never before conceived. Jazzy knew, with a sickening certainty, that the real battle had just begun, and it was being fought not on the streets, but in the silent, unseen depths of the digital ether. The integrity of Tasha's entire world rested on the hope that Anya's discovery was still a secret, and that the ghost in the machine remained just that – a ghost. But the chilling possibility that Silas, or someone even more skilled, had already coaxed it from the shadows was a thought that would haunt Jazzy's waking hours, and her nightmares, for a long time to come. The careful construction of Tasha's empire was proving to be more fragile than any of them had imagined, its strength inversely proportional to the hidden flaws it contained.

Malik's gaze, usually a hard, unyielding obsidian, held a glint of avarice. The whispers of the data breach, the palpable unease radiating from Tasha's inner circle, were not mere background noise to him; they were the overture to his own ascension. He saw not a crisis, but an opportunity, a tempest that threatened to capsize Tasha's vessel, allowing him to seize the helm. The Sterling incident, a crude display of force, had been a necessary prelude, a means to sow discord and highlight Tasha's perceived vulnerabilities. But this digital intrusion, this phantom menace that had penetrated her supposedly impregnable data core, was the real game-changer. It was the unseen wound that promised to bleed Tasha dry, leaving her ripe for the taking.

He didn't need to understand the intricacies of Anya's legacy subroutine, the ghost in the machine Jazzy so feared. Malik's strength lay in leveraging the chaos, in exploiting the fears and uncertainties that such a breach would inevitably engender. He saw how Tasha's focus had been irrevocably diverted from their shared objective – the complete subjugation of the city's elite through the 'Swipe Right' operation – towards damage control and internal investigation. This was precisely the vacuum he intended to fill. His own operatives, though less sophisticated in their digital prowess, were ruthlessly efficient in their execution of his will. They were the blunt instruments he wielded to carve out his domain.

Malik began by subtly amplifying the existing anxieties. He initiated a series of calculated provocations, seemingly unrelated to the data breach but designed to further destabilize Tasha's command structure. He ensured that rumors of Silas's continued, albeit covert, presence within their digital infrastructure reached key individuals within Tasha's organization. These rumors, carefully curated and selectively disseminated, painted a picture of an enemy far more cunning and pervasive than Tasha herself seemed willing to acknowledge. He understood that fear was a potent accelerant, and that doubt, once planted, could take root and choke even the most resilient of leaders.

His primary target was Julian, Tasha's tech strategist and, by extension, the guardian of her digital realm. Malik approached Julian not with threats, but with a chillingly logical proposition. He insinuated himself into Julian's burgeoning paranoia, playing on the analyst's meticulous nature and his inherent fear of failure. "Julian," Malik had said during a clandestine meeting in a nondescript warehouse, the air thick with the metallic tang of industrial solvents, "Tasha is... distracted. She's chasing shadows, worried about what might have been. But the real threat isn't the ghost in her machine; it's the fact that her machine is failing. You built that fortress, Julian. But every fortress has a flaw. And if that flaw is about to be exploited, wouldn't it be wiser to be on the side that can *fix* it, rather than be buried beneath its collapse?"

Malik then subtly offered Julian a lifeline, a carefully veiled 'alternative' plan. He suggested that the breach was not a mere incursion, but a deliberate sabotage, a deeper compromise that Tasha, in her current state, was incapable of rectifying. He hinted that the data, once compromised, would be useless unless it could be meticulously sifted, categorized, and leveraged by someone with a clear, unclouded vision. Malik presented himself as that vision. He painted a picture of a future where the 'Swipe Right' operation would proceed with ruthless efficiency, unburdened by Tasha's increasingly erratic leadership. He subtly positioned himself as the one who could ensure Julian's own contributions were recognized, protected, and ultimately, rewarded. The implication was clear: align with Malik, and ensure your own survival and success in the new order.

To further solidify his position, Malik began to exert his influence on the 'Swipe Right' operation itself. While Tasha was preoccupied with the digital fallout, Malik started to subtly redirect resources. He used his access to key distribution channels and his connections within the city's underbelly to manipulate the flow of information and, more critically, the flow of operatives. He began assigning tasks that directly served his own agenda, often bypassing Tasha's direct authority or framing them as necessary measures to counteract the perceived systemic instability. He would orchestrate situations where his own agents would 'discover' crucial intel, presenting it to Tasha as if it were a fortunate turn of events, thereby showcasing his continued utility while simultaneously undermining her own intelligence-gathering capabilities.

He orchestrated a series of minor setbacks for Tasha's ongoing operations, framing them as consequences of the compromised data. For instance, if a planned rendezvous with a key target was compromised, Malik would be the first to offer a plausible explanation tied to the data breach, emphasizing how critical it was to have a stable, uncompromised leadership guiding their efforts. He would then propose his own alternative strategies, often more aggressive and direct, which would, coincidentally, place more control and visibility into his hands. Each of these maneuvers, though seemingly minor in isolation, served to chip away at Tasha's authority, creating a narrative of her escalating incompetence and his rising indispensability.

Malik also recognized the psychological impact of the breach on Tasha's key lieutenants. He knew that loyalty, while a powerful currency, could also be fragile when faced with existential threats. He began to cultivate relationships with individuals who, he sensed, harbored reservations about Tasha's increasingly erratic leadership. Marcus, with his pragmatic approach to risk management, and Elena, whose legal acumen made her acutely aware of the potential ramifications of compromised data, were prime targets. Malik subtly fed them information that reinforced their existing anxieties, planting seeds of doubt about Tasha's ability to navigate the crisis. He presented himself as a steady hand, a voice of reason in the encroaching storm.

He would arrange 'chance' encounters with Marcus, discussing the operational risks in abstract terms, alluding to the dangers of decentralized command during a security crisis. He'd mention how a singular, decisive leader was crucial to weathering such storms. With Elena, he would touch upon the legal ramifications of data exposure, subtly suggesting that Tasha's current predicament could lead to severe legal repercussions, and that a change in leadership might be the only way to mitigate those risks and ensure the protection of everyone involved. He wasn't overtly betraying Tasha, but rather offering a pragmatic alternative, a path to safety and continued success in a rapidly deteriorating situation.

The 'Swipe Right' operation, designed to be a subtle, pervasive influence, began to transform under Malik's increasingly overt control. Targets identified through Tasha's meticulous profiling were now being approached with a more direct, almost predatory approach. Malik instructed his operatives to leverage the very information that had been compromised, not for long-term leverage, but for immediate, forceful compliance. If a target's secret indiscretion was discovered, Malik's people wouldn't engage in the nuanced manipulation Tasha favored; they would threaten immediate exposure, demanding immediate capitulation. This crude, yet effective, tactic yielded quick results, further demonstrating Malik's ruthlessness and his willingness to discard Tasha's more refined methods.

He began to orchestrate situations where Tasha's operatives would be put in a position where they had to rely on Malik's 'assistance.' For instance, if an operation required accessing a specific piece of information that was known to be within Tasha's compromised systems, Malik's team would 'miraculously' acquire it, presenting it as a fortunate 'leak' that they had managed to intercept. This created a dependency, a subtle reinforcement of the idea that Tasha's own resources were unreliable, and that Malik's network was the only dependable source.

The ultimate goal was not just to usurp Tasha, but to consolidate his own power base within the burgeoning empire. He saw the city's elite as pawns in a much larger game, and Tasha's meticulously crafted network as a means to his own ends. The data breach, in his eyes, was not a threat to be contained, but a weapon to be wielded. He envisioned a scenario where he would control not only the information Tasha had gathered but also the very mechanisms by which it was disseminated and utilized. He wanted to own the narrative, to dictate the terms of engagement, and to ensure that Tasha, and anyone loyal to her, became mere footnotes in his own ascent.

Malik's greed was a corrosive force, eating away at the foundations of their shared enterprise. He saw the chaos as a fertile ground for his ambition, a landscape where the weak would be purged and the strong would inherit. He didn't desire partnership; he desired dominion. The data breach was merely the catalyst, the event that would allow him to dismantle Tasha's fragile control and replace it with his own iron grip. He was not interested in the subtleties of influence or the long game of manipulation. Malik craved immediate power, and the digital vulnerability offered him the perfect opportunity to seize it, unhindered by Tasha's increasingly compromised leadership. He was ready to push his agenda forward, to reshape the 'Swipe Right' operation into his own brutal image, and he saw the escalating crisis as his golden ticket. The digital weakness was not a problem to be solved, but a problem to be exploited. And Malik was a master exploiter.

Detective Cross's world, meticulously constructed on a foundation of deception and calculated anonymity, began to tremble. The whispers of the data breach within Sterling Corp, initially just another abstract threat in the city's underbelly, had suddenly taken on a disturbingly personal resonance. She'd been digging, of course. That was her job, her very existence in this fabricated reality. But her digging had been focused on the shadowy figures orchestrating the city's elite exploitation, the architects of 'Swipe Right.' Now, it seemed, the digital ghost that haunted Sterling Corp's servers was beginning to cast a long, unsettling shadow over her own carefully guarded past.

The information Blackwood had fed her, the cryptic breadcrumbs leading towards a deeper conspiracy, had always felt like a delicate tightrope walk. One wrong step, one misplaced trust, and she'd be plummeting into the abyss. But the breach, if it was what she suspected, was more than a misstep; it was a potential avalanche, threatening to bury her entire operation. Her undercover persona, 'Lena Petrova,' was a carefully crafted shield, designed to deflect suspicion while allowing her unfettered access. But what if the breach wasn't just a digital intrusion? What if it was a surgical strike, meticulously aimed at dismantling the very infrastructure of trust she relied upon?

She felt it in the subtle shifts in the online discourse, the almost imperceptible increase in the scrutiny directed towards anyone associated with Sterling Corp's inner circle. It was as if the digital void had coughed up a million tiny, probing eyes, each one searching for a weakness, a point of entry. And Lena, despite her best efforts to remain a phantom in the digital ether, felt increasingly exposed. Her work with Julian Vance, Sterling Corp's tech strategist, had been instrumental in her infiltration. She'd cultivated a professional, albeit distant, relationship, sharing insights and technical analyses under the guise of assisting with 'system optimizations.' But Julian was no fool. He was the architect of Sterling's digital fortress, and if that fortress was being breached, he would be the first to notice, and the first to suspect.

The breach wasn't merely an abstract problem for Sterling Corp; it was a potential unraveling of everything. Cross knew that any investigation into the breach would inevitably trace back to the internal systems, to the very data streams she'd been feeding into and drawing from. Her own digital footprint, however carefully scrubbed and anonymized, was a tangled web, and a determined investigator, armed with the full scope of Sterling's compromised systems, could potentially untangle it. The thought sent a cold dread through her.

She found herself replaying every interaction with Julian, every shared document, every late-night exchange about system vulnerabilities. Had she been too open? Had she inadvertently revealed a sliver of her true intent? Julian's meticulous nature was both her greatest asset and her most significant liability. He documented everything, logged every access, and analyzed every deviation from the norm. If he discovered even the slightest anomaly in her past interactions, a discrepancy that couldn't be explained by her fabricated persona, it could be enough to trigger a deeper dive.

The irony was not lost on her. She was investigating a data breach, a crime that involved the theft and manipulation of information, and in doing so, she was risking the exposure of her own highly sensitive, covert information. It was a classic case of a mole hunt within a mole hunt, and she was caught squarely in the crosshairs. The breach had created a climate of paranoia within Sterling Corp, a fertile ground for suspicion, and Cross knew that suspicion, once sown, could grow into an unshakeable conviction.

She started receiving encrypted messages from Blackwood, more frequent and more urgent than before. They were terse, filled with coded language that alluded to increased surveillance within Sterling's digital infrastructure and a heightened sense of alert among the city's more unsavory elements. Blackwood was warning her, implicitly, that her window of opportunity was rapidly closing. The deeper the investigation into the breach went, the more likely it was that her own clandestine activities would be uncovered.

Cross felt a growing pressure to act, to either retreat or accelerate her own agenda. Retreat was not an option. She was too deep, too invested in uncovering the full extent of 'Swipe Right' and its puppeteers. Acceleration, however, came with its own set of terrifying risks. She would have to push harder, probe deeper, and potentially expose herself to even greater scrutiny. It was a dangerous gamble, a high-stakes game of digital poker where the ante was her entire clandestine existence.

She decided to take a calculated risk. She needed to get closer to the source of the breach, to understand its mechanics and identify the perpetrators. This meant closer interaction with Julian Vance. She initiated a series of 'troubleshooting' sessions, feigning concern over the increasingly erratic performance of Sterling's internal network. She presented herself as a concerned colleague, eager to assist in identifying the root cause of the instability.

"Julian, the latency on the secure servers is becoming a real issue," she'd said during one such session, her voice carefully modulated to convey professional concern. They were in his sterile, glass-walled office, the hum of powerful servers a constant backdrop. "I've noticed some unusual packet loss, and the system logs are showing intermittent connection drops that don't correlate with any scheduled maintenance."

Julian, hunched over his console, his brow furrowed in concentration, barely looked up. "I'm aware, Lena. We're running diagnostics, but it's proving... elusive. The attack vectors are sophisticated, not the usual brute-force attempts." He paused, his fingers flying across the keyboard. "It's almost as if the system is being interrogated from the inside, subtly, systematically."

Cross's heart gave a slight lurch. 'Interrogated from the inside.' That was precisely what she feared. Was he hinting at something he already knew? Or was this just his professional assessment of a complex problem? She had to tread carefully, to steer the conversation without revealing her own agenda.

"Have you considered the possibility of a compromised access point?" she probed, her gaze fixed on the intricate network diagrams displayed on his multiple monitors. "A rogue device, or perhaps... an internal actor?"

Julian finally turned, his eyes, usually sharp and analytical, now held a hint of weariness. "We've explored every avenue, Lena. Our internal security protocols are robust. And anyone with privileged access has been vetted. Thoroughly." He met her gaze, a flicker of suspicion, or perhaps just professional curiosity, in his eyes. "Why the sudden interest in the network's inner workings, Lena? You're usually more focused on the outreach and profiling aspects of 'Swipe Right'."

The question hung in the air, a tangible manifestation of her precarious position. She needed a plausible explanation, something that would satisfy his professional skepticism without raising further alarms. "It's about the integrity of our data," she replied, forcing a calm, even tone. "If our operational data is compromised, even indirectly, it jeopardizes the entire 'Swipe Right' initiative. I'm concerned about the long-term viability of our profiling algorithms. Any corruption or manipulation at this level could have catastrophic downstream effects."

She watched him closely, searching for any telltale signs of his suspicion. He seemed to accept her explanation, or at least, he didn't immediately dismiss it. He returned to his work, muttering about the need for a complete network sweep, a deep-level forensic analysis.

Cross knew that a deep-level forensic analysis was exactly what she needed to avoid. Her own digital presence within Sterling Corp was a carefully constructed facade, and any thorough examination of the system's history could uncover the anomalies that betrayed her true identity. The more Julian investigated, the higher the probability of her exposure.

She was in a bind. To continue her investigation, she needed to remain embedded within Sterling Corp, to gather intelligence on the 'Swipe Right' operation and its shadowy financiers. But the unfolding data breach was creating an environment of intense scrutiny, a digital dragnet that threatened to ensnare her.

The weight of her dual existence pressed down on her. She was Detective Cross, tasked with dismantling criminal enterprises from the inside. But she was also Lena Petrova, a Sterling Corp analyst, a potential suspect in a widening conspiracy. The lines were blurring, and the danger was escalating with every passing hour.

She had to make a choice. She could either try to subtly derail Julian's investigation, feeding him misinformation or creating diversions to steer him away from her own digital footprint. Or, she could risk a more direct approach, attempting to exploit the breach herself to uncover the perpetrators and perhaps even use the chaos to her advantage. The latter was far more dangerous, a high-wire act with no safety net.

The implications of the breach extended beyond Sterling Corp's digital walls. If the compromised data contained sensitive information about the city's elite, as she suspected, then the fallout could be immense, impacting not only the targets of 'Swipe Right' but potentially destabilizing entire sectors of the city's power structure. She was in a race against time, not just to protect her own cover, but to prevent a catastrophe.

The thought of Silas, the enigmatic figure Blackwood had warned her about, kept resurfacing. Was he involved in this breach? Was he the ghost in the machine that Julian and Tasha were so desperately trying to exorcise? If Silas was indeed pulling the strings, then this was a far more complex operation than she had initially anticipated. Silas was known for his intricate planning and his ability to exploit systemic weaknesses. A data breach of this magnitude would be right in his modus operandi.

She began to work on a contingency plan, a series of protocols designed to extract her if her cover was blown. It involved pre-arranged dead drops, encrypted communication channels, and a network of trusted contacts who owed her favors.

But executing that plan would mean abandoning her mission, leaving the 'Swipe Right' operation unchecked and its perpetrators free to continue their exploitation. That was a price she was unwilling to pay.

The pressure to act intensified. She noticed subtle changes in the way Julian interacted with her. He was polite, professional, but there was a new edge to his inquiries, a more probing nature to his questions about her data analysis techniques and her understanding of Sterling's network architecture. It was as if he were testing her, probing for inconsistencies, for cracks in her carefully constructed facade.

One afternoon, while reviewing a particularly sensitive client profile – data she had acquired through her own clandestine channels, completely separate from Sterling's systems – a flicker of unease settled over her. She had been cross-referencing it with information she'd accessed through her Sterling Corp credentials. As she scrolled through the internal Sterling documents, a timestamp on a server access log caught her eye. It coincided with a period when she had been physically present at Sterling Corp, logged in under her Lena Petrova alias. The entry itself was innocuous, a routine data retrieval. But the sheer volume of data accessed by her alias during that specific timeframe, combined with the nature of the information she was currently reviewing, sent a jolt of alarm through her.

It was a statistical anomaly, a needle in a haystack, but to a meticulous analyst like Julian, it could be the thread that unraveled everything. Had she been too greedy? Had she pushed her access too far, too often, during those early days of her infiltration? The data she was reviewing was highly classified, information that no analyst, even one with her fabricated credentials, should have had a reason to access without explicit, documented authorization.

She felt a growing sense of claustrophobia. The digital walls of Sterling Corp, once her gateway to information, were now closing in on her, threatening to crush her. The breach had acted as a catalyst, accelerating the timeline of her potential exposure. She was no longer just an observer; she was becoming a suspect, a potential link in the chain of the very crime she was investigating.

She knew she couldn't afford to be passive any longer. She had to actively manage the situation, to control the narrative, or at least, to mitigate the damage. This meant taking a bold, and potentially reckless, step. She decided to confront Julian, not with accusations, but with a carefully orchestrated offer of assistance, an attempt to regain his trust and, more importantly, to steer his investigation away from her own vulnerabilities. She would present herself as someone who had discovered something significant, something that could help him understand the true nature of the breach, and in doing so, perhaps deflect his suspicion from herself. The risk was immense, but the alternative – waiting for the inevitable discovery – was even more terrifying. Her investigation, and her very life, hung in the balance. The next move would have to be her own.

The sterile air of Julian Vance's office seemed to thicken with unspoken tension. Detective Cross, inhabiting her Lena Petrova guise, felt the familiar prickle of unease sharpen into a knot of dread. Julian, usually so composed, was a storm of nervous energy, his fingers a blur across the keyboard as he navigated Sterling Corp's compromised network. The data breach, once a shadowy specter, was now a tangible threat, and the closer Cross got to understanding its mechanics, the more she realized how intricately her own carefully constructed world was being pulled into its vortex.

"The intrusion," Julian muttered, his voice strained, "it's not just about the data. It's about the access points. They've exploited vulnerabilities I didn't even know existed. It's like someone knew the blueprints of our digital fortress better than I do." He ran a hand through his already disheveled hair, his eyes fixed on the cascading lines of code on his monitor. "This level of sophistication... it suggests an insider. Someone with intimate knowledge of our system architecture."

Cross swallowed, her throat suddenly dry. An insider. The word echoed ominously. Had her own probing, her attempts to understand the breach, inadvertently painted her as a potential suspect in Julian's eyes? She had to tread a finer line than ever. "An insider, Julian? Are you suggesting a disgruntled employee, or something more... orchestrated?" Her question was a carefully placed probe, designed to gauge his current suspicions without revealing her own precarious position.

Julian finally looked at her, his gaze piercing. "Orchestrated is the word, Lena. This isn't random vandalism. This is surgical. And the terrifying part is," he paused, leaning closer to the screen, "they're not just stealing data. They're subtly altering it. Corrupting logs, rewriting access records... it's an attempt to obscure their tracks, yes, but it's also an attempt to rewrite the narrative of the breach itself."

The implications of his words sent a fresh wave of ice through Cross's veins. Rewriting the narrative. That meant someone was actively trying to control what was discovered, to frame a particular version of events. And if she wasn't careful, that narrative could easily include her. She recalled the anomaly she'd spotted in the server access logs – a fleeting moment of access that, in retrospect, felt less like a mistake and more like a calculated risk she had taken. Now, Julian's words painted that risk in a much more sinister light.

Suddenly, her comms buzzed, a discreet vibration against her thigh. An encrypted message from Blackwood. She subtly shifted, feigning a stretch to retrieve her phone from her pocket. The message was brief, cryptic, as always: "Jazzy compromised. Watch your six. Malik's making moves."

Jazzy. The name sent a jolt of pure shock through her. Jazzy was an informant, a street-smart kid with an uncanny knack for navigating the city's underground data networks. He'd been a valuable, albeit unreliable, asset in gathering information on 'Swipe Right's' digital footprints. If Jazzy was compromised, it meant the breach had implications far beyond Sterling Corp's servers. It meant the tentacles of this operation were reaching into the very foundations of her intelligence network.

Her mind raced. How could Jazzy be involved? He operated on the fringes, a digital ghost content with his small-time gigs, never a part of the high-stakes world of corporate espionage. Unless… unless someone had specifically targeted him, either to silence him or to use him. Malik. The name Blackwood mentioned sent a chill down her spine. Malik was a ghost, a phantom operative rumored to be the enforcer for the shadowy figures behind 'Swipe Right.' If Malik was involved with Jazzy, it meant the situation had escalated dramatically, and Cross herself was now in direct danger.

"Is everything alright, Lena?" Julian asked, his sharp eyes catching her momentary distraction.

"Yes, just… a personal matter," she replied, forcing a professional smile. "I need to step away for a moment, Julian. I'll need to access some of the older archived data from the Q3 security audits to see if there are any patterns that might correlate with the current breaches. I'll be in touch." She exited his office, her mind a whirlwind of calculations. Jazzy was compromised. Malik was involved. And the data breach at Sterling Corp was inextricably linked to her own informant's predicament.

She found a quiet corner in a deserted hallway, her heart pounding. She activated a secure channel to Blackwood. "Report. What do you mean Jazzy is compromised? And Malik?"

Blackwood's voice, a low rasp through the encrypted line, was grim. "Jazzy was flagged by a phishing attempt a few days ago. Went for the bait, hook, line, and sinker. Seems to have been a sophisticated social engineering ploy. The source pointed towards Malik's network. They didn't just steal his data; they're using his access. He was running a parallel investigation into some of Sterling's early data acquisition protocols, unrelated to your current focus. He stumbled onto something, Lena. Something that connected Sterling's profiling data to offshore financial transfers. Malik's people got to him. They're forcing him to cooperate, to provide access to his own encrypted channels and the backdoor he'd built into Sterling's legacy systems."

Cross's mind flashed back to Jazzy's last few messages to her. He'd been unusually cagey, hinting at a major breakthrough, something that would 'shake the foundations.' She'd dismissed it as his usual hyperbole, but now… now it all made a horrifying kind of sense. He'd found the connection between Sterling's data harvesting and the illicit financial flows, the very core of the 'Swipe Right' operation. And Malik, the silent predator, had found him first.

"What kind of access does Jazzy have?" she asked, her voice tight with urgency.

"His backdoor," Blackwood replied. "It's a piece of code he embedded years ago, a contingency for his own retrieval needs. It bypasses some of Sterling's internal firewalls, giving him limited but deep access to specific archival databases. He was using it to trace the origins of the stolen data, to see where it was being routed. If Malik has him, and is forcing him to use it… they can access Sterling's historical data, potentially pre-breach, and manipulate it without triggering current security alerts. It's a goldmine for them, Lena. And a terrifying liability for you, if your own digital footprints intersect with any of Jazzy's activities."

The implications were staggering. If Malik and his associates were using Jazzy's backdoor, they could potentially access and alter records that might contain traces of Cross's own clandestine activities within Sterling Corp. Her own carefully curated digital history could be rewritten, erased, or worse, fabricated to implicate her in ways she couldn't even imagine. The breach at Sterling was no longer just a corporate security incident; it was a weapon being wielded against her, and Jazzy was the unwilling conduit.

She had to get to Jazzy. Not just to save him, but to understand the extent of the compromise and to prevent Malik from using his access against her. But how? Going in directly would be suicide. Malik's people were professional, ruthless. She needed leverage, a way to outmaneuver them.

Her gaze fell on a sleek, discreet data drive she'd kept hidden in her jacket pocket, a sample of the proprietary data analysis software Sterling Corp was developing – the same software Julian had been so proud of. It was a powerful tool, capable of sifting through vast datasets with unprecedented speed and precision. If she could get her hands on Jazzy's backdoor code, she could use this software to analyze its function, its access points, and potentially find a way to neutralize it, or even to trace its usage in real-time.

But getting the software out of Sterling Corp's secure servers without raising any flags was a monumental task. It would require a level of access and technical finesse that even Lena Petrova, with her fabricated credentials, didn't possess. Unless... unless she could leverage Julian.

A daring, almost reckless, plan began to form in her mind. She would have to exploit the very paranoia Julian was experiencing. She would present herself not as a detective investigating a crime, but as a colleague deeply concerned about the integrity of Sterling's proprietary technologies, technologies that were now at risk of falling into the wrong hands.

She returned to Julian's office, her demeanor a carefully constructed blend of urgency and intellectual curiosity. "Julian," she began, her voice lower, more intense than before, "I've been thinking about your insider theory. It's not just about access to the network; it's about access to Sterling's proprietary research. Specifically, the Aether algorithm."

Julian's head snapped up, his eyes widening slightly. The Aether algorithm was Sterling's crown jewel, a revolutionary AI-driven predictive analytics engine that was the backbone of 'Swipe Right.' "Aether? What about it?"

"If someone could gain control of Aether, or even just its underlying data streams, they wouldn't just be stealing information. They could be manipulating the entire predictive model. Imagine if they could subtly influence the profiling, steer targets towards specific outcomes, or even... erase certain individuals from its historical analysis." She paused, letting the implications sink in. "This breach feels less like a simple data theft and more like an attempt to subvert Aether itself."

Julian was visibly intrigued, his professional instincts kicking in. He nodded slowly. "You might be right, Lena. The anomalies we're seeing in the data processing... they could be indicators of Aether being compromised from within. But Aether is sandboxed, heavily isolated. Accessing its core functions requires multi-factor authentication and specific clearance levels far beyond what a general system exploit would achieve."

"Exactly," Cross pressed, seeing her opening. "Which is why I think the threat might be more insidious. I've been reviewing some of our own internal diagnostic tools, specifically a prototype data analysis suite we developed for deep-dive diagnostics. It's designed to operate with high-level system privileges, allowing for a granular examination of data flow and algorithmic behavior, even within sandboxed environments." She was referring to the drive in her pocket. "It's still in beta, and it's incredibly sensitive, but if we could use it to analyze the Aether data streams... we might be able to identify the corrupted code or the manipulated inputs. But it requires a direct, albeit temporary, integration with the Aether sandbox. It's risky, but if Aether is being subverted, we need to know *how*."

Julian's gaze narrowed, a flicker of suspicion warring with his professional curiosity. "That prototype... it's not authorized for external use, Lena. And integrating it directly with Aether's core... that's a highly sensitive operation. We'd need explicit authorization, and a very clear justification."

"The justification is Aether's integrity, Julian," Cross said, her voice firm. "And the fact that the breach might be targeting it specifically. We're talking about potentially handing over control of Sterling's entire predictive infrastructure. If this 'insider' has access to Aether, then every piece of data we've collected, every profile we've built, could be compromised or turned against us. I believe the breach is a diversion, Julian. A smokescreen for a more targeted attack on Aether itself." She was layering her own fears onto the situation, making it seem like a shared concern for Sterling's future.

Julian remained silent for a long moment, his fingers drumming a restless rhythm on his desk. Cross could almost see the wheels turning in his analytical mind. He was faced with a catastrophic potential threat to his life's work, and she was offering him a tool, a solution, albeit a risky one, that might just save it.

"This prototype..." he finally said, his voice low, "what exactly does it do?"

"It allows for an unprecedented level of forensic analysis on data processing," Cross explained, choosing her words carefully. "It can trace the origin of data points, identify anomalies in processing patterns, and even reconstruct fragmented data. If there's malicious code or manipulated data affecting Aether, this tool could flag it. But it requires direct access to the source data streams, and it's designed to operate with minimal footprint to avoid detection. If we're right about the Aether compromise, then anything less would be like trying to find a needle in a haystack with a blindfold on."

She watched him, holding her breath. He was making a decision. The risk of her exposing herself was enormous, but the potential fallout if Aether was truly compromised was even greater. He was a man who valued control, and the idea of his creation being subtly manipulated, subverted, would be an unbearable affront to his professional pride.

Finally, Julian sighed, a weary exhalation. "Alright, Lena. I'll authorize a limited, one-time integration. But you'll be in the room with me, every step of the way. And if anything goes sideways, anything at all, you're the one who has to explain it." He met her gaze, his expression serious. "This is a massive risk. We're walking into a firestorm, but if you're right... we can't afford not to."

Cross felt a surge of adrenaline, a mixture of relief and trepidation. She had successfully maneuvered herself into a position to access the tools she needed, but now she was directly tethered to Julian's investigation, her every move scrutinized. The game had just become infinitely more dangerous, with Jazzy's fate, her own cover, and potentially the entire Sterling Corp operation hanging precariously in the balance. The ghost in the machine, it seemed, was becoming increasingly corporeal, and its presence was casting a long, chilling shadow over everyone involved. She was no longer just an observer of the breach; she was now an active participant, a pawn in a game she desperately needed to win, even if it meant playing with fire.

The digital echoes of Sterling Corp's breach, once confined to the hushed, sterile environment of Julian Vance's office, were already beginning to resonate in darker, far less regulated spaces. Detective Cross, still operating under the guise of Lena Petrova, knew that compromised data of this magnitude rarely stayed confined to corporate servers or even national networks. It was currency, a potent and sought-after commodity in the shadowy underbelly of the internet, a place where information was traded, bartered, and weaponized with terrifying efficiency. The illicit marketplaces, often referred to as "dark markets" or "bulletin boards," were the arteries through which such valuable information flowed, connecting anonymous sellers with even more anonymous buyers. These were not mere online forums; they were complex ecosystems, built on layers of encryption, untraceable cryptocurrencies, and a shared understanding of operational security that would make national intelligence agencies envious.

Julian's mention of an "insider" and the subtle corruption of data logs had painted a grim picture, but the chilling realization that this breach was about to enter the black market amplified the danger tenfold. This wasn't just about stolen corporate secrets;

it was about potentially weaponized personal data, financial records, intellectual property, and any other sensitive information that could be exploited for profit or power. The implications for Tasha's operation, for Cross herself, and indeed for countless individuals whose data might have been swept up in the initial breach, were profound. The carefully constructed digital world of Sterling Corp was about to be exposed to the harsh, unforgiving realities of the criminal underworld.

Cross understood that the black market wasn't a monolithic entity. It was a fractured landscape, populated by a diverse array of actors, each with their own motivations and methods. There were the data brokers, faceless entities that specialized in acquiring, verifying, and reselling datasets to the highest bidder. They operated with a chilling professionalism, their operations akin to sophisticated supply chains, ensuring the quality and integrity of their illicit wares. Then there were the nation-state actors, covert operatives seeking leverage, intelligence, or the means to destabilize rival economies. For them, the stolen Sterling data could represent a treasure trove of strategic information, offering insights into technological advancements, market trends, or even vulnerabilities in critical infrastructure.

Beyond these organized players were the individual predators: hackers for hire, blackmailers, and those seeking to exploit personal information for financial gain or sheer malice. The prospect of Sterling's data, particularly any personal identifiable information or financial details, appearing on these markets was a nightmare scenario. It meant that the meticulously crafted profiles Tasha had been building, the very foundation of her operation, could now be accessible to anyone with the right amount of cryptocurrency and a willingness to delve into the digital abyss.

Cross knew she couldn't afford to simply wait and see what happened. The breach at Sterling Corp was no longer an isolated incident; it had morphed into a clear and present danger to her own intelligence network, a threat that required immediate and decisive action. The information Blackwood had relayed about Jazzy's compromise and Malik's involvement was a stark indicator that the breach was not merely about data extraction. It was about control, about leveraging compromised assets to gain access to deeper, more valuable information – and potentially, to silence anyone who stood in their way.

Her mind raced, piecing together the fragments of information. Jazzy, a digital ghost who navigated the city's underbelly, had stumbled onto something significant – a connection between Sterling's data harvesting practices and illicit offshore financial transfers. This was the very nexus of the 'Swipe Right' operation, the dirty money trail that Tasha had been trying to expose and disrupt. Malik, the feared enforcer, had clearly moved in to protect his organization, first by compromising Jazzy, and then by forcing him to exploit his backdoor into Sterling's legacy systems. This backdoor, a relic of Jazzy's own operational history, was the key. It offered a way into Sterling's older, less secured archives, a place where data predating the current, more robust security measures might still reside. If Malik could access and manipulate this older data, he could potentially rewrite the digital history of Sterling Corp, erasing any incriminating evidence of Tasha's activities or, more ominously, framing individuals like Cross herself for crimes she hadn't committed.

The potential for this stolen data to be weaponized on the black market was staggering. Imagine credit card numbers being sold in bulk, allowing fraudulent transactions to skyrocket. Imagine sensitive personal details being used for identity theft on a massive scale, leaving victims financially ruined and their lives in tatters. Imagine trade secrets and proprietary research being leaked, undermining Sterling Corp's competitive advantage and potentially impacting global markets. The breach wasn't just a leak; it was a potential detonation, with shrapnel capable of reaching far beyond the immediate confines of Sterling's corporate walls.

Cross's thoughts drifted back to the data drive in her pocket, the prototype Sterling Corp analysis software Julian had been so proud of. This software, designed for deep-dive diagnostics and capable of operating with high-level system privileges, was her only hope. If she could gain access to Jazzy's backdoor code, she could potentially use this tool to dissect its functionality, understand its access points, and perhaps even trace its usage in real-time. It was a long shot, a risky gambit, but it was the only path forward that offered any chance of understanding the true extent of the compromise and mitigating the damage.

Her strategy to leverage Julian's paranoia was a delicate dance. By framing the issue as a threat to Sterling's proprietary technologies, specifically the Aether algorithm, she was appealing to his deepest professional insecurities. Aether, the AI-driven predictive engine, was the heart of 'Swipe Right,' and the idea of it being subtly manipulated, its predictive models altered, was a terrifying prospect for its creator. Cross had to present it not as a data breach, but as an existential threat to Sterling's core intellectual property.

"This prototype…" Julian's voice had been hesitant, laced with a mixture of professional curiosity and suspicion, "what exactly does it do?"

"It allows for an unprecedented level of forensic analysis on data processing," Cross had explained, choosing her words with extreme care. "It can trace the origin of data points, identify anomalies in processing patterns, and even reconstruct fragmented data. If there's malicious code or manipulated data affecting Aether, this tool could flag it. But it requires direct access to the source data streams, and it's designed to operate with minimal footprint to avoid detection. If we're right about the Aether compromise, then anything less would be like trying to find a needle in a haystack with a blindfold on." She had deliberately emphasized the need for direct access, knowing it was the only way to get the prototype out of Sterling's secure servers and into her possession, even if only temporarily.

Julian's agreement, to authorize a limited, one-time integration, was a victory, but a fragile one. It meant she was now directly tethered to his investigation, every move scrutinized, every keystroke potentially observed. The plan was audacious, bordering on reckless, but it was her only chance to intercept the flow of compromised data before it hit the black market, before Jazzy's backdoor became a fully operational pipeline for Malik and his associates to exploit Sterling's past, and potentially rewrite her own future.

The realization that the stolen data would inevitably surface on the black market was a chilling confirmation of her worst fears. It meant that Tasha's meticulously gathered intelligence, the very foundation of her operation, was now vulnerable to exposure. The data wasn't just bytes and code; it represented lives, relationships, and the intricate web of influence that Tasha had been working to unravel. If this information fell into the wrong hands, it could be used to blackmail, to destroy reputations, or worse, to facilitate further criminal enterprises.

Cross's mind immediately went to the vendors who operated on these illicit markets. They were the unseen hand that guided the flow of stolen information, the facilitators of digital crime. These weren't your typical street-level dealers; they were sophisticated operators who understood the value of data and the importance of anonymity. They would procure the Sterling data, vet it for authenticity and usability, and then list it for sale, often using encrypted marketplaces accessible only through specialized browsers like Tor. The pricing would be dictated by the perceived value and sensitivity of the information, with personal financial data, access credentials, and proprietary algorithms commanding the highest premiums.

The process of selling compromised data on the black market was a science in itself. Sellers would often package the data into discrete bundles, sometimes targeting specific industries or types of information. For example, a bundle might consist of thousands of compromised customer records from a specific company, complete with personal contact details, purchase histories, and payment information. These bundles would be advertised with cryptic descriptions, hinting at the contents without revealing too much, enticing potential buyers with promises of exclusivity and high profit margins. The transactions themselves would typically be conducted using cryptocurrencies like Bitcoin or Monero, further obscuring the identities of both buyer and seller. Once the payment was confirmed, the data would be delivered through secure, encrypted channels, often via peer-to-peer file sharing networks or temporary file-hosting services that quickly purged the data after download.

The consequences of this data entering the black market were far-reaching. For Sterling Corp, it meant a catastrophic loss of trust and potentially significant financial penalties for data protection violations. For the individuals whose data was compromised, it opened the door to a cascade of risks, from identity theft and financial fraud to reputational damage and personal harassment. Cross knew that Tasha's operation relied on the integrity of the data she gathered. If that data was corrupted, leaked, or discredited through its presence on the black market, the entire operation could be jeopardized.

The involvement of Malik and his forces, as Blackwood had indicated, added another layer of complexity and danger. Malik wasn't just a street-level enforcer; he was a strategic player, someone who understood the value of information not just for its immediate resale potential, but for its long-term strategic implications. If Malik was leveraging Jazzy's backdoor to access older Sterling data, he wasn't just looking to offload data onto the black market. He was likely seeking to identify and manipulate information that could be used to further his organization's goals, to silence opposition, or to gain an insurmountable advantage over competitors. This could involve anything from altering financial records to planting false intelligence or even orchestrating the digital erasure of individuals deemed a threat.

Cross's current predicament, needing Julian's cooperation to access the prototype analysis software, was a testament to how intricately her own investigation was now intertwined with the fallout of the Sterling Corp breach. She had to tread a fine line, presenting herself as a concerned colleague while secretly working to mitigate a threat that originated from a source she was still trying to fully understand. The pressure was immense. Any misstep, any deviation from her fabricated persona, could expose her and shatter the delicate balance she had so carefully constructed.

The urgency of the situation was amplified by the knowledge that time was a critical factor. The longer Malik and his associates had access to Jazzy's backdoor, the more data they could acquire, manipulate, and potentially distribute. Every moment that passed increased the likelihood of that sensitive information hitting the black market, becoming a weapon in the hands of countless unknown actors. She had to move quickly, to exploit the window of opportunity Julian had provided, and to find a way to neutralize the threat before it spiraled further out of control. The black market bid for Sterling's compromised data was not a hypothetical scenario; it was a looming reality, and Cross was now in a desperate race against time to prevent it from becoming a devastating fait accompli. The digital arteries of the criminal underworld were about to pulse with the stolen lifeblood of Sterling Corp, and her mission was to reroute that flow, or at the very least, to understand its ultimate destination before it could cause irreparable harm. The game had evolved, and the stakes had just been raised to an unimaginable level.

5: Collateral Damage

The digital tendrils of Tasha's operation, once a meticulously guarded secret, were beginning to fray, and the consequences were manifesting in the lives of those who had inadvertently become entangled. The Sterling Corp breach, a catastrophic event in itself, had acted as a catalyst, exposing not just corporate secrets, but the hidden underpinnings of Tasha's vast network. Individuals who had sought Tasha's expertise, her ability to manipulate systems and expose hidden truths, were now finding themselves on the wrong side of a very dangerous equation. Their trust had been misplaced, their vulnerability exploited, and the fallout was proving to be devastatingly personal.

Consider the case of Eleanor Vance, the wife of Julian Vance. While Julian was consumed by the intricacies of Sterling Corp's data security and the looming threat of its compromised algorithms, Eleanor had inadvertently become a pawn in a far more insidious game. Her engagement with Tasha had begun innocuously, a desperate attempt to uncover evidence of Julian's clandestine affairs, a suspicion fueled by his increasingly erratic behavior and late nights at the office. Tasha, ever the pragmatist, had seen an opportunity, not just to satisfy Eleanor's request, but to subtly gather intelligence on Julian himself. Eleanor, unaware of the true nature of Tasha's methods, had provided access to Julian's personal devices, his cloud storage, and even his social media accounts, believing she was merely helping a private investigator sift through digital detritus. What she didn't realize was that in doing so, she was opening a backdoor, not just into Julian's digital life, but into the core systems of Sterling Corp, a backdoor that Malik's operatives would soon exploit.

The information Tasha had gathered for Eleanor was damning enough – emails, financial records, and geolocation data that painted a clear picture of Julian's infidelity. But it was the additional data, inadvertently swept up in the process, that proved to be Eleanor's undoing. Julian, in his obsessive pursuit of the Aether algorithm's predictive capabilities, had been using Eleanor's personal cloud storage as a secure, off-network repository for his most sensitive research data. He had created a hidden partition, encrypted and masked, believing it to be beyond the reach of any external intrusion. He was wrong. Tasha, with her sophisticated data-mining tools, had uncovered it, extracting not just evidence of his affairs, but terabytes of proprietary Sterling Corp data, including early iterations of Aether and critical blueprints for upcoming projects.

This data, now compromised, was exactly what Malik's network craved. It wasn't just financial or personal information; it was the intellectual property that Sterling Corp held dear, the very engine of its future profitability. Malik, through his access to Jazzy's backdoor, had managed to locate and siphon this data from Eleanor's seemingly innocuous cloud account. The implications were chilling. Eleanor, who had simply wanted proof of her husband's betrayal, was now unknowingly harboring a treasure trove of stolen corporate secrets.

The first sign of trouble for Eleanor came not as a direct threat, but as a subtle, unsettling shift in her digital life. Her online banking alerts, previously a mundane stream of notifications, began to flag unusual activity. Small, almost imperceptible transactions, appearing and disappearing from her account with alarming regularity. Then came the phishing attempts, more sophisticated and targeted than anything she had encountered before. They were disguised as official communications from Sterling Corp, asking her to verify account details or update personal information, clearly leveraging fragments of data that had been leaked. Eleanor, initially dismissing them as annoyances, soon found herself in a terrifying situation when her credit cards were suddenly declined, and her bank account was frozen due to suspected fraudulent activity. The small transactions had been a prelude, a test run before the full-scale assault.

The black market, the very place where this stolen Sterling data was about to surface, was a hungry beast, and Eleanor's compromised information, coupled with Julian's data, became its sustenance. Data brokers, operating in the shadowy corners of the internet, would have quickly identified the value in Julian's research data. They would have meticulously verified its authenticity, cross-referenced it with other stolen datasets, and then packaged it for sale. For Eleanor, this meant her personal financial details, her social security number, her date of birth – all the identifiers that constituted her digital identity – were now circulating amongst criminals, ready to be exploited for identity theft, loan fraud, or even to create fabricated identities for illegal activities.

The psychological toll on Eleanor was immense. She was a woman who had prided herself on her discretion, her quiet, orderly life. Now, she was living in a constant state of anxiety, her privacy violated, her financial security shattered. The blame, she felt, was hers. She had been the one who, in her pursuit of marital truth, had inadvertently provided the access. The very act of seeking justice had led her down a path of ruin. She was a victim of Tasha's calculated moves, a collateral casualty in the war for information waged by Sterling Corp and Malik's empire.

Beyond Eleanor, there were others. Take, for instance, Marcus Bellweather, a mid-level analyst at Sterling Corp who had, in a moment of financial desperation, agreed to Tasha's offer of a substantial sum in exchange for access to internal project reports. He had been promised anonymity, assured that his small act of digital indiscretion would remain just that – small, isolated, and untraceable. Tasha, as always, had kept her word, ensuring that Marcus's involvement was masked by layers of obfuscation. However, the subsequent breach had rendered his actions anything but isolated.

The data Marcus had provided, concerning early-stage market research and competitor analysis, was now in the hands of Malik's network. These were not just abstract figures; they represented potential market advantages, strategies for product development, and information that could be used to preemptively undercut Sterling Corp's future ventures. Malik, a man who operated with ruthless efficiency, didn't just sell this information; he leveraged it. He would identify Sterling's upcoming product launches, understand their marketing strategies, and then manipulate the market to his advantage, often through shell corporations that appeared to be legitimate competitors.

For Marcus, the direct consequences were not immediate financial ruin, but a creeping paranoia. He began to notice subtle changes in his work environment. Colleagues would speak in hushed tones when he approached. His access to certain databases, previously unrestricted, was suddenly curtailed. He received an anonymous email, a single sentence that chilled him to the bone: "We know what you did." This wasn't a threat of exposure; it was a statement of fact, a chilling reminder that his actions, however carefully masked, had created a ripple effect, and that effect had now come back to find him.

He understood, with a dawning horror, that his attempt to alleviate his financial woes had placed him squarely in the path of Malik's influence. Malik's network, by acquiring and utilizing the data Marcus had provided, was actively working to undermine Sterling Corp. This meant that Marcus, by extension, was now a liability, a known point of compromise. The very systems he had helped to expose were now being used against his employer, and he was a silent accomplice. The anonymous email was a warning, a subtle implication that Malik's reach extended beyond the digital realm, a hint that his newfound silence was not a guarantee of safety, but a precarious temporary reprieve. His reputation within Sterling Corp began to erode, his career prospects dimmed, and the isolation he felt was a far greater punishment than any financial gain he had sought.

The human cost was also evident in the case of Amelia Chen, a graphic designer who had, months earlier, hired Tasha to investigate a potential copyright infringement on her artwork. Amelia, an independent artist struggling to make ends meet, had discovered that a large corporation, with whom Sterling Corp had recently partnered, was using her distinctive artistic style without her consent. Tasha, seeing the potential for leverage and further intelligence gathering on Sterling's associates, had taken on the case. She had, as part of her investigation, accessed Sterling's internal communications, revealing not only the extent of the partnership but also the fact that Sterling's legal department was aware of the infringement and had actively chosen to ignore it, deeming the artist insignificant.

This information, once unearthed by Tasha, was intended to be used to pressure Sterling's partner into a favorable settlement for Amelia. However, the Sterling Corp breach had changed everything. The communications Amelia's case had inadvertently revealed, detailing Sterling's complicity in the infringement, were now part of the compromised data that Malik's network was trading. This meant that Amelia's artistic integrity, her livelihood, and the evidence of Sterling's unethical behavior were now public commodities.

The fallout for Amelia was devastating. When fragments of the Sterling Corp data began to surface on the black market, her name, and the details of her dispute, appeared in hacker forums. Those who dealt in reputational damage and blackmail saw an opportunity. Anonymous individuals began contacting Amelia, threatening to release fabricated stories about her, accusing her of plagiarism herself, or threatening to expose her financial struggles in a malicious light. They demanded large sums of money, leveraging the very information that Tasha had gathered on her behalf.

Amelia, once a hopeful artist seeking justice, found herself in a nightmarish scenario. Her personal life was under attack, her artistic reputation tarnished by baseless accusations. She was too afraid to go to the authorities, knowing that her initial contact with Tasha, while for a legitimate purpose, had involved unauthorized access to Sterling Corp systems. She was trapped, a victim of a data breach she had no direct part in, but whose consequences had ensnared her through Tasha's operations. Her creative spirit was being crushed under the weight of digital exploitation.

These were not isolated incidents. They were the stark, human manifestations of the collateral damage wrought by the complex, often brutal, world Tasha navigated, a world that had now been irrevocably breached by Sterling Corp's vulnerabilities and Malik's predatory instincts. The pursuit of power, the manipulation of information, and the relentless drive for profit had created a chain reaction, leaving a trail of ruined lives and shattered trust in its wake. Eleanor, Marcus, and Amelia were just a few faces in a growing crowd of individuals caught in the crossfire, their personal stories serving as grim testaments to the devastating human cost of the games played in the shadows of corporate espionage and organized crime. The digital whispers of Sterling Corp's compromised data were becoming screams of despair for those who had the misfortune of being within earshot.

Tasha watched the rain lash against the reinforced glass of her secure loft, each droplet a tiny hammerblow against her fraying composure. The city lights below, usually a comforting tapestry of human endeavor, now seemed like a thousand accusing eyes, reflecting the chaos that had erupted in her meticulously constructed world. The Sterling Corp breach, a storm she had anticipated but underestimated, had not only torn through the corporate behemoth but had also ripped through the lives of those who had placed their trust, however tentatively, in her capabilities. Eleanor Vance, Marcus Bellweather, Amelia Chen – their stories, relayed through hushed, urgent channels, were not just collateral damage; they were sharp, agonizing shards of glass embedded in her own conscience.

She had always operated in the shadows, a phantom weaving through the digital ether, extracting truths, exposing secrets, and occasionally, subtly reshaping narratives. Her business, built on a foundation of discretion and results, had attracted a specific clientele: those seeking justice, protection, or simply a way to level a playing field tilted against them. And often, these clients were women, vulnerable in ways the male-dominated corporate world rarely acknowledged, navigating treacherous waters with few allies. Tasha had offered them a lifeline, a digital shield, and for a time, it had worked. But the Sterling Corp breach, amplified by Malik's predatory reach, had turned her protective measures into conduits of disaster.

The moral calculus of her operations had always been a tightrope walk. She justified her actions by focusing on the injustice her clients faced, the systemic inequities she helped to dismantle. But the escalating fallout was forcing a brutal re-evaluation. Was her pursuit of justice worth the crushing weight of unintended consequences? Malik's network, a hydra of illicit operations, had proven to be far more agile and ruthless than she had anticipated. They didn't just steal data; they weaponized it, turning personal vulnerabilities into instruments of blackmail and ruin. And her clients, the women who had sought her aid, were now the primary targets of this digital predation.

Eleanor Vance's story was a particularly bitter pill. Tasha had seen Eleanor's initial request – to expose her husband's infidelity – as a minor diversion, a way to access Julian Vance's digital life and glean intelligence on Sterling Corp's inner workings. The access Eleanor unwittingly provided, through her personal cloud, had been a golden ticket, a backdoor into Sterling's most prized secrets. Tasha had believed she was mitigating the risk, carefully extracting the necessary data while minimizing Eleanor's exposure. But Julian, in his arrogance, had used Eleanor's storage as a secondary cache for his Aether research. Tasha had retrieved it, unaware that Malik's agents were already scanning those same digital spaces. The subsequent freeze of Eleanor's bank accounts, the rampant identity theft – it was a direct consequence of Tasha's intrusion, amplified by Malik's opportunism. Eleanor, a woman caught between a philandering husband and a devastating data breach, was now facing financial ruin, her digital identity fractured. Tasha felt a cold dread pool in her stomach; she had promised discretion, but had delivered catastrophe.

Marcus Bellweather's situation was equally disturbing. His desperation for cash, a common thread among those who found their way to Tasha, had led him to provide internal project reports. Tasha had ensured his digital footprint was scrubbed clean, his involvement masked by a complex web of anonymizing proxies. But the sheer volume and nature of the data compromised in the Sterling breach meant that Malik's network had effectively mapped out Sterling's future strategies. Marcus's information, though seemingly minor, had contributed to a larger picture, allowing Malik to anticipate product launches, disrupt market entry, and sow discord. The anonymous email Marcus received – "We know what you did" – was a chilling testament to Malik's pervasive surveillance. It wasn't just about the data anymore; it was about the human element, the quiet dismantling of careers, the insidious erosion of trust. Marcus, a man who had only wanted to alleviate his financial burden, was now living in a constant state of paranoia, his career at Sterling Corp teetering on the brink of collapse, his very presence a liability. Tasha had intended to be his silent protector, but had inadvertently made him a marked man.

And then there was Amelia Chen, the artist whose creative integrity had been violated. Tasha's intervention had been meant to secure justice for Amelia, to expose Sterling Corp's complicity in a copyright infringement. The digital breadcrumbs Tasha had followed had revealed Sterling's awareness and deliberate inaction. This information, potent in the hands of Amelia's legal representation, had been inadvertently spilled into the digital black market through the Sterling breach. Amelia's name, her financial struggles, and the details of her dispute were now fodder for blackmailers, her artistic reputation threatened by fabricated accusations. The very people Tasha had sought to protect were now being exploited using the information she had painstakingly gathered. Amelia's fear, her inability to approach authorities for fear of implicating herself, was a reflection of the compromised, morally ambiguous landscape Tasha inhabited. Tasha had always seen herself as an agent of justice, but the current reality painted a starkly different picture: she was becoming an unwitting architect of her clients' downfall.

The magnitude of the external pressure was undeniable. Malik's network was actively exploiting the Sterling data, and the ripple effects were devastating for her clients. But the internal pressure was equally crushing. Tasha's own ethical compass was spinning wildly. Her business, built on the promise of empowerment and protection, was now the source of her clients' deepest fears. She had curated a network of women who sought to reclaim agency, to fight against systems that sought to control or exploit them. Now, those very systems, amplified by Malik's machinations, were using her network against them.

She paced the length of her loft, the polished concrete cool beneath her bare feet. The carefully curated calm of her existence was shattered. The technology that had been her fortress was now her greatest vulnerability. Malik's ability to penetrate Sterling's defenses, and by extension, to access the data Tasha had collected, meant that her entire operation was under immense scrutiny. Every client, every piece of information, every carefully constructed digital ghost was potentially exposed.

The question that gnawed at her, the one that had kept her awake for nights, was no longer about mitigating damage. It was about fundamental choices. Could she continue to operate in this volatile environment, knowing the price her clients were paying? Or was it time to dismantle her empire, to retreat from the front lines and protect herself and the few remaining loyalists she had? The thought of walking away felt like a betrayal of the women who still believed in her, who were still reaching out for help. But the thought of continuing, of risking further devastation, felt like a descent into a moral abyss.

She replayed the conversations, the whispered pleas, the desperate hopes. Eleanor's frantic calls, Marcus's increasingly erratic messages, Amelia's tearful silence after a phishing attempt. These were not abstract data points; they were human lives unraveling. Tasha had always operated with a detached pragmatism, viewing her work as a series of complex puzzles to be solved. But the Sterling breach had stripped away that detachment, revealing the raw, emotional cost of her clandestine war.

Malik represented a new breed of adversary, one who operated with a chilling blend of technological prowess and primal greed. He saw the digital world not as a space for information exchange or justice, but as a hunting ground, a marketplace for secrets and influence. His network was a parasite, feeding on the vulnerabilities of corporations and individuals alike. And Sterling Corp, with its hubris and its cutting-edge algorithms, had inadvertently provided the perfect feeding ground. Tasha, in her attempt to expose Sterling, had inadvertently guided Malik's predators to the very heart of the beast, and by extension, to the vulnerabilities of her own network.

The question of control was paramount. Could she regain control of the narrative, of the compromised data, of Malik's narrative of Tasha's network? The sheer scale of the Sterling breach suggested it was a near impossibility. Malik's agents were likely already disseminating fragments of her clients' information across various black markets, each transaction a fresh wound. Trying to claw back that data would be like trying to collect spilled mercury.

Perhaps the only true way out, the only way to salvage what remained of her principles, was to disappear. To sever all ties, to erase her digital presence, and to let the storm rage without her. But the thought of abandoning her clients, of leaving them exposed to Malik's relentless pursuit, was a visceral pain. She had built this network, this sanctuary, and now it was crumbling. Could she truly walk away from the wreckage?

Her mind raced, sifting through strategies, contingencies, escape routes. The carefully constructed walls of her operation were porous. The connections she had forged, once her strength, were now potential weaknesses. Malik was not just after Sterling Corp's data; he was interested in destabilizing any operation that threatened his own lucrative enterprises. Tasha, with her ability to disrupt corporate secrecy and expose illicit dealings, was a prime target.

She thought of the women who had relied on her. Not just clients, but associates, informants, individuals who had been drawn into her orbit by a shared desire to fight back. Were they also at risk? Had Malik's agents identified her network as a valuable target for infiltration or elimination? The paranoia that had gripped Marcus Bellweather was beginning to infect her own thoughts.

The weight of responsibility settled on her shoulders, heavy and suffocating. She had always believed in the power of information, in its ability to level the playing field. But information, in the wrong hands, could be a weapon of mass destruction. And Malik's hands were undoubtedly the wrong hands.

She considered reaching out to her most trusted confidantes, but the risk of further compromise was too great. Every digital interaction, every coded message, could be monitored. The silence of her loft was deafening, broken only by the persistent drumming of the rain, a relentless rhythm that seemed to mock her attempts at control.

The choice before her was stark: continue the fight, risking further devastation to herself and her network, or abandon her empire, sacrificing her hard-won position and potentially leaving her clients to fend for themselves against a predator of unparalleled cunning. There was no easy answer, no clear path to victory. Only the grim understanding that every decision, every action, carried a price, and the collateral damage of this war was mounting with terrifying speed. Tasha knew that the reckoning was not just external; it was internal, a deep, soul-searching confrontation with the consequences of her own ambition and the human cost of playing in the shadows. The rain continued its assault, mirroring the tempest brewing within her. She had to decide, and quickly, whether to shore up her defenses and fight for control, or to dismantle everything she had built, even if it meant sacrificing her empire to save herself and those she could still protect. The cost of continued operation was becoming immeasurable, and the temptation to simply disappear, to melt back into the anonymity from which she had emerged, was growing with every passing, rain-swept minute.

The relentless drumming of rain against the city's glass arteries was a soundtrack to Lena's inner turmoil. Each drop, a tiny, insistent voice whispering accusations, amplified the hollowness that had begun to consume her. Detective Cross, a title that had once resonated with a sense of purpose, now felt like a shroud, a label that had entangled her in a web far more complex and dangerous than any criminal conspiracy she had ever investigated. The Sterling Corp breach, a vortex of digital corruption, had not only ensnared corporate giants but had also dragged her, with chilling precision, into its murky depths. The initial thrill of uncovering a sophisticated cyber-attack had long since evaporated, replaced by a gnawing dread, a constant hum of anxiety that vibrated beneath her skin. She was no longer merely an observer, a detached investigator meticulously piecing together a case; she was a participant, irrevocably bound to the unfolding disaster by threads of her own making.

Her personal entanglement, a secret she guarded with the ferocity of a cornered animal, was the fulcrum upon which her entire world now balanced precariously. It was a relationship, or perhaps a situation, that defied easy definition, a clandestine dance in the shadows that had blurred the lines between professional duty and private obligation. The identity of the person at the center of this entanglement remained her most guarded secret, a vulnerability she couldn't afford to expose. But their existence, their very vulnerability, had become her Achilles' heel, the single point through which the machinations of Malik's network could breach her defenses. The knowledge that her actions, her choices, could have dire consequences not just for herself but for someone she deeply cared about, had twisted her moral compass into a desperate knot. The pursuit of justice, once a clear, unwavering beacon, had become a treacherous maze, each turn potentially leading her further away from her objective and closer to a devastating personal loss.

The pressure to compromise was immense, a constant, insidious whisper suggesting easier paths, more expedient solutions. Malik's operatives, like phantom limbs of a larger, unseen entity, had begun to exert their influence not through overt threats, but through subtle, calculated maneuvers that targeted her most sensitive points. She'd received anonymous packages, seemingly innocuous gifts delivered to her precinct, each containing a veiled message, a chilling reminder of their awareness. A vintage fountain pen, identical to one her mentor, the retired Detective Harding, had gifted her years ago, accompanied by a cryptic note: "Some debts are harder to pay than others." It was a reminder of her past, a subtle attempt to leverage her history against her present. Then there was the incident with her sister's car – a minor fender bender, easily explained away as coincidence, but the timing, the way the other driver had lingered, his eyes too observant, had sent a cold shiver down Lena's spine. These weren't random occurrences; they were carefully orchestrated chess moves designed to isolate her, to force her hand.

She found herself constantly looking over her shoulder, the familiar corridors of the police department now feeling alien and hostile. Every hushed conversation, every sideways glance, felt loaded with suspicion. Was she being watched? Were her communications being monitored? The paranoia was a corrosive agent, eating away at her resolve. She had always prided herself on her objectivity, her ability to remain impartial, but now, her personal stake had irrevocably tainted her judgment. The desire to protect the person at the heart of her entanglement warred with her ingrained sense of duty.

The information she had managed to extract about Sterling Corp's deep involvement with Malik's operations, particularly their culpability in the development of advanced surveillance technology, was damning. It was the kind of evidence that could dismantle entire organizations, bring down powerful individuals. But to bring it to light, she needed to navigate a minefield of internal corruption and external threats. Whispers within the department spoke of officers on Malik's payroll, of sensitive information being leaked to the very criminals they were supposed to be pursuing. The realization that her own colleagues might be compromised, that her investigation could be sabotaged from within, was a bitter pill to swallow.

Her personal entanglement had begun innocently enough, or so she had told herself. A chance encounter, a shared vulnerability, a spark of connection that had ignited in the sterile environment of her investigations. But that connection had deepened, evolving into something she couldn't easily disentangle herself from, something that made her question every professional decision she made. Now, the very person she sought to protect was unknowingly tied to the dangerous currents of the Sterling Corp scandal. And Malik, with his uncanny ability to sniff out weakness, had undoubtedly sensed it.

She remembered a recent late-night conversation with Marcus Bellweather, a low-level Sterling Corp employee who had provided crucial intel on the company's data handling protocols. Marcus, a man drowning in debt, had seemed genuinely terrified. He'd mentioned an anonymous email he'd received, a chillingly specific threat that referenced details only someone with deep access could know. "They know I talked to you, Detective," he'd stammered, his voice cracking. "They know about... about everything." Lena had tried to reassure him, to offer protection, but even as she spoke, a cold dread had settled in her stomach. Had her connection to Marcus, however tenuous, also exposed him to Malik's predatory gaze? Had her efforts to protect her own secret inadvertently placed others in peril?

The thought of her sister, Eleanor Vance, was another constant thorn in her side. Eleanor, a woman caught in the crossfire of her husband's corporate treachery and her own burgeoning awareness of Sterling's darker dealings, was increasingly fragile. Lena's attempts to guide Eleanor, to subtly steer her towards safety, felt clumsy and inadequate. Eleanor's frantic calls about suspicious activity on her bank accounts, her growing fear of being watched, echoed Tasha's own anxieties. Lena had initially approached Eleanor hoping to gain insight into Julian Vance's activities, but had inadvertently provided Malik with a backdoor into Eleanor's personal digital life. The irony was a bitter draught. She had sought to be a guardian, but had become an unwitting accomplice to her clients' unraveling. The vulnerability Lena felt wasn't just for herself, but for those who had stumbled into her orbit, those who had trusted her instincts and her badge.

The moral quagmire Lena found herself in was a suffocating reality. Every action she took was fraught with consequence. If she pursued the Sterling Corp leads aggressively, she risked exposing her personal entanglement, jeopardizing the safety of the person she cared about. If she pulled back, if she prioritized her own safety and the safety of her loved one, she would be betraying her oath, allowing Malik and his network to continue their insidious operations unchecked. The very fabric of her identity as a detective was being tested, stretched to its breaking point. She was no longer just a law enforcement officer; she was a woman making impossible choices, weighing the lives and security of others against her own deeply personal attachments.

The weight of this duality was crushing. She'd spent sleepless nights poring over encrypted files, cross-referencing financial records, piecing together the intricate web of deceit that ensnared Sterling Corp. Yet, interspersed with these professional endeavors were frantic, coded messages to the person who held her heart, reassurances, desperate attempts to maintain a semblance of normalcy in a world that was rapidly descending into chaos. The duality was exhausting, a constant battle between the detective and the woman, between duty and desire.

Her investigation had led her to a critical junction. The evidence against Sterling Corp was substantial, pointing towards a disturbing symbiosis with Malik's illicit operations, particularly concerning the development and weaponization of advanced AI surveillance systems. These systems, designed to predict and preempt criminal activity, were in reality being used by Malik to identify and exploit vulnerabilities in his targets, both corporate and personal. Sterling Corp's culpability wasn't merely in providing the infrastructure, but in actively collaborating with Malik to refine these invasive technologies, all under the guise of corporate security and innovation. The breach hadn't been an accident; it was a deliberate act of espionage, a test run for a far more sinister agenda.

The difficulty lay in presenting this evidence without revealing the source of some of her most crucial intel – information that had been obtained through means that bordered on, if not outright crossed, the ethical boundaries of her profession, all driven by her need to protect her personal connection. There were moments when she had to make impossible choices: to reveal a piece of information that would unequivocally prove Sterling's guilt, but which also carried the risk of exposing her own compromised position, or to withhold it, thereby protecting herself but allowing the criminals to escape justice.

The choice between pursuing justice and protecting herself, or rather, protecting someone intrinsically linked to her own life, was no longer theoretical. It was a stark, immediate reality. Malik's network had demonstrated a chilling capacity for retribution, not just against their targets but against anyone who posed a threat. She'd received an anonymous tip, delivered through a burner phone she'd acquired for clandestine communications, warning her that her personal life was now "under active surveillance." The message was chillingly specific, referencing a private conversation she'd had with the person she cared about, a conversation held in the supposed privacy of her own home. This was no longer about uncovering a corporate crime; it was about survival.

Lena found herself contemplating actions that would have been unthinkable just weeks prior. She considered planting evidence, a tactic she'd always abhorred, to create a narrative that would protect her sources and, by extension, herself and her loved one. She thought about orchestrating a rival's downfall, a carefully planned smear campaign to divert Malik's attention away from her own vulnerabilities. These were the thoughts of a woman cornered, a detective whose moral compass had been shattered, leaving her to navigate a landscape of shifting ethics and desperate measures.

The investigation into Sterling Corp had become a dual-purpose mission. On one hand, she was determined to expose the corruption at its core, to bring justice to those who had been harmed by the breach and its subsequent fallout. On the other, she was engaged in a clandestine battle for her own survival, and for the survival of someone who had inadvertently become entangled in her dangerous world. The stakes had never been higher. Every step forward was a calculated risk, every decision a potential precipice. The integrity she had always held dear was now a fragile commodity, constantly bartered against the primal urge to protect what she held most dear. The rain outside continued its relentless rhythm, each drop a reminder of the storm that raged within her, a storm that threatened to drown her in a sea of moral compromise. She was no longer just a detective hunting criminals; she was a woman caught in a desperate fight for her life, and for the life of another, a fight where the lines between right and wrong had become irrevocably blurred. The question was no longer *if* she would compromise, but *how much* she was willing to sacrifice to emerge from this darkness, and what would be left of her if she did.

The silence in the car was heavy, a palpable thing that pressed in on Jazzy from all sides. Outside, the city lights smeared into streaks of neon and amber as the rain intensified, drumming a frantic tattoo on the windshield. It had been hours since she'd seen Lena, hours since that fraught, whispered conversation in the damp alleyway. Lena's words echoed in Jazzy's mind, each syllable a hammer blow against her carefully constructed complacency. "They know about you, Jazzy. They know about us." The implication was a cold dread that had settled deep in her gut, far colder than the damp chill that had seeped into her bones.

For weeks, Jazzy had been a ghost in her own life, a silent observer of a game she didn't fully understand, played by forces she couldn't quite comprehend. She'd been content, or perhaps just resigned, to remain on the periphery, a passive recipient of Lena's clandestine interventions. Her role had been simple: be available, be discreet, and most importantly, be unaware. Lena had been the one navigating the treacherous currents, the one making the dangerous calls. Jazzy had been the collateral, the unintended consequence, the secret Lena was desperately trying to protect. But Lena's desperate plea had shattered that illusion of safety, that comforting distance. The danger wasn't a theoretical construct anymore; it was a tangible threat, a shadow stretching out to engulf her.

She gripped the steering wheel, knuckles white. The sleek, black sedan, a gift from Lena that now felt like a gilded cage, hummed beneath her. It was a symbol of the life Lena had tried to build for her, a life insulated from the harsh realities Lena herself faced daily. But that insulation had proven to be as fragile as spun glass. The breach at Sterling Corp, the digital phantom Malik and his network had conjured, had ripple effects that reached far beyond the sterile boardrooms and encrypted servers. It had reached into the quiet anonymity of Jazzy's existence, turning her into a target.

The memories of the past few days played on a loop in her mind. The unsettling feeling of being watched, the almost imperceptible shifts in the rhythm of the city that now seemed to scream danger. A few days ago, it had been a black SUV that seemed to materialize in her rearview mirror on two separate occasions, its tinted windows offering no glimpse of its occupants. Then, the anonymous package left on her doorstep – a small, intricately carved wooden bird, unsettlingly similar to one she'd owned as a child, a treasured memento from a time before Lena, before all of this. The accompanying note, penned in elegant, looping script, had been even more unnerving: "Some birds sing the song of freedom, others are caged. Be careful which you choose." It was a veiled threat, a chilling reminder that her very existence was known, her choices being scrutinized.

Lena had been trying to shield her, to keep her out of the crosshairs. But in doing so, she had also, inadvertently, made Jazzy a liability. Jazzy was the Achilles' heel, the soft underbelly that Malik's network could exploit to hurt Lena. The thought sent a fresh wave of fear through her. She thought of Lena's strained voice, the weariness etched into her features the last time they'd met. Lena wasn't just fighting a case; she was fighting for Jazzy's life, and that was a burden too heavy for anyone to bear alone.

This was the crux of it, the precipice Lena had spoken of. Jazzy could remain on the sidelines, a pawn passively waiting to be moved, or worse, sacrificed. She could continue to exist in the shadow of Lena's investigation, hoping that Lena's actions would be enough to keep the wolves at bay. That was the path of least resistance, the path of self-preservation, albeit a fragile, precarious one. It meant continued silence, continued ignorance, a surrender of agency in exchange for a fleeting sense of security. But the words "they know about you" had irrevocably altered that equation. Ignorance was no longer a shield; it was a blindfold, and the precipice was directly ahead.

Or, she could choose a different path. A path that meant stepping out of the shadows, out of Lena's protective embrace, and into the blinding glare of the danger itself. This wasn't about being a hero; it was about survival, about taking control of a narrative that was rapidly spiraling out of her grasp. It meant actively seeking a way out, not just for herself, but perhaps even for Lena. It meant confronting the reality that Lena's efforts, while valiant, might not be enough. Malik's network operated with a ruthlessness that transcended conventional law enforcement. They were masters of manipulation, of exploiting weakness, and Jazzy's existence was Lena's greatest vulnerability.

The options, stark and terrifying, presented themselves like diverging paths in a dark forest. Path one: continue as Lena's protected secret, hoping for the best, bracing for the worst. Path two: actively seek escape, to remove herself from the board entirely, to become an unreadable variable. And then, a more radical, terrifying option began to form in the recesses of her mind: to actively influence the outcome, to become an agent of change rather than a victim of circumstance.

She pulled the car over to the side of the deserted, rain-slicked road, the wipers swishing rhythmically, a metronome counting down her moments of indecision. The city skyline, a distant, glittering promise of normalcy, seemed impossibly far away. She thought of her life before Lena, a life of quiet routine, of predictable days and uneventful nights. It seemed like a dream now, a phantom limb of memory. Lena had brought passion, danger, and a love that had rewritten her world. But that rewriting had come at a cost, a cost Jazzy was now forced to confront head-on.

The passive route felt like a betrayal of Lena, a silent abdication of their shared bond. If Lena was willing to put herself on the line, to risk everything, then Jazzy couldn't simply sit by and wait to be saved. It felt cowardly. It felt like allowing Malik to win by default. The knowledge that she was the leverage, the key to hurting Lena, was a potent motivator. If she was the weakness, then perhaps she could also be the solution.

Escape. The word tasted like freedom, but also like abandonment. To disappear, to create a new identity, a new life far from the tendrils of Sterling Corp and Malik's reach. It was a tempting thought, a siren call promising oblivion from the present danger. But could she truly escape? Malik's network seemed to permeate every aspect of the city, every digital shadow. And even if she did escape, what of Lena? Lena would still be in the thick of it, still a target, and Jazzy would be leaving her alone to face it. The guilt of that possibility was a heavy weight.

Then came the idea, insidious and powerful, born from Lena's own desperate situation. What if Jazzy wasn't just a victim to be protected, but an asset to be utilized? Lena had managed to extract information, to navigate the system from within, albeit at great personal risk. Could Jazzy do the same? Could she leverage her proximity, her perceived innocence, to gather her own intelligence, to find a way to disrupt Malik's operations from an unexpected angle? It was a terrifying prospect, one that would require Lena's guidance, but also one that would put Jazzy directly in harm's way. It was the riskiest choice of all, the one that required actively engaging with the very danger she desperately wanted to avoid.

She closed her eyes, taking a deep, ragged breath. The rain was a torrent now, blurring the world outside into an abstract wash of light and shadow. She saw Lena's face in her mind, the fierce determination warring with a profound fear. Lena had made her choice: to fight, to uncover the truth, no matter the cost. Now, Jazzy had to make hers.

The choice wasn't about Lena anymore, not entirely. It was about her own self-preservation, yes, but it was also about a fundamental shift in her own existence. She could no longer be defined by her relationship with Lena, by her role as the protected secret. She had to forge her own path, make her own choices, even if those choices were fraught with peril.

She started the engine, the low thrum vibrating through the car. The decision had been made, not with a triumphant flourish, but with a quiet, grim resolve. She wouldn't be a passive bystander any longer. She would actively seek to control her own destiny. The question was, what form would that active participation take? Would she run, or would she fight? And if she fought, what would be her weapon? Her knowledge, her intuition, or something more... desperate?

The initial impulse was to disappear. To vanish from the city, from Lena's life, from the very awareness of Malik's network. It was the instinct of prey, the primal urge to flee from the predator. She could drive, just drive until the city lights were a distant memory, until she was a nameless face in a forgotten town. She could change her name, her appearance, and build a new life, one where Sterling Corp and Malik were just distant echoes of a nightmare she'd narrowly escaped. But Lena's words, her plea for help, her desperate warning, held her captive. Lena had confided in her, trusted her with a burden that was clearly crushing her. To abandon Lena now, when she was most vulnerable, felt like an unthinkable betrayal. It was a betrayal of their love, their connection, and the trust Lena had placed in her.

The alternative was far more daunting. It involved actively engaging with the very forces that threatened to engulf her. It meant shedding the passive role she had unconsciously adopted, the role of the protected innocent. She had seen the evidence Lena had gathered, the chilling details of Sterling Corp's complicity in Malik's sinister operations, the development of AI surveillance systems that preyed on human vulnerability. She had also seen the human cost of this digital warfare – the fear in the eyes of Marcus Bellweather, the growing paranoia in Eleanor Vance. These were not abstract concepts; they were the lived realities of people caught in Malik's web.

Jazzy was not a detective, not a hardened investigator like Lena. Her skills lay in observation, in understanding human behavior, in navigating the subtle nuances of social interactions. Could those skills be repurposed, weaponized against Malik's network? The idea was audacious, bordering on suicidal. To infiltrate, to gather intelligence, to become a spy in her own right, all while being the very vulnerability Lena was trying to shield. It was a tightrope walk over an abyss, with no safety net.

Lena had mentioned the possibility of Malik leveraging her personal life, using her as a means to an end. That was the key, the pivot point. If she was the leverage, then perhaps she could also be the lever. The anonymous messages, the subtle threats – they weren't just designed to intimidate Lena; they were designed to control her, to force her into submission. And Jazzy was the primary tool for that control.

She thought about the risks. Discovery meant not just her own demise, but potentially Lena's as well. It meant catastrophic failure for Lena's investigation. The consequences were staggering. Yet, the alternative – remaining a passive target, a pawn in Malik's game – felt like a slow, inevitable defeat. It meant letting Malik dictate the terms of her existence, and by extension, Lena's.

The rain seemed to wash away the last vestiges of her indecision. She couldn't outrun this. Not truly. Not without abandoning the person who meant everything to her. And she couldn't simply wait for Lena to resolve it all. This was her fight too, now. The realization settled over her, cold and stark, but also, surprisingly, empowering. She had been given a choice, however terrifying, and she would not squander it.

Her mind began to race, cataloging the information she possessed, the subtle observations she'd made during her limited interactions with Lena's world. She remembered overhearing snippets of conversations, noticing details Lena might have dismissed as insignificant. The way a certain code was referenced, the almost imperceptible hesitation in Lena's voice when discussing specific data points. These were fragments, but in the right hands, or with the right context, they could become something more.

The immediate goal wasn't to dismantle Malik's empire single-handedly. It was to survive, to remove herself from the immediate danger, or at least, to make herself a harder target. But simply fleeing felt like a defeat. She needed to be proactive. She needed to create distance, but not necessarily sever the connection entirely. She could become a more informed, more strategic player, rather than a passive victim.

Perhaps she could use the very tools Malik's network employed. Deception, misdirection, information warfare. She wasn't equipped for direct confrontation, but she was adept at observation and adaptation. The idea of creating a decoy, of manipulating the perception of her own vulnerability, began to take shape. If Malik believed she was a simple, terrified victim, easily controlled through Lena, then she could use that assumption to her advantage.

This would require Lena's explicit cooperation, a dangerous proposition given the risks to both of them. But Lena had already acknowledged the severity of the situation. Lena had already identified Jazzy as the weak point. If Jazzy could present a plan, a way to turn that weakness into an advantage, a way to gather crucial intelligence without directly exposing herself or Lena, then perhaps they could forge a new strategy, one that moved beyond mere protection and into active counter offense.

She thought of the anonymous wooden bird, the cryptic message. "Be careful which you choose." It wasn't just about choosing between escape or remaining. It was about choosing her role in this unfolding drama. Was she the singing bird of freedom, soaring away from the cage, or was she the caged bird, subtly manipulating her captors from within? The latter felt more aligned with the desperate reality they faced.

The path forward was not clear, not by a long shot. It was a labyrinth of shadows and whispers, a minefield of consequences. But for the first time since Lena's warning, Jazzy felt a flicker of agency. She wasn't just a piece on the board anymore. She was a player, albeit one forced into the game by circumstance, but a player nonetheless. The choice had been made. She would not be a passive casualty. She would actively seek a way through this darkness, a way to protect not only herself but the person who had irrevocably intertwined her fate with this dangerous world. The question now was not *if* she would act, but *how* she would act, and what unforeseen repercussions her choices would unleash. The rain continued to fall, washing over the city, over her, a baptism into a new, perilous reality.

Malik's gaze, sharp and unyielding, swept across the opulent boardroom, each face a carefully chosen mask of deference and ambition. The air, thick with the scent of expensive cologne and veiled avarice, crackled with an unspoken tension. He held court, a king surveying his domain, his fingers drumming a slow, deliberate rhythm on the polished mahogany table. His empire, built on the fractured foundations of data and deception, was on the cusp of a monumental expansion. 'Swipe Right', the dating behemoth he'd systematically hollowed out, was to be his ultimate prize, the crown jewel in his crown of digital conquest. Its vast repository of intimate user data, a goldmine of behavioral patterns and predictive algorithms, represented not just power, but the keys to unprecedented societal control.

He leaned forward, his voice a low, resonant hum that commanded absolute attention. "The final integration is scheduled for forty-eight hours. All systems must be optimized. Any… anomalies," he paused, letting the word hang in the air, a subtle threat, "will be dealt with. Swiftly. Permanently." A faint smile, devoid of any warmth, touched his lips. He saw the flicker of apprehension in the eyes of Thorne, his chief lieutenant, a man whose loyalty was as unwavering as his ambition was naked. Thorne, however, was a tool, a sharp, effective one, but a tool nonetheless. Malik knew how to wield him, just as he knew how to discard him when his utility waned.

The recent acquisition of 'Swipe Right' had been anything but smooth. Lena Petrova, the tenacious cybersecurity expert, had been a persistent thorn in his side, a digital phantom that had eluded his grasp for far too long. Her interference, her uncanny ability to anticipate his moves, had cost him valuable time and resources. He'd underestimated her, a mistake he wouldn't repeat. Her resilience, however, had inadvertently highlighted a critical vulnerability within his own meticulously crafted network: Jazzy. The woman, so seemingly insignificant, so utterly detached from the high-stakes game of corporate espionage and digital warfare, had become an unintended focal point. Lena's protectiveness of her, a maternalistic instinct that Malik found both predictable and exploitable, had presented him with a new, more intimate avenue of pressure.

He recalled the intelligence reports, the whispers from his operatives planted within Sterling Corp's less savory departments. Jazzy, an artist, a woman of quiet routines and predictable habits, was Lena's anchor, her emotional Achilles' heel. The thought was almost... amusing. To think that such a fragile connection could be the linchpin in Lena's grand defense. Malik's own emotional landscape was a barren wasteland, devoid of such sentimental attachments. Love, loyalty, empathy – these were weaknesses he had long since purged from his own operating system, and he sought to exploit them in others with surgical precision.

The pressure on Lena needed to intensify, but not in a way that would break her too soon. He wanted her to feel the tightening noose, to experience the gnawing dread of imminent defeat. He had orchestrated the anonymous threats, the unsettling packages, the chilling messages. Each was a calculated step, designed to isolate her, to sow seeds of doubt, and to remind her that no matter how skilled she was, she was not beyond his reach. The wooden bird, a seemingly innocent trinket, was a deliberate echo of her childhood, a subtle reminder that he knew her intimately, her past as well as her present. He reveled in the psychological warfare, the quiet dismantling of his opponent's mental fortitude.

His strategy was simple, brutal, and ruthlessly efficient: isolate, intimidate, and neutralize. Jazzy was the perfect tool for this phase of his operation. By making Jazzy the collateral damage, by threatening her safety, he could manipulate Lena into making rash decisions, into sacrificing her own integrity for the sake of the woman she cared for. He envisioned a scenario where Lena would be forced to compromise, to hand over crucial data, or to betray her own principles, all to ensure Jazzy's survival. The thought of Lena, the brilliant strategist, the formidable adversary, brought to her knees by a simple act of familial affection, was a particularly satisfying prospect.

He leaned back, a satisfied smirk playing on his lips. Thorne shifted nervously in his seat. "Sir," Thorne began, his voice carefully modulated, "there are… complications. Petrova's activity has increased. She's accessing older encrypted channels, ones we thought were dormant."

Malik's eyes narrowed, a predator sensing a shift in the wind. "Complications are for the unprepared, Thorne. And we are never unprepared." He waved a dismissive hand. "Her increased activity is a symptom, not a cause. She's cornered, desperate. She's looking for an escape route that doesn't exist. We have her trapped." He paused, letting the weight of his words settle. "What about Jazzy? Is she proving to be a useful leverage point?"

Thorne hesitated, his gaze dropping to the table. "Her movements are… erratic. She's not following the patterns we've established. There's a new element of… agency. She's not simply waiting to be a victim."

The revelation struck Malik like a shard of ice. Agency? Jazzy? That was… inconvenient. He had envisioned her as a passive pawn, a tragic damsel in distress whose fear would be the lever to pry Lena's secrets loose. The idea of her actively participating, of her making her own moves, was an unwelcome disruption to his carefully orchestrated plan. It suggested a level of resourcefulness, a potential for independent action, that he had not accounted for.

"Erratic movements?" Malik's voice hardened, the subtle amusement replaced by a dangerous edge. "Define erratic, Thorne. What is she doing?"

"She's been accessing public transit records, cross-referencing them with older traffic camera feeds. She's been… tracing her own movements, looking for surveillance." Thorne swallowed, his usual confidence faltering. "And she's been researching secure communication methods, untraceable networks. It's subtle, but it's there."

Malik's jaw tightened. Jazzy was not supposed to be engaging in such proactive measures. She was supposed to be terrified, paralyzed by fear, a helpless hostage. This newfound resourcefulness was a betrayal of his meticulously constructed narrative. It meant that Lena might have already briefed her, might have equipped her with the knowledge to evade him. This was not just a complication; it was a potential unraveling of his strategy.

He stood abruptly, his chair scraping loudly against the floor. The entire room fell silent, all eyes fixed on him. He began to pace, his footsteps echoing in the unnerving quiet. "She's not supposed to be capable of this," he muttered, more to himself than to anyone else. "She's not a player in this game."

"Perhaps," Thorne ventured cautiously, "she's not the passive element we believed her to be. Petrova may have underestimated her as well."

Malik stopped pacing, his gaze fixing on Thorne with a chilling intensity. "Underestimation is a luxury I cannot afford. And if Jazzy is indeed exhibiting… independent thought, then she becomes a threat. Not just to Lena, but to the integrity of our operation. We cannot have loose ends, Thorne. We cannot have unpredictable variables in play." His voice dropped to a menacing whisper. "Find out precisely what she's been doing. Trace her digital footprint, her physical movements. I want to know who she's been meeting with, what information she's accessed. If she's trying to escape, we need to intercept her. If she's trying to gather information, we need to neutralize that threat before it can fester."

He walked to the floor-to-ceiling window, looking out at the sprawling cityscape, a glittering tapestry of lights that represented his dominion. He had built his empire on the principle of control, on the absolute eradication of chaos. And Jazzy, in her unexpected awakening, represented a form of chaos he could not tolerate.

"Thorne," he said, his voice resonating with cold authority, "I want her contained. Not eliminated, not yet. Contained. Make her understand that her perceived agency is an illusion. Remind her of her true position in this equation. If she resists, if she proves difficult, then you have my authorization to escalate. Use whatever means necessary. I will not have this operation jeopardized by a foolish artist playing spy." His eyes, like chips of obsidian, scanned the distant lights. "And if Petrova interferes directly, if she attempts to shield Jazzy in any significant way, then she too becomes an obstacle. One that requires immediate and permanent removal."

He turned back to face his lieutenant, the predatory glint in his eyes undimmed. "The acquisition of 'Swipe Right' is paramount. Every piece of data, every user profile, every algorithmic insight must be secured. This is not merely about profit, Thorne. It is about shaping the future. And anyone who stands in the way of that future will be… erased."

Malik's ruthlessness wasn't a sudden development; it was the culmination of years spent navigating the murky underbelly of corporate power. He had started with nothing, a sharp mind and an insatiable hunger for more. Betrayal was not a moral failing; it was a strategic necessity. Allies were merely stepping stones, to be discarded once their purpose was served. He remembered Thorne's rise through the ranks, a man whose ambition mirrored his own, yet lacked the crucial element of foresight. Thorne was predictable, a quality Malik despised in anyone but himself. He was useful, undeniably so, but Malik was already mapping out Thorne's eventual obsolescence. The man was a tool, and like any tool, it would eventually be replaced by a more efficient model.

The data from 'Swipe Right' was the ultimate prize. It wasn't just about understanding dating patterns; it was about understanding human desire, human vulnerability, human predictability on a mass scale. With that data, Malik could influence elections, manipulate markets, even dictate social trends. 'Swipe Right' was the gateway to a level of power most people couldn't even comprehend, and Malik intended to hold the key. His ambition was a ravenous beast, constantly demanding to be fed, and 'Swipe Right' was the feast he had been anticipating.

He thought of the internal politics at Sterling Corp, the board members who had initially resisted his takeover. He had played them, leveraged their own greed and fear against them. He'd orchestrated discreet 'accidents', conveniently timed leaks of damaging information, and subtly manipulated stock prices. Thorne had been instrumental in some of those maneuvers, his direct, unthinking brutality a valuable asset. But Malik was the architect, the puppeteer pulling the strings from the shadows. He reveled in the complexity of his schemes, the intricate dance of deception and power.

The pressure on Lena needed to be amplified. He decided to shift tactics. Instead of merely threatening Jazzy, he would create a scenario where Jazzy herself could be used to betray Lena. He recalled a past operation where he had implanted a sleeper agent within a rival's inner circle, a man driven by debt and a thirst for revenge. The agent had been expertly groomed, his motivations carefully exploited. Could Jazzy be similarly manipulated? The idea was audacious, bordering on perverse, but it resonated with Malik's particular brand of genius.

He summoned Thorne back to his private office, the city lights a cold, distant backdrop to their clandestine meeting. The room was minimalist, designed to project an aura of cold efficiency. A single, abstract painting hung on the wall, its chaotic strokes a stark contrast to the calculated order Malik imposed on his world.

"Thorne," Malik began, his voice smooth as polished steel, "I've been reconsidering our approach to Jazzy. Direct intimidation is proving... inefficient. She's developing a resilience we didn't anticipate. This suggests that Lena may be preparing her, perhaps even giving her tools to resist us." He paused, letting the implication sink in. "We need a more... subtle method of control."

Thorne, ever the pragmatist, nodded. "What do you have in mind, sir?"

"We turn her. Or at least, we make her believe she has no other choice but to cooperate with us. We isolate her from Lena, create a situation where she feels abandoned, unprotected. Then, we offer her an alternative. A way to ensure her own safety, a way to escape this situation, but at a cost. A cost that involves a minor... betrayal of Lena's trust." Malik's eyes gleamed with a chilling calculation. "We feed her information, Thorne. Carefully curated misinformation that makes her believe Lena is using her, or that Lena is about to be apprehended. We make her believe that her only salvation lies with us."

Thorne looked genuinely surprised. "That's... ambitious, sir. And incredibly risky. If Petrova discovers this, she'll move heaven and earth to stop it."

"Petrova is currently focused on securing the 'Swipe Right' data. Her resources are stretched thin. She believes she's containing Jazzy, keeping her safe. She's blind to the fact that she's making Jazzy a more valuable asset to *us* if she's willing to betray her." Malik smiled thinly. "We'll exploit Jazzy's fear, her desperation, her inherent desire for self-preservation. We'll make her believe that her own survival hinges on cooperating with us."

Malik elaborated on his plan, detailing the subtle psychological manipulations, the carefully planted breadcrumbs of misinformation. He spoke of creating a false sense of urgency, of manufacturing a crisis that would force Jazzy to make a desperate choice. He envisioned a scenario where Jazzy would be fed fragmented data, seemingly innocuous at first, but designed to slowly erode her trust in Lena. Perhaps a misdirected communication, a fabricated digital footprint that suggested Lena was sacrificing her to protect herself. The goal was to sow discord, to shatter the fragile bond that made Jazzy a liability.

"We'll need to create a scenario where Jazzy believes she's being actively hunted by Lena's enemies, and that the only way to survive is to trust our protection," Malik explained, his voice taking on a low, hypnotic cadence. "We'll feed her information that makes her question Lena's motives, perhaps hinting that Lena has already cut her loose, or that Lena's plan involves her inevitable capture. We'll position ourselves as the only viable option for her safety."

Thorne, though visibly unnerved by the sheer audacity of the plan, understood the strategic brilliance. If they could turn Jazzy into a reluctant informant, a double agent even, it would be a devastating blow to Lena's efforts. It would provide them with direct access to Lena's plans, her vulnerabilities, her next moves. It would also serve as a powerful form of psychological warfare, crippling Lena from the inside.

"And if she refuses?" Thorne asked, his voice a low murmur. "If she remains loyal to Petrova?"

Malik's expression darkened. The veneer of calm composure fractured, revealing the chilling ruthlessness beneath. "Then she becomes an unrecoverable asset. A liability that needs to be managed. You will initiate contingency protocol Gamma-7. It's... unpleasant, but effective. We cannot afford to have loose ends, Thorne. Not now, not when 'Swipe Right' is within our grasp. The data must be secured. The operation must proceed. Jazzy's loyalty, or her lack thereof, will not be the determining factor. The outcome will be."

He looked Thorne directly in the eye, his gaze pinning the man in place. "I want you to understand something, Thorne. Sentiment is a weakness. Loyalty is a commodity. And survival... survival is the only true currency. Jazzy is a variable. And all variables must be accounted for, controlled, or eliminated. Ensure she understands the true nature of power, the true cost of resistance. Make her understand that her life, and Lena's, are merely pieces on my board. And when I decide to move them, they will fall exactly as I command."

The pursuit of 'Swipe Right' was more than just a business acquisition; it was a testament to Malik's unshakeable belief in his own destiny. He saw himself as a force of nature, a modern-day titan shaping the digital landscape. The data within 'Swipe Right' was the raw material of a new world order, an order he intended to architect. He was a man who believed in his own exceptionalism, a conviction that fueled his relentless ambition and justified his increasingly brutal methods. He viewed human lives as expendable resources, their hopes and dreams mere data points to be analyzed and exploited. Jazzy, in her unwitting entanglement, represented an irritating but ultimately surmountable obstacle. Her burgeoning independence was a statistical anomaly, a minor deviation from his predicted outcomes, and like any deviation, it would be corrected. The concept of collateral damage was not a moral failing for Malik; it was an accepted cost of doing business, a necessary byproduct of progress. He would dismantle Lena's defenses, exploit her emotional ties, and seize control of 'Swipe Right' with an unwavering resolve, leaving a trail of broken lives and shattered trusts in his wake. The stakes were too high, the prize too grand, for any consideration beyond his ultimate victory.

6: The Showdown

The sterile, echoey chambers of Sterling Corp's subterranean data vault hummed with a low, omnipresent thrum – the heartbeat of Malik's digital empire. It was a place of absolute control, where every byte of information was meticulously cataloged, scrutinized, and weaponized. Tonight, however, the usual symphony of servers was being drowned out by a discordant overture of escalating tension. Malik, a phantom in the periphery of his own creation, observed the unfolding chaos with a detached, almost clinical curiosity. His focus, however, was no longer solely on the acquisition of 'Swipe Right'. A new, more unpredictable element had entered his meticulously calculated equation: Jazzy.

Her deviation from the expected behavioral models had been a mere statistical anomaly, a glitch in his otherwise flawless predictive algorithms. But Thorne's reports had painted a far more disturbing picture. Jazzy, the unassuming artist, the emotional anchor for Lena Petrova, was no longer a passive piece on his chessboard. She was moving, thinking, actively seeking to disrupt his carefully laid plans. The intelligence Thorne had procured painted a disquieting portrait: Jazzy meticulously tracing her own digital footprint, cross-referencing public transit data with archived traffic camera feeds, searching for the invisible tendrils of surveillance that ensnared her. She was researching secure communication methods, exploring untraceable networks. It was a nascent rebellion, a spark of agency in a life he had presumed to be under his absolute dominion.

Malik stood by the observation window, his gaze sweeping over the rows of blinking lights and humming machinery, the physical manifestation of his power. He'd always prided himself on his ability to anticipate, to control, to predict. Lena Petrova, with her sharp intellect and her unyielding defiance, had been a worthy adversary, a formidable opponent who had forced him to adapt. But Jazzy… Jazzy was an oversight. An emotional variable he had underestimated, dismissing her as a pawn to be sacrificed. Now, she was proving to be an independent agent, a wildcard that threatened to unravel the entire operation.

"She's not supposed to be capable of this," Malik murmured, his voice a low growl that barely disturbed the ambient hum. "She's not a player in this game." His carefully constructed narrative of her helplessness, of her predictable fear, was crumbling. Lena, he surmised, must have armed her, perhaps even briefed her, equipping her with the knowledge to evade his grasp. This was no longer a minor complication; it was a critical vulnerability.

Thorne, ever the obedient subordinate, shifted his weight, his face a mask of professional concern. "Perhaps, sir, she's not the passive element we believed her to be. Petrova may have underestimated her as well."

Malik turned, his eyes, usually pools of calculated indifference, now glinting with a dangerous edge. "Underestimation is a luxury I cannot afford. And if Jazzy is indeed exhibiting... independent thought, then she becomes a threat. Not just to Lena, but to the integrity of our operation. We cannot have loose ends, Thorne. We cannot have unpredictable variables in play." He paced the length of the observation deck, his footsteps unnervingly silent on the polished floor. "Find out precisely what she's been doing. Trace her digital footprint, her physical movements. I want to know who she's been meeting with, what information she's accessed. If she's trying to escape, we need to intercept her. If she's trying to gather information, we need to neutralize that threat before it can fester."

His mind raced, formulating new strategies, new contingencies. Jazzy wasn't just a person; she was a potential exploit, a lever he could use against Lena. If she was actively trying to evade them, then she was already afraid. And fear, as Malik knew intimately, was a potent motivator.

"Thorne," he commanded, his voice regaining its chilling authority, "I want her contained. Not eliminated, not yet. Contained. Make her understand that her perceived agency is an illusion. Remind her of her true position in this equation. If she resists, if she proves difficult, then you have my authorization to escalate. Use whatever means necessary. I will not have this operation jeopardized by a foolish artist playing spy." His gaze, cold and unyielding, settled on Thorne. "And if Petrova interferes directly, if she attempts to shield Jazzy in any significant way, then she too becomes an obstacle. One that requires immediate and permanent removal."

The pursuit of 'Swipe Right' was more than a mere business acquisition for Malik; it was a testament to his unshakeable belief in his own destiny. He saw himself as a force of nature, a modern-day titan shaping the digital landscape. The data within 'Swipe Right' was the raw material of a new world order, an order he intended to architect. He was a man who believed in his own exceptionalism, a conviction that fueled his relentless ambition and justified his increasingly brutal methods. He viewed human lives as expendable resources, their hopes and dreams mere data points to be analyzed and exploited. Jazzy, in her unwitting entanglement, represented an irritating but ultimately surmountable obstacle. Her burgeoning independence was a statistical anomaly, a minor deviation from his predicted outcomes, and like any deviation, it would be corrected. The concept of collateral damage was not a moral failing for Malik; it was an accepted cost of doing business, a necessary byproduct of progress. He would dismantle Lena's defenses, exploit her emotional ties, and seize control of 'Swipe Right' with an unwavering resolve, leaving a trail of broken lives and shattered trusts in his wake. The stakes were too high, the prize too grand, for any consideration beyond his ultimate victory.

His thoughts turned to the intricate web of deception he had woven around 'Swipe Right'. The acquisition had been a masterclass in corporate warfare, a calculated dismantling of Sterling Corp's defenses from the inside out. He had leveraged Sterling's own internal politics, their board members' insatiable greed and their crippling fear, against them. Discreet 'accidents' had befallen those who resisted, conveniently timed leaks had crippled key departments, and subtle manipulations of stock prices had paved his path to dominance. Thorne, with his brute force and unwavering loyalty, had been an invaluable instrument in these maneuvers, a blunt instrument wielded with precise intent. But Malik was the architect, the puppeteer pulling the strings from the shadows. He savored the complexity of his schemes, the intricate dance of deception and power, the way he could orchestrate the downfall of an entire organization with a few well-placed whispers and a carefully timed financial maneuver.

The pressure on Lena needed to be amplified, but not through brute force. Direct confrontation, as Jazzy's unexpected defiance had shown, could breed resilience. Malik's mind, a constantly churning engine of strategy, began to formulate a more insidious approach. He would turn Jazzy's own strengths, her perceived weaknesses, against her. He recalled a past operation, a delicate maneuver involving a sleeper agent embedded within a rival's inner sanctum. This agent, driven by a potent cocktail of crippling debt and a burning desire for revenge, had been meticulously groomed, his motivations carefully exploited until he was putty in Malik's hands. Could Jazzy, the artist, the seemingly innocent bystander, be similarly manipulated? The thought was audacious, bordering on perverse, but it resonated with Malik's particular brand of genius. The idea of corrupting innocence, of turning a victim into a willing accomplice, was a particularly satisfying prospect.

He summoned Thorne back to his private office, a sterile space designed to project an aura of cold efficiency. The city lights outside, a glittering tapestry of Malik's dominion, seemed distant and indifferent. A single, abstract painting, its chaotic strokes a stark contrast to the calculated order Malik imposed on his world, hung on the wall, a silent witness to the machinations that transpired within.

"Thorne," Malik began, his voice smooth as polished steel, "I've been reconsidering our approach to Jazzy. Direct intimidation is proving... inefficient. She's developing a resilience we didn't anticipate. This suggests that Lena may be preparing her, perhaps even giving her tools to resist us." He paused, letting the implication sink in. "We need a more... subtle method of control. We need to fracture her trust in Petrova. We need to plant seeds of doubt so deep that they blossom into full-blown suspicion."

Thorne, ever the pragmatist, nodded, his gaze steady. "What do you have in mind, sir?"

"We turn her. Or at least, we make her believe she has no other choice but to cooperate with us. We isolate her from Lena, create a situation where she feels abandoned, unprotected. Then, we offer her an alternative. A way to ensure her own safety, a way to escape this situation, but at a cost. A cost that involves a minor... betrayal of Lena's trust." Malik's eyes gleamed with a chilling calculation. "We feed her information, Thorne. Carefully curated misinformation that makes her believe Lena is using her, or that Lena is about to be apprehended. We make her believe that her only salvation lies with us."

Thorne looked genuinely surprised, a rare flicker of something akin to astonishment crossing his features. "That's... ambitious, sir. And incredibly risky. If Petrova discovers this, she'll move heaven and earth to stop it."

"Petrova is currently focused on securing the 'Swipe Right' data. Her resources are stretched thin. She believes she's containing Jazzy, keeping her safe. She's blind to the fact that she's making Jazzy a more valuable asset to *us* if she's willing to betray her." Malik smiled thinly, a predatory curve of his lips. "We'll exploit Jazzy's fear, her desperation, her inherent desire for self-preservation. We'll make her believe that her own survival hinges on cooperating with us."

Malik elaborated on his plan, detailing the subtle psychological manipulations, the carefully planted breadcrumbs of misinformation that would lead Jazzy down a path of suspicion and fear. He spoke of creating a false sense of urgency, of manufacturing a crisis that would force Jazzy to make a desperate choice, a choice that would irrevocably sever her ties to Lena. He envisioned a scenario where Jazzy would be fed fragmented data, seemingly innocuous at first, but designed to slowly erode her trust in Lena. Perhaps a misdirected communication, a fabricated digital footprint that suggested Lena was sacrificing her to protect herself. The goal was to sow discord, to shatter the fragile bond that made Jazzy a liability, and transform her into an unwitting pawn in his grander design.

"We'll need to create a scenario where Jazzy believes she's being actively hunted by Lena's enemies, and that the only way to survive is to trust our protection," Malik explained, his voice taking on a low, hypnotic cadence that seemed to coil around Thorne. "We'll feed her information that makes her question Lena's motives, perhaps hinting that Lena has already cut her loose, or that Lena's plan involves her inevitable capture. We'll position ourselves as the only viable option for her safety, the only sanctuary in a world that is rapidly closing in around her."

Thorne, though visibly unnerved by the sheer audacity and the chilling implications of the plan, understood the strategic brilliance. If they could turn Jazzy into a reluctant informant, a double agent even, it would be a devastating blow to Lena's efforts. It would provide them with direct access to Lena's plans, her vulnerabilities, her next moves. It would also serve as a powerful form of psychological warfare, crippling Lena from the inside out, forcing her to confront the devastating consequences of her perceived failures.

"And if she refuses?" Thorne asked, his voice a low murmur, tinged with a hint of apprehension. "If she remains loyal to Petrova, despite our efforts?"

Malik's expression darkened, the veneer of calm composure fracturing, revealing the chilling ruthlessness that lay beneath. "Then she becomes an unrecoverable asset. A liability that needs to be managed. You will initiate contingency protocol Gamma-7. It's... unpleasant, but effective. We cannot afford to have loose ends, Thorne. Not now, not when 'Swipe Right' is within our grasp. The data must be secured. The operation must proceed. Jazzy's loyalty, or her lack thereof, will not be the determining factor. The outcome will be."

He looked Thorne directly in the eye, his gaze pinning the man in place, a silent assertion of absolute authority. "I want you to understand something, Thorne. Sentiment is a weakness. Loyalty is a commodity. And survival... survival is the only true currency. Jazzy is a variable. And all variables must be accounted for, controlled, or eliminated. Ensure she understands the true nature of power, the true cost of resistance. Make her understand that her life, and Lena's, are merely pieces on my board. And when I decide to move them, they will fall exactly as I command."

The pursuit of 'Swipe Right' had transcended mere acquisition; it had become a crusade, a testament to Malik's unshakeable conviction in his own exceptionalism. He viewed himself as a force of nature, a modern-day titan reshaping the digital landscape according to his own grand design. The vast trove of data within 'Swipe Right' was not simply information; it was the raw material of a new world order, an order he intended to architect with absolute precision. His ambition was a ravenous beast, constantly demanding to be fed, and 'Swipe Right' represented the feast he had been anticipating for years. He believed in his own destiny, a conviction that fueled his relentless drive and justified his increasingly brutal methods. Human lives, in his calculus, were expendable resources, their hopes and dreams mere data points to be analyzed, exploited, and ultimately, discarded. Jazzy, in her unwitting entanglement, represented an irritating but ultimately surmountable obstacle. Her burgeoning independence was a statistical anomaly, a minor deviation from his meticulously calculated outcomes, and like any deviation, it would be corrected with ruthless efficiency. The concept of collateral damage was not a moral failing for Malik; it was an accepted cost of doing business, a necessary byproduct of progress. He would dismantle Lena's defenses, exploit her emotional ties, and seize control of 'Swipe Right' with an unwavering resolve, leaving a trail of broken lives and shattered trusts in his wake. The stakes were too high, the prize too grand, for any consideration beyond his ultimate, unassailable victory.

The convergence was now absolute. Tasha, unaware of the true stakes, had agreed to meet Detective Cross at a discreet, off-the-grid location within the city's sprawling industrial district – an abandoned shipping depot, its skeletal remains a stark contrast to the gleaming towers of corporate power. Her goal was simple: to pass on the fragmented intelligence she had managed to unearth, the whispers of Malik's true intentions, the devastating scope of his plan to weaponize personal data. She believed she was acting on Lena's behalf, a loyal operative in a complex but ultimately understandable fight for privacy. She had no idea that her actions, her every move, were being meticulously tracked, not just by Malik's surveillance network, but by an even more insidious force.

Malik, however, had his own agenda for this nexus point. He had orchestrated the gathering, a calculated move to draw out his disparate enemies, to corral them into a single, contained environment where he could observe and, if necessary, neutralize them. He knew Tasha was meeting Cross. He also knew Lena was on her way, a calculated risk he was willing to take. She was too invested, too desperate to protect Jazzy, to stay away. For Malik, this convergence was not an accident; it was the apex of his plan, the moment all the threads he had so painstakingly woven would finally come together, creating a tapestry of his absolute control. The abandoned shipping depot, with its labyrinthine corridors and its cavernous, echoing spaces, would serve as the perfect stage for the final act. The air, thick with the metallic tang of rust and the lingering scent of sea salt, would soon be charged with a far more volatile tension

– the raw energy of a showdown where loyalties would be tested, and lives would be irrevocably altered.

As Tasha navigated the derelict landscape, her senses on high alert, the gnawing unease intensified. The silence here was not peaceful; it was a pregnant, suffocating quiet, the kind that preceded a storm. She clutched the encrypted drive containing her findings, its weight a physical manifestation of the danger she was in. She had seen the flicker of something sinister in Malik's eyes during their brief, chilling encounter, a depth of ruthlessness she hadn't fully comprehended until now. Lena had warned her, but Tasha, fueled by a sense of justice and a fierce protectiveness for the digital frontier, had pushed forward. Now, standing amidst the decaying remnants of commerce, she felt a primal fear prickle her skin. This was no longer just about data privacy; it was about survival.

Across town, Lena Petrova was en route to the same location, her mind a whirlwind of tactical considerations and desperate hopes. Jazzy's cryptic messages, her increasingly sophisticated attempts to communicate through secure, untraceable channels, had confirmed Malik's insidious plan. He wasn't just after 'Swipe Right'; he was targeting Jazzy directly, using her as leverage, a pawn in his elaborate game of manipulation. Lena's protective instincts, her fierce maternal love for Jazzy, had overridden her usual cautious approach. She had to reach her, to protect her, to dismantle Malik's operation before he could inflict irreparable damage. She knew the risks, but the thought of Jazzy falling prey to Malik's machinations was a terror she could not endure. The shipping depot, a known neutral zone in the city's underbelly, seemed like the only plausible meeting point, a place where communication could potentially occur away from Malik's omnipresent digital surveillance. She had reached out to Cross, entrusting him with a portion of her findings, hoping he could provide the necessary backup, the legitimate force to counter Malik's illicit power.

Detective Cross, a man whose weary cynicism masked a core of unwavering integrity, was already on his way. The information Tasha had provided, though fragmented, painted a chilling picture of Malik's reach and his disregard for human life. The encrypted drive, a digital Pandora's Box, hinted at a conspiracy far grander and more terrifying than he had initially imagined. He knew Sterling Corp's acquisition of 'Swipe Right' was more than a hostile takeover; it was a prelude to something far more devastating. He had seen the patterns, the anomalies in the data, the whispers of illegal surveillance and manipulation. He recognized Malik as a predator operating at the highest echelms of power, a man who wielded information as a weapon of mass destruction. The shipping depot meeting was a calculated risk, a desperate attempt to gather concrete evidence, to confront Malik's operation head-on. He was going in blind, armed with limited intelligence and a badge, stepping into a hornet's nest with the hope of bringing down the queen bee. He knew Tasha would be there, a vital source of information, and he felt a grim responsibility for her safety. The convergence was inevitable, a collision course of protagonists and antagonists, each driven by their own desperate motives, all converging on a single, volatile point. The fate of countless individuals, their privacy and their very autonomy, hung precariously in the balance, about to be decided within the decaying embrace of the abandoned shipping depot. The air crackled with anticipation, the quiet hum of the city outside a stark contrast to the brewing storm within.

The acrid scent of decaying canvas and stagnant brine clung to Tasha as she navigated the labyrinthine interior of the abandoned shipping depot. Each echoing footstep amplified her isolation, a stark counterpoint to the controlled chaos she was accustomed to within Sterling Corp's digital fortress. She clutched the encrypted drive containing her findings, its cold metal a tangible symbol of the truth she was about to expose. Lena had entrusted her with this, a crucial piece of the puzzle, and the weight of that responsibility pressed down on her, heavy and suffocating. She'd been so focused on the data, on the insidious ways Malik intended to weaponize personal information, that she hadn't fully anticipated the personal peril. Her belief in the inherent goodness of her mission, the righteousness of exposing Malik's depravity, had blinded her to the machinations unfolding in the shadows, the subtle poisons of betrayal that could seep into even the most virtuous of alliances.

The instructions from Lena had been precise: meet Detective Cross at this location, pass him the drive, and disappear. A simple exchange, designed to be a surgical strike against Malik's sprawling empire of corruption. But as she moved deeper into the cavernous space, the air growing colder, a prickle of unease that had been growing since her initial encounter with Malik began to solidify into a cold dread. The silence wasn't empty; it felt pregnant with unseen eyes, with a malevolent awareness of her presence. She replayed the brief, chilling exchange with Malik in her mind – the almost imperceptible tremor in his voice when he spoke of 'contingencies,' the predatory gleam in his eyes that had promised far more than mere corporate rivalry. He had alluded to disruptions, to unforeseen variables that could alter the course of his grand design. Had he known about this meeting? Had he orchestrated this very moment, not to be exposed, but to witness the unraveling of those who dared to oppose him?

A sudden movement in the periphery of her vision sent a jolt of adrenaline through her. She froze, her heart hammering against her ribs like a trapped bird. It was just a rat, a scuttling shadow disappearing into the gloom, but the visceral reaction was a stark reminder of how far she had strayed from the sterile safety of her digital world. Lena had insisted on Tasha's involvement, recognizing the artist's unique perspective, her ability to see patterns where others saw only noise. But Tasha, in her naiveté, had underestimated the sheer ruthlessness of the players involved. She had believed Lena's careful plans, her meticulous strategies, were enough. Now, the ground beneath her feet felt unstable, the carefully constructed edifice of trust she had placed in her allies beginning to crumble.

Across town, Lena Petrova gripped the steering wheel of her nondescript sedan, her knuckles white. Jazzy's latest communication had been more than just a message; it had been a desperate cry for help, encrypted within layers of digital obfuscation that spoke of a rapidly escalating threat. Malik wasn't just acquiring 'Swipe Right'; he was actively targeting Jazzy, using her as a psychological weapon, a means to break Lena's resolve. The confirmation of her worst fears sent a surge of cold fury through her. She had tried to protect Jazzy, to shield her from the devastating reality of Malik's machinations, but in doing so, she had inadvertently made her a more potent target. The thought of Jazzy, vulnerable and alone, falling into Malik's clutches was a terror that gnawed at her, a primal instinct that demanded immediate action, overriding her usual cautious, calculated approach. The shipping depot, a recognized blind spot in the city's omnipresent surveillance grid, had seemed like the only viable rendezvous, a place where a brief window of unmonitored communication might exist. She had reached out to Detective Cross, a man whose reputation for integrity was as solid as the city's foundations, entrusting him with a partial decryption of Malik's master plan, hoping his authority could provide the necessary muscle to counter Malik's illicit power.

Detective Cross, his face etched with the weariness of a thousand sleepless nights and a hundred thankless investigations, navigated the pre-dawn streets with a grim determination. The fragmented intel from Tasha, a digital whisper of Malik's true intentions, had confirmed his deepest suspicions. The acquisition of 'Swipe Right' wasn't just a hostile takeover; it was the prelude to a systematic dismantling of privacy on an unprecedented scale. He had seen the subtle anomalies, the whispers of illegal surveillance and data manipulation that Lena's team had managed to unearth. Malik was no mere businessman; he was a predator, a phantom architect of digital control, wielding information as a weapon of mass destruction. The rendezvous at the shipping depot was a calculated risk, a desperate gamble to obtain irrefutable evidence, to finally confront Malik's operation head-on. He was walking into the lion's den, armed with limited intelligence and a badge, hoping to bring down the apex predator. He knew Tasha would be there, a vital conduit of information, and a significant part of him felt responsible for her safety. The convergence was inevitable, a collision course of individuals driven by disparate motives, all converging on a single, volatile point. The fate of countless individuals, their privacy and their autonomy, hung precariously in the balance, about to be decided within the decaying embrace of the abandoned shipping depot.

As Tasha edged closer to the designated meeting point, a hulking, rust-streaked container with the faded insignia of a long-defunct shipping line, a chilling realization began to dawn. The intelligence she possessed was more than just data; it was a testament to Lena's meticulous planning, her unwavering dedication to exposing Malik. But Tasha had also noticed subtle inconsistencies in Lena's instructions, small hesitations, almost imperceptible shifts in tone that, in retrospect, hinted at a deeper layer of concern, a carefully guarded apprehension. Was Lena truly as in control as she seemed? Or was she, like Tasha, being manipulated, her own carefully laid plans potentially compromised? The thought was a bitter pill to swallow. Trust, once a bedrock, now felt like shifting sand.

Then, she saw him. Detective Cross, a silhouette against the weak predawn light filtering through a grimy window. He was exactly as Lena had described him – unassuming, yet radiating an aura of quiet authority. Relief, sharp and sudden, flooded through her, momentarily eclipsing her growing unease. She moved towards him, her pace quickening, the drive held tightly in her hand.

"Detective Cross?" she called out, her voice a little too loud in the vast emptiness.

He turned, his expression unreadable in the dim light. "Tasha?" His voice was a low rumble, devoid of inflection.

She nodded, extending the drive. "I have it. Everything I could find. Malik's plan, the scope of his surveillance, the way he intends to use 'Swipe Right'—"

He took the drive, his fingers brushing hers. The contact was brief, but Tasha felt an odd stillness in his touch, a peculiar lack of urgency. It was as if he already knew what was on the drive, as if this meeting was merely a formality.

"Lena briefed me," Cross said, his gaze sweeping over her, not with curiosity, but with a strange, detached assessment.

Tasha's relief faltered, replaced by a fresh wave of suspicion. "She did? So she knows I'm here?"

"She knows you're making the exchange," he confirmed. "And she also knows the risks involved." He paused, the silence stretching between them, punctuated only by the distant groans of the aging structure. "Risks that, perhaps, you haven't fully appreciated."

Before Tasha could press him, a new sound cut through the stillness – the heavy clang of metal on concrete. Multiple footsteps, echoing and purposeful, approached from the opposite end of the depot. Tasha's breath hitched. This wasn't the sound of Cross's backup. This was something else, something more coordinated, more... predatory.

Cross remained unnervingly calm. "It appears our time is limited," he said, his voice retaining that same unnerving detachment. He slipped the drive into his jacket pocket. "Lena anticipated this possibility."

The approaching figures emerged from the shadows – not police officers, but burly, grim-faced men, clad in dark tactical gear. Their leader, a man with a scar bisecting his left eyebrow, stopped a few yards away, his gaze fixed on Cross.

"Detective," the scarred man's voice was a gravelly rasp. "Mr. Malik appreciates your cooperation."

Tasha's blood ran cold. Cooperation? Malik? The words slammed into her with the force of a physical blow. Her gaze snapped to Cross, searching his face for a flicker of betrayal, a hint of the conspiracy she now suspected. His expression remained impassive, a perfect mask.

"It seems there's been a misunderstanding," Cross said, his voice steady. "I'm here to secure the data and ensure Tasha's safety."

The scarred man let out a low chuckle. "Mr. Malik is a generous employer, Detective. He believes in rewarding loyalty. And in ensuring that valuable assets are properly accounted for." He gestured with his chin towards Tasha. "Especially assets that have proven... resourceful."

Tasha stumbled back, the world tilting on its axis. Resourceful? She was an asset? She looked at Cross, her eyes wide with dawning horror. He wasn't here to help her; he was here as a gatekeeper, a facilitator of Malik's twisted agenda.

"Lena," Tasha whispered, the name catching in her throat. "Lena sent you?"

Cross's gaze finally met hers, and in that brief, chilling moment, she saw it – not malice, but a profound weariness, a resignation that spoke volumes. "Lena's plans were… compromised, Tasha. Malik anticipated this meeting. He anticipated your involvement. And he made me an offer I couldn't refuse." His voice dropped, laced with a hint of something Tasha couldn't quite decipher – regret, perhaps, or a chilling pragmatism. "He's been watching us, Tasha. All of us. He knows about your drive. He knows about Lena. And he knows that sometimes, the best way to control the narrative is to control the players."

The scarred man took a step forward, his hand resting on the butt of a sidearm. "Mr. Malik wants a direct dialogue with Ms. Petrova. He believes she needs a… clearer understanding of her position. And he believes you, Tasha, can help facilitate that."

Tasha's mind reeled. Betrayal. It had come from the most unexpected quarter. Cross, the man Lena had trusted, the detective who was supposed to be her shield, was now an agent of her tormentor. The realization was a physical blow, stealing her breath. Lena had warned her about unforeseen variables, about Malik's capacity for deception, but she had never imagined this – a betrayal from within their own fragile alliance.

"You're working for Malik?" she managed to choke out, the words thick with disbelief.

Cross didn't answer directly. He simply inclined his head towards the scarred man. "Mr. Malik is… persuasive. He offered me a way out of a very difficult situation. A way to protect certain… sensitive information I've been holding onto. Information that could be very damaging to my career, to my pension." He finally looked at Tasha, his eyes holding a flicker of something that might have been apology. "He knew I was compromised, Tasha. He knew about my… vulnerabilities. And he exploited them. Just as he's trying to exploit Lena's."

The implications slammed into Tasha with brutal force. Cross's compromised state, Lena's subtle hesitations – it all clicked into place. Malik hadn't just anticipated the meeting; he had orchestrated it, leveraging an informant within their own ranks. And the informant wasn't some faceless subordinate; it was the man they had turned to for help.

"So this whole thing..." Tasha gestured wildly around the depot, her voice rising with a desperate edge. "This was a trap. You led me right into it."

"Malik wanted you delivered," Cross said, his voice flat. "He wants to send a message to Lena. That her attempts to resist are futile. That he controls every aspect of this... situation." He took a step back, a clear signal that his part in this charade was complete. "He'll be in touch with Lena. He'll explain the terms."

As the tactical team began to advance on Tasha, she knew that her efforts, her dangerous journey into the heart of Malik's operation, had led not to exposure, but to her own capture. The drive, clutched so tightly just moments before, was now in the hands of her enemy's ally, its contents twisted and weaponized against the very people it was meant to protect. The carefully constructed facade of trust had crumbled, revealing the stark, brutal reality of Malik's influence, an influence that reached into the most unexpected corners, turning allies into adversaries and hope into despair. The betrayal was absolute, a chilling testament to Malik's insidious power, leaving Tasha stranded in a darkness far deeper than the shadows of the abandoned depot.

Meanwhile, Lena, en route to the same location, experienced a sudden, chilling premonition. The radio crackled with static, a burst of unintelligible chatter from a police frequency. It wasn't a direct threat, but it was enough to prick her instincts. Cross was supposed to be a ghost in the system, an unseen hand working from the shadows. Any indication of official involvement, any hint of discovery, would be disastrous. She tried to contact him, her fingers flying across the console of her encrypted comms unit, but there was only silence. A dead channel. A void where Cross's steady presence should have been.

A cold dread began to coil in her stomach. Cross had confirmed the meeting, had acknowledged receiving the intel. His silence now was deafening. Had Malik intercepted their communications? Had he somehow anticipated this last-ditch effort? Or was something far worse at play? The thought, a venomous whisper, began to take root: had Cross been compromised? The idea was abhorrent, a violation of the fundamental trust she had placed in him. But Malik's modus operandi was precisely this – to exploit vulnerabilities, to turn trusted individuals into unwitting pawns.

She pushed the thought away, refusing to entertain it. She had to believe in Cross, in his integrity. He was their only hope for external support, for any chance of leveling the playing field against Malik's overwhelming resources. But the silence persisted, a growing chasm of doubt that threatened to swallow her resolve. She accelerated, her focus sharpening, the city lights blurring into streaks of color as she navigated the increasingly deserted streets. The shipping depot was still her target, the last known location for both Tasha and Cross. If her fears were realized, if Cross had indeed fallen, then Tasha would be utterly alone, exposed and vulnerable.

As Lena neared the industrial district, the familiar hum of the city began to fade, replaced by an unnerving quiet. The streetlights grew sparse, casting long, distorted shadows that danced with a life of their own. She spotted the distinctive silhouette of the abandoned shipping depot against the bruised pre-dawn sky. It loomed like a skeletal behemoth, a monument to decay and forgotten purpose. She slowed her vehicle, her senses on high alert, scanning the perimeter for any sign of activity, any deviation from the expected desolation.

Then she saw it – a flicker of movement near one of the larger, rust-eaten cargo containers. It was too deliberate to be random, too subtle to be accidental. Her heart leaped into her throat. Was it Tasha, signaling her arrival? Or was it a trap? She cut her engine, the sudden silence amplifying the thudding of her own pulse. Peering through the grimy windshield, she could make out figures moving in the gloom. Not just one or two, but a small, organized group, clad in tactical gear. They were positioned strategically, forming a perimeter around the very area she suspected Tasha and Cross would be meeting.

Her premonition solidified into a chilling certainty. Malik had anticipated this. He had turned the meeting into a trap, and it seemed he had secured the cooperation of the very detective she had entrusted with her desperate plea for help. The betrayal, if it was true, was a bitter poison, a testament to Malik's insidious reach. She saw the glint of metal, the purposeful movements, and a knot of dread tightened in her chest. Tasha would be there, a crucial witness, an innocent caught in the crossfire of Malik's ruthless ambition. Lena had to reach her, to pull her out of this deadly embrace, even if it meant exposing herself directly to the danger.

Her hands trembled as she reached for the ignition, her mind racing through desperate scenarios. If Cross had been turned, then any hope of official intervention was gone. She was on her own, with Tasha's safety hanging precariously in the balance. The data on Tasha's drive was vital, a key to dismantling Malik's operation, but Tasha's life was paramount. She couldn't let Malik silence her, couldn't let him extinguish the spark of truth that Tasha had so bravely carried.

As Lena began to inch her car forward, preparing to create a diversion, to draw the attention of Malik's men away from Tasha, she noticed something else. A single, unmarked black sedan parked at a distance, its tinted windows obscuring the occupants. It was too still, too deliberate in its placement, to be a casual observer. A chill snaked down her spine. Was Malik himself present? Or was this another layer of his intricate deception? The game had escalated, the stakes had been raised, and the arena was no longer a sterile data vault, but the gritty, unforgiving reality of the city's underbelly. The betrayals were unfolding, the hidden agendas were being unveiled, and Lena found herself at the precipice of a showdown where trust was a currency easily debased, and survival depended on anticipating the next devastating move of an enemy who seemed to be everywhere, and knew everything.

Jazzy's breath hitched, the sharp intake of air a stark contrast to the controlled stillness she had forced upon herself. The oppressive silence of the interrogation room, a stark, metallic echo chamber, had been her prison for what felt like an eternity. Malik's men, brutish and unimaginative, had seen her as little more than a pawn, a key to unlocking Lena's secrets, a bargaining chip to be discarded once its value was extracted. They had underestimated her. They had always underestimated her. They saw the 'artist,' the 'muse,' the vulnerable woman adrift in a world of corporate titans and digital espionage. They had never seen the strategist, the observer, the one who meticulously cataloged every tremor of fear, every flicker of arrogance, every misplaced word.

Malik's overture, delivered through the grim-faced enforcer with the unnervingly precise movements, had been a crude attempt at manipulation. Offer her freedom, leverage her against Lena, and then presumably, dispose of her once she was no longer useful. It was a predictable tactic, one born of a mind that saw everything through the lens of acquisition and control. But Jazzy had spent years navigating the treacherous currents of human psychology, not just in her art, but in her own survival. She had learned to read the subtle cues, the unspoken intentions, the hollow spaces behind the bravado. And in the enforcer's eyes, behind the veneer of duty, she had glimpsed a flicker of something else – a weariness, a resignation. He was a cog, as much a prisoner of Malik's empire as she was.

Her 'confession,' a carefully constructed tapestry of half-truths and strategic omissions, had been delivered with a practiced vulnerability. She had painted a picture of a naive artist, accidentally caught in the crossfire, eager to escape the machinations of a powerful woman she barely understood. She had hinted at Lena's desperation, her perceived instability, planting seeds of doubt about her rival's mental fortitude. It was a delicate dance, a tightrope walk over an abyss of consequence. One wrong step, one misplaced word, and she would have been erased. But she had held her ground, her gaze unwavering, her voice steady, even as her heart hammered a frantic rhythm against her ribs.

The enforcer, whose name she'd gleaned as 'Silas' from hushed conversations beyond her cell door, had reported back to Malik. She had heard the muffled voices, the rise and fall of their tones, the sharp, authoritative pronouncements that were undoubtedly Malik's. And then, silence. A pregnant pause that stretched her nerves taut. She had expected them to come for her, to extract whatever final morsel of information they believed she possessed. Instead, they had left her there, in the cold, sterile confines of the room, the heavy steel door a solid barrier between her and the world.

But this was not a defeat. This was a calculated pause, a breath before the plunge. Jazzy had been observing, analyzing. The guards outside her door were not the same ones who had initially brought her in. Their routines were different, their conversations more guarded. Malik's inner circle was in flux, a testament to the pressure Lena and her allies were exerting. More importantly, she had noticed a subtle shift in the security protocols during Silas's brief visits. A momentary lapse in the constant surveillance, a fractional delay in the response time of the electronic locks. It was a minuscule crack, almost imperceptible, but it was enough.

She began to work, her movements slow and deliberate, feigning continued despair. From a loose thread pulled from the frayed edge of her worn jumpsuit, she began to meticulously pick at the rivets securing the ventilation grate. Her fingers, calloused from years of wielding paintbrushes and chisels, now worked with a surgeon's precision. The rough metal scraped against the delicate fibers, a grating sound that seemed impossibly loud in the stillness. She had to be careful, to time her efforts with the infrequent patrols outside. Each tiny scrape was a gamble, each moment of silence a victory.

Hours blurred into a haze of focused effort. The jumpsuit offered little protection against the biting cold of the metal, and her muscles screamed in protest, but Jazzy pushed through the discomfort, fueled by a simmering rage and a fierce determination to reclaim her agency. The small grate, barely wide enough for her to slip through, was her ticket out of this suffocating tomb. Malik thought he had broken her, thought he had stripped her of her power. He was wrong. He had merely forged her in a hotter fire.

As the first of the rivets gave way, a quiet sense of triumph coursed through her. She wasn't just an artist anymore; she was a survivor, a strategist. She had gathered what she could from the limited interactions – the layout of this particular facility, the shift changes of the guards, the general direction of the main exits. It was fragmented knowledge, incomplete, but it was a starting point.

Her plan wasn't about brute force or open confrontation. She couldn't outfight Malik's men, nor could she outmaneuver them in a direct chase through the labyrinthine corridors of his stronghold. Her strategy had to be one of calculated disruption, of sowing chaos where there was order, of exploiting the very system Malik had built to control her. She needed to be a phantom, a whisper in the machine, a ghost in the code.

She managed to pry the grate open, revealing a narrow, dusty shaft. The air within was stale, thick with the accumulated grime of years. Without hesitation, she squeezed through the opening, her body scraping against the rough metal. The grate, with a soft click, settled back into place, obscuring her escape. She was now in the bowels of the facility, a network of service tunnels and ventilation shafts that, if her deductions were correct, would lead her away from the main security hubs.

Her progress was slow and arduous. She crawled through narrow spaces, the darkness absolute, the silence broken only by the rhythmic pounding of her own heart and the scuttling of unseen vermin. She had no light source, relying on her sense of touch and the faint, metallic scent that permeated the air, a scent that spoke of hidden machinery and electrical conduits. She remembered fragments of conversations she had overheard, hints about the facility's infrastructure, about critical systems that ran beneath the surface. Malik was obsessed with efficiency, with redundancy. And redundancy, she knew, often created exploitable vulnerabilities.

She found a junction, a nexus of several smaller ducts. One of them seemed to lead upwards, towards the hum of heavier machinery. This was it. This was where the core systems would likely be housed, where she could potentially access something, anything, that could disrupt Malik's operations or, at the very least, create a diversion significant enough for her to slip away entirely.

Navigating the vertical shaft was even more challenging. She used the protruding pipes and joints as handholds, her body trembling with exertion. The metallic scent grew stronger, tinged with the ozone smell of active electronics. She could hear the low thrum of powerful generators, the whirring of cooling fans. She was getting closer.

She reached a wider section of the shaft, a grating overlooking a vast, dimly lit chamber. Below, rows upon rows of servers blinked with an array of colored lights, a digital nervous system throbbing with life. This was the heart of Malik's data empire, the repository of all the information he had so ruthlessly compiled. And within this chamber, she knew, was the key to unlocking her own liberation.

Her plan, however, was not to destroy the servers. That would be too overt, too easily traced. Her objective was far more subtle, far more insidious. She needed to leverage her understanding of Malik's motivations, his obsession with control and perception. He thrived on manufactured narratives, on projecting an image of invincibility. Her move had to shatter that image, to expose the cracks in his carefully constructed facade, and to do so in a way that would resonate with Lena and her allies.

Jazzy had observed the guards' routines, their brief moments of distraction. She had noted the timing of the supply deliveries, the arrival and departure of personnel. And she had a secret weapon, a small, intricately crafted EMP device she had managed to construct from salvaged components within the interrogation room. It was crude, a testament to her resourcefulness, and its range was limited, but its potential impact was enormous.

She waited, her eyes scanning the chamber below. A lone technician, hunched over a console, was the only human presence. He was engrossed in his work, oblivious to the precarious situation unfolding above him. Jazzy took a deep breath, centering herself. This was her moment. She couldn't afford to hesitate.

With a silent prayer, she activated the device. A faint, high-pitched whine emanated from it, a sound that would be lost in the ambient noise of the server room to anyone not listening for it. She dropped it into the shaft. It tumbled downwards, a small, dark projectile against the glowing cascade of server lights.

The EMP hit its target with a barely audible *thump*. For a fraction of a second, nothing happened. Then, as if a giant hand had reached in and flicked a switch, the chamber plunged into darkness. The cacophony of whirring fans and blinking lights ceased abruptly. The technician yelped in surprise, fumbling for his flashlight.

But Jazzy wasn't finished. She had planned for this. As the EMP pulsed through the server room, it would also trigger a cascading failure in a secondary system – the automated lockdown protocols. These protocols, designed to isolate any breach, would now trap the very people Malik had tasked with maintaining order. And more importantly, they would trigger a silent alarm, a digital distress signal that, if Lena's network was still operational, would be noticed.

She didn't linger to observe the full effect of her actions. Her immediate goal was escape. The EMP would buy her precious minutes, creating confusion and diverting attention. She retraced her path, crawling back through the ventilation shafts, her movements now fueled by the adrenaline of her successful gambit. The silence that had previously been terrifying now felt like a cloak of invisibility.

She emerged from the ventilation system into a dimly lit corridor, far from the initial interrogation area. The air here was different, colder, carrying the faint scent of exhaust fumes. She could hear the distant echo of shouting, the sounds of alarm bells beginning to clang, a discordant symphony of chaos. Her move had worked. The meticulously ordered world of Malik's stronghold was unraveling, and she was a part of that unraveling.

Her path to the exterior was still fraught with danger, but now, she had a fighting chance. She moved with a newfound speed and purpose, her senses heightened, her mind sharp. She encountered a small group of security personnel, their faces a mixture of confusion and alarm as they reacted to the ongoing lockdown. Jazzy didn't engage. She melted into the shadows, using the environment to her advantage, a phantom in the storm she had created.

She reached a loading bay, the large metal doors ajar, revealing the pre-dawn gloom outside. The air was cool and crisp, a welcome balm against her raw nerves. But freedom was not yet secured. As she moved towards the opening, a figure emerged from the shadows, blocking her path. It was Silas, the enforcer.

His expression was unreadable, but his stance was weary. He didn't raise his weapon, but his presence was a formidable obstacle. "You shouldn't be here," he said, his voice low and gravelly.

Jazzy met his gaze, her own unwavering. "And you shouldn't be working for a monster," she replied, her voice surprisingly steady. She saw the conflict in his eyes, the internal struggle. He was not a monster, but a man caught in a trap of his own making, much like herself.

"Malik won't let you go," Silas stated, a grim certainty in his tone. " He doesn't let anyone go."

"Then you should have thought of that before," Jazzy retorted, her gaze flicking past him towards the opening. "And maybe you should think about your own choices,

Silas."

She didn't wait for his response. With a burst of speed, she lunged, not at Silas, but at a control panel near the loading bay door. Her fingers flew across the buttons, activating the emergency opening sequence. The massive doors began to groan, slowly grinding upwards.

Silas moved to intercept her, but Jazzy was already in motion. She had anticipated this, had factored in his presence. As the doors opened wider, revealing the rain-slicked tarmac outside, she tossed a small, metallic object towards him – a compact data chip, encrypted with a message she had prepared earlier, a message intended for Lena. It contained details of Malik's operation, specific vulnerabilities she had gleaned during her captivity, and a coded warning about the compromised security personnel she had encountered.

"This is for Lena," she said, her voice carrying over the rising din of the alarms. "Tell her I'm not a pawn anymore."

Silas, momentarily distracted by the flying chip, hesitated. It was the opening Jazzy needed. She sprinted past him, out into the biting rain, the cold water a shock against her skin. The loading bay doors continued to rise, providing her with a brief window of opportunity.

Behind her, she heard the shouts of approaching guards, the sound of Silas's own alarm being raised. But she was already moving, a shadow in the downpour, disappearing into the labyrinthine sprawl of the industrial district. She was free, not because of Malik's leniency, but because she had rewritten the rules of the game, proving that even in the darkest of cages, the human spirit could forge its own escape, its own path to defiance. Her calculated move had not only secured her own freedom but had also struck a blow against Malik's seemingly impenetrable fortress, a signal flare in the darkness, a testament to Lena's resilience, and to Jazzy's own indomitable will. She was no longer a victim, but a force to be reckoned with, a ghost in the machine, ready to rejoin the fight on her own terms.

The stale air of the interrogation room clung to Lena's senses like a shroud. She could still feel the phantom weight of the restraints, the sterile chill of the steel table beneath her fingertips. Jazzy's escape, a ghost story whispered through the facility's ventilation shafts, had sent ripples of panic through Malik's ranks, but it had also tightened the noose around Lena's own neck. Silas, the enforcer whose weary eyes had held a flicker of something akin to pity, was now a silent testament to the collateral damage of Malik's paranoia. He had relayed Jazzy's message, the data chip a digital grenade tossed into the heart of their carefully constructed world. And Lena, trapped in the gilded cage of her own making, was now facing the precipice.

Malik, when he finally appeared, was a storm contained within a Savile Row suit. His presence filled the room, radiating an icy fury that promised retribution. The forced calm in his voice was more terrifying than any outburst. "Jazzy has always been... unpredictable, Detective," he said, the words dripping with condescension. He paced the length of the room, his polished shoes clicking against the linoleum floor like a metronome of impending doom. "A volatile artist, prone to dramatic gestures. Her recent actions, however, are an unfortunate, and I might add, highly inconvenient, testament to her instability."

Lena watched him, her own emotions carefully banked. She knew the game he was playing. Jazzy's escape, coupled with the data chip, was a seismic event, threatening to expose the intricate web of illegal activities that Malik had so meticulously woven. The EMP, the lockdown, the subsequent chaos – these were all tangible consequences that Lena, as the supposed mastermind behind Lena's operations, would be held accountable for. Her career, her reputation, her very freedom, hung precariously in the balance.

"Instability is a matter of perspective, Mr. Malik," Lena replied, her voice steady, betraying none of the tremor that threatened to seize her. "Ms. Dubois demonstrated remarkable resourcefulness and an acute understanding of your operational vulnerabilities. Perhaps that's a sign of intelligence, not instability." She leaned forward slightly, her gaze locking with his. "And the data chip she delivered... that contained details, didn't it? Details that paint a very different picture than the one you've so carefully curated."

Malik stopped pacing, his eyes narrowing. The mask of polite disdain began to crack, revealing the predator beneath. "You have a remarkable capacity for self-deception, Detective. Or perhaps, a death wish." He gestured to a guard standing impassively by the door. "You see, Ms. Dubois's 'gift' has inadvertently placed you in a rather... precarious position. The evidence she presented, while sensational, is merely circumstantial. Unless, of course, you can corroborate it. With your own... insider knowledge."

The implication was clear. Malik was offering her a lifeline, a way out of the mess, but it came at a steep price: her complicity. He wanted her to validate Jazzy's findings, to confirm the illicit nature of his operations, but on his terms. He wanted her to be the witness who would solidify his downfall, but also the one who would implicate herself beyond redemption. It was a Hobson's choice, a trap sprung with the precision of a seasoned killer.

Lena's mind raced. She could deny everything, cling to the narrative of a naive detective caught in the crossfire. But Jazzy's actions had blown holes in that carefully constructed facade. The EMP that disabled the server room, the triggered lockdowns – these weren't random acts of vandalism. They were targeted strikes, executed with a clear understanding of the facility's infrastructure. And the data chip, brimming with encrypted files, was a ticking time bomb. If it fell into the wrong hands, or if its contents were fully decrypted by Lena's allies, Malik's empire would crumble.

She looked at Malik, at the cold calculation in his eyes. He was willing to sacrifice everything and everyone to protect his empire, and she was now just another variable in his equation, one he intended to neutralize. The thought of Jazzys's escape, of her defiant act of rebellion, fueled a spark within Lena. Jazzy had risked everything to strike a blow against Malik. Lena couldn't let that effort be in vain.

"You underestimate me, Mr. Malik," Lena said, her voice gaining a new edge of steel. "You think this is about self-preservation. About saving my career, my life. But it's not." She paused, allowing the weight of her words to settle. "It's about justice. And about ensuring that people like you, who prey on the vulnerable and operate outside the law, are brought to account."

Malik let out a short, humorless laugh. "Justice? You are a police officer, Detective. Your job is to uphold the law, not to enact some personal vendetta. And as for account – you will be held accountable for your association with Ms. Dubois, for your complicity in her... insurrection." He gestured towards the data chip that had been placed on the table between them, a sleek, metallic object that pulsed with latent power. "You can either hand that over to me, and we can discuss a... mutually beneficial arrangement where your part in this unfortunate incident is... minimized. Or," he continued, his voice dropping to a near whisper, "you can refuse, and face the consequences of aiding and abetting a fugitive. And believe me, Detective, the consequences for you will be far more severe than any Ms. Dubois could ever imagine."

The choice was stark, and the clock was ticking. Lena's eyes scanned the room, not for an escape route, but for an advantage. She knew that Malik's men were closing in, that Jazzy's actions had alerted the entire facility. The chaos Jazzy had unleashed was spreading, and Lena needed to use that to her own benefit.

"Mutually beneficial?" Lena echoed, a sardonic smile playing on her lips. "What could possibly be mutually beneficial in this situation, Mr. Malik? You've already made it clear that my complicity is a liability you intend to erase." She met his gaze directly, her own eyes blazing with a newfound resolve. "I'm not going to help you bury the truth. Jazzy was right to expose you, and I intend to see that her efforts are not in vain."

She reached out, not for the data chip, but for her own personal tablet, which had been confiscated earlier. She had anticipated this possibility, had a contingency plan in place. While the guards had been focused on Jazzy, Lena had been subtly observing their communications, their routines. She had managed to activate a hidden beacon on her tablet, a silent distress signal designed to reach a trusted contact within the department – a contact who was not beholden to Malik's influence.

Malik's smile faltered. He had assumed her fear, her desperation, would make her pliable. He had miscalculated. "You're making a grave mistake, Detective," he said, his tone hardening. "This facility is now on lockdown. No one enters, no one leaves. You have nowhere to run."

"Perhaps," Lena conceded, her fingers flying across the tablet's screen, initiating a series of commands. "But I'm not trying to run, Mr. Malik. I'm trying to bring you down." She looked up, her expression resolute. "Jazzy gave me the ammunition. Now, I'm going to be the one to pull the trigger."

The guards flanking Malik shifted uneasily. They had heard the hushed whispers of Jazzy's escape, the reports of system failures. The confidence they had exuded moments before was now tinged with apprehension. Lena's calm defiance was an anomaly, a disruption to the carefully controlled narrative Malik had attempted to impose.

"You think you can do this?" Malik scoffed, trying to regain control of the situation. "You're one woman against an entire organization. You're outmatched, outgunned, and out of time."

"Am I?" Lena challenged, her gaze unwavering. "Jazzy proved that your security is not impenetrable. And the data on that chip… it implicates more than just you, doesn't it? It implicates people in positions of power, people who have been looking the other way. People who will be very eager to silence anyone who knows too much." She let that sink in, watching Malik's expression shift from anger to something akin to concern. He understood the implications. Jazzy hadn't just attacked his operation; she had potentially unraveled a much larger conspiracy.

Suddenly, a new sound pierced the tense silence – the distant wail of sirens. Malik's eyes widened in disbelief, then narrowed with fury. "Impossible!" he hissed, turning to his guards. "How is this happening?"

Lena allowed herself a small, triumphant smile. Her hidden beacon had worked. It wasn't a full tactical response, not yet, but it was enough to alert external forces, to draw attention to the situation. It was the first domino, poised to fall and bring down the entire structure.

"It seems, Mr. Malik," Lena said, her voice laced with a quiet satisfaction, "that I'm not out of time after all. And I'm certainly not outmatched. Because I have allies who believe in justice, people who aren't afraid to stand up to tyranny, even when it wears a designer suit."

The guards exchanged nervous glances. They were caught between their loyalty to Malik and the undeniable reality of the approaching sirens. The air crackled with anticipation, the outcome of the confrontation hanging precariously in the balance. Lena, despite her compromised position, had managed to turn the tables, to orchestrate her own defense from within the very walls of her captivity. She had made her choice, and it was a choice to fight, to expose, to dismantle Malik's empire, no matter the personal cost. Her defiance was a testament to her unwavering commitment to her principles, a powerful counterpoint to the corruption that threatened to engulf them all. The confrontation was far from over, but Lena had secured her first victory, a small, yet significant, triumph against overwhelming odds. She had refused to be a pawn, and in doing so, had become a queen, ready to play her hand in the dangerous game that lay ahead. The sirens grew louder, closer, a symphony of justice echoing in the halls of power.

The sterile interrogation room, moments ago a stage for Lena's calculated defiance, now felt like a prelude to a much larger, more violent act. The distant wail of sirens, once a beacon of hope, now echoed with the grim promise of escalation. Malik's composure had fractured, replaced by a predatory glare that promised to leave no stone unturned, no ally unaccounted for. Lena's gamble, activating the hidden beacon, had bought her time, but time was a currency that Malik had always dealt in lavishly, and he was not about to let a single detective dictate its value. His empire, a labyrinth of digital tendrils and illicit influence, was far from toppling, and Lena's audacious move had merely alerted him to the precise location of the most significant threat: herself.

The data chip, still resting innocuously on the table, was the nexus of this unfolding disaster. It was a Trojan horse, meticulously crafted by Jazzy, and Lena was now its unwitting guardian. Malik's gaze flickered to it, then back to Lena, a cold calculation dawning in his eyes. He understood the leverage it represented, the potential for widespread exposure. But more than that, he understood Lena. He knew her tenacity, her unwavering belief in justice, a quality he found both pathetic and dangerous. He had underestimated her once; he wouldn't make that mistake again.

"Sirens," Malik mused, a slow, dangerous smile spreading across his face. "A desperate cry from a drowning mouse. You think this changes anything, Detective? You think a few flashing lights will dismantle years of careful planning, of absolute control?" He took a step closer, his voice dropping to a low, menacing growl. "This facility is a fortress, Lena. And the reinforcements I've called in are far more... accommodating than your departmental allies. They understand loyalty. They understand the value of silence."

Lena's heart hammered against her ribs, but her outward demeanor remained a mask of steely resolve. She had anticipated that Malik would have layers of security, contingency plans for precisely this kind of external interference. The sirens were a signal, yes, but also a potential trap, drawing the attention of those who served Malik's darker interests – the ones who operated far beyond the reach of any standard police procedure. "You're overconfident, Malik," she replied, her voice unwavering. "You've built your empire on secrets and fear. But fear is a fragile foundation. And secrets, eventually, have a way of surfacing."

The guards, flanking Malik, shifted their weight, their eyes darting towards the door. The tension in the room was palpable, a coiled spring ready to unleash a devastating kinetic force. They were professional, trained to follow orders, but the escalating situation, the distant but growing sound of approaching vehicles, was clearly unsettling them. Lena had managed to inject a note of uncertainty into their unwavering loyalty, a seed of doubt that could blossom into mutiny if the pressure continued to mount.

Malik, sensing the wavering resolve of his own men, decided to shift tactics. The direct confrontation, the veiled threats, had failed to break Lena. He needed to appeal to something else, something he believed was her fundamental weakness: her desire to protect others. "Jazzy, for all her theatrics, was a nuisance," Malik said, his tone shifting, becoming almost conversational, yet laced with venom. "A loose end. And you, Lena, are fast becoming another. But unlike her, you have... dependents, don't you? People you care about. People who might find themselves in... unfortunate circumstances if you continue down this path."

The veiled threat struck Lena like a physical blow. She knew he was referring to her younger sister, Sarah, who lived a quiet life miles away, blissfully unaware of the dangerous world Lena navigated. Malik had a chilling ability to identify and exploit vulnerabilities, and Sarah was Lena's most significant. "You wouldn't," Lena whispered, her voice betraying the first hint of genuine fear.

"Wouldn't I?" Malik countered, his smile widening, a cruel victory gleaming in his eyes. "You've seen what I'm capable of, Detective. Your friend Silas, for instance. A man who had a family, who made the mistake of showing you a sliver of empathy. Where is he now, I wonder? Perhaps enjoying a prolonged vacation. Or perhaps... he's been reassigned to a more permanent, less comfortable post. Just a thought."

The mention of Silas, the enforcer who had shown Lena a flicker of humanity before being summarily dealt with, sent a fresh wave of dread through her. Malik was a master manipulator, expertly threading the needle between plausible deniability and outright intimidation. He was painting a stark picture: her defiance would not only endanger her but also those she held dear. The weight of that responsibility settled heavily on her shoulders, threatening to crush her resolve.

Just as the silence threatened to become suffocating, a sharp crack echoed through the hallway, followed by a series of muffled shouts. The guards flanking Malik reacted instantly, their stances shifting from passive observation to active defense. Malik himself turned, his eyes narrowing, a flicker of annoyance crossing his features. The disruption was growing, the carefully controlled environment Malik had established within the facility fraying at the edges.

"What is going on out there?" Malik barked, his voice laced with impatience.

One of the guards, a burly man with a scar bisecting his left eyebrow, stepped forward, his radio crackling to life. "Sir, we have... multiple breaches. Unidentified personnel are advancing through Sector Gamma. They're armed, and they're not responding to hails."

Malik's face contorted with fury. "Breaches? Gamma? That's impossible! The lockdown is absolute!" He turned his icy gaze back to Lena, a horrifying realization dawning on him. "This wasn't just Jazzy. You... you orchestrated this, didn't you? You brought them here."

Lena didn't answer, her focus now on the subtle shifts in Malik's demeanor. His arrogance, his belief in his own invincibility, was his greatest weakness. He had become so accustomed to being in control, to operating in the shadows, that any external force, any act of defiance that he hadn't personally sanctioned, was an affront he couldn't comprehend.

The sounds of fighting grew louder, closer. Gunfire, not the controlled, professional crack of Malik's men, but a more chaotic, desperate symphony of struggle. Lena's contact, the one she had activated with her beacon, must have understood the gravity of the situation, had rallied their own forces. It wasn't a full-scale military invasion, but it was enough to sow discord, to create the very chaos that Lena needed to exploit.

"You've made a terrible mistake, Lena," Malik snarled, his voice a low, dangerous rumble. He gestured to the data chip. "That chip is your only bargaining chip. And now, with this...cursion, it's become a liability. I can't let it fall into the wrong hands. I can't let them decipher its contents."

He reached out, his fingers brushing the cool, metallic surface of the chip. Lena reacted instinctively, slamming her hand down on top of his, her own fingers curling around the small device. "It's mine now, Malik," she said, her voice firm, imbued with a newfound authority. The confrontation had evolved. It was no longer about Lena's survival, or even Jazzy's exposé. It was about control of the narrative, control of the truth.

Malik stared at her, his eyes burning with a mixture of rage and disbelief. He had always seen Lena as a pawn, a valuable asset to be managed, manipulated, and ultimately, discarded if necessary. He had never considered the possibility that she might become the player, the one who dictated the terms of the game. He had underestimated her intelligence, her courage, and her unwavering commitment to her principles.

"You think you can win this, Detective?" Malik spat, his voice dripping with contempt. "You think you can walk out of here with that chip and expose me? My reach is far greater than you can possibly imagine. This facility may be under siege, but the network remains intact. The information on that chip will be buried, and you will be erased."

Suddenly, the heavy steel door to the interrogation room burst open with a deafening bang. Standing in the doorway, silhouetted against the flickering emergency lights of the hallway, was Tasha. Her face was a mask of grim determination, her signature tactical gear bearing the marks of recent skirmishes. Behind her, a squad of heavily armed operatives, clad in the same dark, nondescript uniforms, fanned out into the room, weapons raised, eyes scanning for threats.

Malik's eyes widened in shock, a flicker of genuine alarm finally piercing his carefully constructed facade. Tasha. Of all the people, it was Tasha who had arrived to confront him. The irony was not lost on him. She was the one he had groomed, the one he had trusted to inherit his empire, and now she stood before him, an unlikely ally to his captive detective.

"Malik," Tasha's voice was low and steady, devoid of emotion, yet carrying the weight of a thousand unspoken betrayals. "It's over."

"Tasha?" Malik stammered, his voice rough with disbelief. "What are you doing here? Who do you think you are, coming into my facility, dictating terms?"

Tasha ignored his outburst, her gaze fixed solely on Lena. A brief, almost imperceptible nod passed between them, a silent acknowledgment of the alliance forged in the crucible of Malik's tyranny. "I'm here to finish what Jazzy started, Malik," Tasha said, her voice hardening. "And to reclaim what you stole."

The air in the interrogation room crackled with a new kind of tension, one born not of fear, but of confrontation. The empire Malik had so painstakingly built was now caught between two formidable forces: Lena, the detective who refused to be silenced, and Tasha, the protégé who had chosen justice over power. The fate of the Swipe Right empire, and the lives of everyone entangled within its web, now hung precariously in the balance, awaiting the outcome of this ultimate showdown. Malik's reign of control was teetering, and the architects of his downfall had finally arrived.

Malik's gaze darted from Lena, still clutching the data chip, to Tasha, her stance unwavering, her operatives fanned out with chilling efficiency. He had always viewed Tasha as a tool, an extension of his will, meticulously molded to serve his insatiable ambition. He had taught her, nurtured her, and ultimately, he believed, controlled her. The realization that she had turned against him, that she was now actively aiding his prisoner, was a betrayal that cut deeper than any physical wound.

"Tasha, you fool," Malik hissed, his voice laced with a venom that promised retribution far more potent than any physical threat. "Do you truly believe you can win this? Do you think you can simply waltz in here and dismantle everything I've built? This is my empire! My creation! You owe me your loyalty, your life!"

Tasha took a slow, deliberate step forward, her eyes never leaving Malik's. The faint glow of the data chip pulsed in Lena's hand, a silent testament to the truth it contained. "You taught me many things, Malik," Tasha replied, her voice calm, yet resonant with an authority that seemed to echo the very foundations of the facility. "You taught me how to build. How to control. How to survive. But you also taught me the price of unchecked greed. And you taught me that loyalty, when it's built on fear and coercion, is as fragile as glass."

She gestured to her operatives, who moved with silent, synchronized precision, securing the exits, neutralizing any remaining pockets of resistance within the immediate vicinity. The sounds of the skirmish in the hallways had died down, replaced by a tense, expectant hush. The swiftness and professionalism of Tasha's team were a testament to the depth of her planning, the extent of her preparedness. She hadn't just decided to intervene; she had orchestrated a meticulously planned operation.

Malik let out a harsh, disbelieving laugh. "Fragile? My loyalty is absolute! I am the architect of this world, Tasha. Without me, it crumbles. And you, my dear protégé, will be crushed beneath its ruins." He glanced at Lena again, a flicker of something akin to desperation in his eyes. "She is a threat, Tasha. A dangerous anomaly. She will expose everything. Us. Our work. You know what that means. The consequences will be dire, for all of us."

"The only dire consequence, Malik," Tasha countered, her gaze hardening, "is letting you continue. You've become a cancer, spreading corruption and desolation wherever you touch. Your empire is built on a foundation of broken promises and exploited lives. It's time for it to be purged." She extended a hand towards Lena, a gesture of solidarity. "Jazzy's sacrifice, Lena's courage... they won't be in vain. We will bring the truth to light."

Lena, understanding Tasha's intent, slowly rose from her seat, her eyes locked with Malik's. The data chip was a small, seemingly insignificant object, yet it held the power to unravel everything. Malik, cornered and facing the ultimate betrayal from his most trusted lieutenant, made a desperate move. He lunged forward, not towards Tasha, but towards Lena, his aim to snatch the chip from her grasp.

But Tasha was faster. With a practiced, fluid motion, she intercepted his lunge, her body positioning itself between Malik and Lena. A swift, precise strike to his jaw sent

Malik staggering back, his balance compromised. The carefully constructed veneer of control he had maintained for so long finally shattered, revealing the desperate, cornered animal beneath.

"You can't win, Tasha," Malik snarled, his face contorted with rage and pain. "You're just like me. You understand the necessity of certain... compromises. You can't escape that part of yourself."

"No, Malik," Tasha replied, her voice laced with a cold finality. "I understand the necessity of choosing who you compromise *for*. And I choose not to compromise for you, or for your twisted vision of power." She turned to her operatives. "Secure him."

Two of Tasha's team moved forward, their movements efficient and professional, disarming Malik and escorting him away. He offered no further resistance, his earlier fury replaced by a stunned, bewildered silence. The empire, it seemed, had finally fallen, not with a bang, but with the quiet, calculated efficiency of a coup.

Lena watched as Malik was led away, his gaze lingering on her, a silent promise of future vengeance in his eyes. The battle for the Swipe Right empire was over, but the war for justice, for the dismantling of the corrupted systems Malik had embedded himself within, was far from concluded. Tasha approached Lena, her expression a complex mix of relief and grim determination.

"Are you alright, Detective?" Tasha asked, her voice softening, the hard edge of command giving way to a more genuine concern.

Lena nodded, her hand still clutching the data chip. "I'm alright. Thanks to you." She looked at Tasha, a new understanding dawning between them. They were two women who had navigated the treacherous underbelly of power, each in their own way, and found common ground in their rejection of its corrupting influence.

"Jazzy would have wanted this," Tasha said, her gaze drifting towards the exit, as if picturing the defiant artist who had ignited this firestorm. "She believed in truth. And she believed that everyone deserved a chance to be free from people like him."

Lena met Tasha's gaze, a silent pact forming between them. The Swipe Right empire, a symbol of Malik's unchecked ambition and ruthlessness, was now in their hands. The data chip contained not just evidence of his crimes, but the keys to unlocking the vast network of corruption he had cultivated. The path ahead would be fraught with peril, with powerful enemies who would undoubtedly try to silence them, but for the first time in a long time, Lena felt a sense of hope. The empire's fate was still uncertain, but for now, it had been wrested from the clutches of a tyrant, and placed in the hands of those who dared to believe in something more. The showdown had concluded, but the real work, the painstaking process of rebuilding and seeking true justice, had only just begun. The future of the empire, and the people within it, would be forged in the fires of their newfound alliance.

7: The Aftermath

The heavy steel door of the interrogation room, now hanging precariously on its hinges, groaned in protest as Lena stepped over its threshold. The air outside was thick with the acrid scent of ozone and the faint, metallic tang of blood. Tasha followed, her movements efficient and controlled, even as the adrenaline from the recent confrontation began to recede, leaving behind a bone-deep weariness. The hallway, moments before a theater of desperate action, was now eerily silent, save for the distant hum of emergency generators and the methodical sweep of Tasha's operatives securing the area. Each step echoed, a stark reminder of the violence that had just erupted, the visceral clash of wills that had culminated in Malik's swift and ignominious downfall.

Lena's gaze swept over the scene. The pristine, almost sterile elegance of the facility had been marred by the brutal efficiency of the encounter. Scorch marks marred the polished marble floors, testament to stray energy blasts from Tasha's team. A shattered display case, once showcasing Malik's ostentatious collection of rare antiquities, lay in glittering shards, its contents scattered like forgotten memories. A fine dusting of debris coated everything, a visible shroud over the remnants of a reign of terror. It wasn't the grand, operatic destruction one might expect from a cinematic climax, but rather a stark, brutal testament to a desperate struggle for survival, a quiet devastation that settled heavily on the senses.

The data chip, still clutched in Lena's hand, felt like a lead weight, a tangible anchor to the unfolding reality. The weight of what it represented, the years of corruption, the hidden networks, the lives ruined or manipulated, pressed down on her. The euphoria of victory, if it could even be called that, was tempered by the grim understanding of the immensity of the task that lay ahead. Malik was neutralized, his immediate power broken, but the tendrils of his empire, the insidious web he had woven, were vast and deeply entrenched. Disentangling them would be a Herculean effort, one that would surely leave its own indelible marks.

Tasha approached a fallen guard, his uniform still bearing the faint insignia of Malik's inner circle. He was unconscious, not dead, a testament to the restraint her team had exercised. "He's stable," Tasha reported, her voice devoid of triumph, her focus already shifting to the next immediate concern. "We've secured all key personnel and neutralized any immediate threats. The facility is ours." She paused, her gaze meeting Lena's, a shared acknowledgment passing between them. "But the fight… it's far from over, Detective."

Lena nodded, her throat tight. "I know. This is just the beginning." She looked at the data chip again, its surface cool against her palm. It was a Pandora's Box, and she had just lifted the lid. The information within would not only dismantle Malik's operations but would also expose the dark underbelly of institutions and individuals who had either enabled him or profited from his illicit activities. The fallout would be immense, rippling through industries, governments, and lives across the globe.

The immediate aftermath was a stark contrast to the explosive confrontation. The adrenaline that had fueled their actions, sharpening their senses and pushing them beyond their limits, began to ebb, replaced by a gnawing exhaustion. Lena felt a phantom ache in muscles she hadn't realized she'd strained, a throbbing in her head that spoke of sleep deprivation and sheer mental exertion. The taste of copper, a lingering echo of a near miss, coated her tongue. Every nerve ending felt raw, exposed, attuned to the smallest sound, the slightest shift in the air.

Tasha, ever the pragmatist, began issuing quiet commands to her operatives, coordinating the next stages of their operation: securing Malik, documenting the scene, initiating preliminary data extraction from the chip. Her voice, usually sharp and commanding, now carried a subtle undertone of weariness, a hint of the emotional toll the ordeal had taken. Lena watched her, a flicker of admiration mixed with a dawning understanding. Tasha, the protégé, had not only matched Malik's ruthlessness but had surpassed it in her pursuit of justice. She had been forged in the crucible of his empire, and in doing so, had discovered her own strength, her own unwavering moral compass.

Lena's gaze drifted to the opulent furnishings, now in disarray. A plush velvet armchair was overturned, its stuffing spilling out like entrails. A delicate porcelain vase lay shattered on the floor, its intricate floral pattern obscured by dust and debris. These were the spoils of Malik's illicit empire, a stark reminder of the disparity between the facade of power and the grim reality of its foundation. Lena had always operated in the shadows, accustomed to the grime and grit of her own world, but this was different. This was the deliberate, almost gleeful, flaunting of wealth built on the exploitation and suffering of others.

The silence that now permeated the hallway was not peaceful, but pregnant with the weight of unsaid words, of unspoken trauma. Lena closed her eyes for a brief moment, picturing Jazzy's fierce, defiant gaze, her unwavering commitment to the truth. Jazzy's sacrifice had been the catalyst, the spark that ignited this inferno. And now, Lena carried that torch, the responsibility a heavy burden, yet also a source of profound purpose. The scars of this showdown were not merely physical; they were etched onto their very souls, a testament to the battles fought, the betrayals endured, and the lives irrevocably altered.

The taste of victory was undeniably bitter. Lena felt a profound sense of loss, not just for Jazzy, but for the innocence she had once possessed, the naive belief that justice was a straightforward pursuit. The reality was a messy, brutal affair, stained with compromise and sacrifice. She thought of Silas, his brief moment of humanity a distant memory, now lost in the annals of Malik's collateral damage. Had he found peace? Or was his fate another grim secret buried within the labyrinthine depths of Malik's operations? The questions gnawed at her, adding another layer to the emotional residue of the confrontation.

Tasha approached, a medical kit in her hand. "You need to get that cut on your arm cleaned, Detective," she said, her tone gentle, professional. The small, superficial wound on Lena's forearm, a memento from a close encounter with a shard of glass, suddenly felt like a beacon, a physical manifestation of the danger she had faced. As Tasha meticulously cleaned and dressed the wound, Lena looked at her, a question forming in her mind, a curiosity about the woman who had so decisively turned the tide.

"How did you know?" Lena asked softly, her voice barely above a whisper. "How did you know I was here? Or that I needed help?"

Tasha secured the bandage with a strip of medical tape. "Jazzy. She trusted you. And she knew, perhaps better than anyone, how deep Malik's rot went. She had contingency plans, fail-safes, for everything. Including her own potential demise. She reached out to me, Lena. She believed you were the only one who could finish what she started."

Lena absorbed this, a wave of emotion washing over her. Jazzy, even in her final moments, had been orchestrating this, a meticulous planner leaving no stone unturned. It was a testament to her foresight, her unwavering dedication. "She was… remarkable," Lena managed, her voice thick.

"She was," Tasha agreed, her own voice tinged with a somber respect. "And she believed in you. I believed in her. And now,,, we have to believe in this." She gestured around the damaged hallway, encompassing the remnants of Malik's fallen empire. "This is our inheritance, Lena. The mess he left behind. We have to clean it up. For Jazzy. For all the others he hurt."

The weight of Tasha's words settled on Lena's shoulders. The immediate threat was gone, but the long, arduous journey of dismantling Malik's network, of bringing his collaborators to justice, and of protecting the integrity of the data chip, stretched out before them like an uncharted, treacherous terrain. The scars of this showdown were not just the physical wounds or the shattered opulence, but the profound understanding of the deep-seated corruption they had only just begun to confront.

As Tasha's operatives began to move Malik, now secured and disoriented, towards a waiting vehicle, Lena watched, her gaze fixed on the man who had orchestrated so much pain. His eyes, when they met hers, held a flicker of contempt, a promise of future retribution. But there was also a dawning realization of his own defeat, a stark understanding that his reign of absolute control had been irrevocably shattered.

The silence in the hallway was no longer just the absence of noise; it was the sound of a world irrevocably changed. The opulent setting, once a symbol of Malik's immense power and influence, was now a stark monument to his downfall, a silent testament to the devastating consequences of unchecked ambition and ruthless exploitation. The debris scattered across the floor, the scorch marks on the walls, the overturned furniture – each element served as a stark reminder of the raw, brutal survival instinct that had played out within these walls. Lena felt the lingering tremor of fear, the phantom sensations of close calls, the emotional residue of betrayal and desperate action.

Tasha returned to Lena's side, her expression composed but her eyes holding a depth of understanding that transcended words. "We need to move, Lena. Get the chip to a secure location. The information on it is critical, and there are many who would want to silence us before we can bring it to light." Her voice was calm, professional, but carried an urgency that underscored the precariousness of their situation.

Lena nodded, her grip tightening on the data chip. It was small, unassuming, yet it represented the downfall of a titan and the potential liberation of countless others. The weight of it, both literal and figurative, was almost overwhelming. She felt a profound sense of exhaustion, a weariness that went beyond the physical, settling deep into her bones. The adrenaline had faded, leaving behind a raw, exposed vulnerability.

"Where do we go?" Lena asked, her voice raspy, unused for a prolonged period.

"I have a secure location," Tasha replied. "Off the grid. It will be the safest place for the chip until we can properly secure the evidence and prepare for dissemination."

She paused, her gaze meeting Lena's, a silent acknowledgment of the shared burden they now carried. "This was never going to be easy, Detective. Malik's empire was built on layers of protection, on a network of complicity. We've struck a blow, but the war is far from over."

Lena's eyes scanned the hallway, the silent figures of Tasha's operatives moving with practiced efficiency, securing the perimeter, ensuring the transport of the captured Malik. The sterile opulence of the facility now seemed to mock the darkness that had festered within it. The silence was not one of peace, but of anticipation, of the calm before a storm that was sure to follow. The repercussions of Malik's downfall would be far-reaching, and Lena knew, with a chilling certainty, that she and Tasha were now prime targets.

The emotional scars were already beginning to manifest. Lena felt a flicker of anger resurface, not just at Malik, but at the systemic failures that had allowed his empire to flourish. She thought of the countless victims, their lives shattered by his machinations, and a fierce resolve hardened within her. This wasn't just about justice for Jazzy anymore; it was about justice for all of them. The fight had taken on a new, broader dimension, one that demanded not just the dismantling of an empire, but the purging of the corruption that had allowed it to exist.

Tasha placed a reassuring hand on Lena's shoulder. "We did what we had to do, Lena. For Jazzy. For ourselves. But the path ahead is dangerous. We need to be prepared for anything." Her words were a stark reminder that survival, in the aftermath of such a violent confrontation, was a fragile state, easily shattered by the enemies who remained.

Lena met Tasha's gaze, a shared understanding passing between them. They were two women, brought together by tragedy and a shared determination to expose the truth. The scars of this showdown were a testament to their resilience, their courage, and their willingness to face the darkness head-on. The immediate aftermath was a somber tableau, a stark reminder of the cost of their actions, but it also held the promise of a future where justice, however hard-won, might finally prevail. The opulent setting, now a scene of quiet devastation, served as a powerful backdrop to the dawning realization that their battle had only just begun, and the true fight lay in the meticulous, dangerous work of unearthing and exposing the full extent of Malik's corrupt legacy. The silence that followed the echoes of gunfire and shouted commands was not an end, but a pause, a moment to breathe before plunging into the uncertain, perilous waters that lay ahead. Lena felt a deep ache, not just in her body, but in her very soul, a weariness born from witnessing the brutal realities of power and the devastating toll it took. The opulence around her was now a grim mockery, its gilded surfaces tainted by the violence that had unfolded, a constant reminder of the price paid for this precarious victory.

The sterile, almost clinical chill of the safe house seeped into Jazzy's bones, a stark contrast to the humid, pulsating heat of the underground complex she had only recently escaped. Each breath felt measured, a conscious effort to control the tremor that still vibrated beneath her skin. The adrenaline, a volatile mistress, had finally receded, leaving behind a hollow ache and the disquieting quiet of survival. Lena and Tasha had ensured her extraction, a feat that still felt surreal, a phantom limb of a life she had almost lost. Now, she was adrift in a sea of anonymity, a ghost in a world that had tried to swallow her whole.

The room was sparse, functional. A cot, a small table, a single chair. The bareness was intentional, a deliberate stripping away of the opulent, deceptive veneer of Malik's world. Yet, even in this austerity, the shadows seemed to cling to the corners, whispering remnants of the life she had been forced to lead. Had she truly escaped? Or had she merely traded one cage for another, albeit one with less gilded bars? The question echoed in the silence, a constant, gnawing companion. She traced the faint scar on her wrist, a tangible reminder of a desperate gamble, a moment of sheer terror that had irrevocably altered her trajectory.

Tasha had been clear. "You're out, Jazzy. Clean slate. But you're not invisible. Not yet." The implication hung heavy in the air. Malik's network was vast, his influence insidious. Even in his downfall, the tendrils of his empire could still reach, could still ensnare. Jazzy understood. The information she had risked everything to obtain, the data chip Lena now possessed, was a weapon, a double-edged sword. It had been the key to unlocking Malik's secrets, but it also made her a liability, a loose end that many would want to tie off permanently.

She remembered the controlled chaos of the extraction, the hushed urgency in Tasha's operatives' voices, the fleeting glimpse of Lena's determined face as she was ushered into a nondescript vehicle. They had been precise, efficient, a well-oiled machine designed to operate in the liminal spaces, the grey zones where loyalty and survival often collided. But Jazzy had seen more than just their professional detachment. She had seen a flicker of something else in Tasha's eyes – a shared understanding, a grudging respect born from navigating similar treacherous waters. Tasha, too, had been forged in the crucible of Malik's operations, a survivor who had found a new purpose in dismantling the very system that had once sought to control her.

The days that followed were a blur of enforced stillness. Jazzy wrestled with the memories, the faces of those she had been forced to betray, the compromises she had made to stay alive. The allure of Malik's power, the intoxicating whisper of influence, had once seemed a necessary evil, a means to an end. But the reality had been far more corrosive, a slow erosion of her own moral compass. She had become adept at deception, a master of camouflage, shedding identities like discarded skin. Now, stripped bare, she wondered if she could ever reclaim the person she had been before.

One evening, a soft knock echoed through the small apartment. Jazzy's heart leaped into her throat, her hand instinctively reaching for the small, utilitarian knife Tasha had provided. The door opened to reveal Tasha, her presence commanding even in the mundane setting. She carried a small, plain bag.

"Thought you might be getting restless," Tasha said, her voice a low, steady hum. She placed the bag on the table. "Supplies. And… this." She pulled out a slim, unmarked burner phone. "For emergencies. Or if you decide you want to talk. I'm not going to pretend this is easy for you, Jazzy. What you went through… it changes a person."

Jazzy looked at the phone, then at Tasha, her gaze searching. "You… you didn't have to. I was just… a pawn."

Tasha's lips curved into a ghost of a smile, a rare, almost hesitant expression. "No one is just a pawn, Jazzy. Everyone has a choice. You made yours. And you chose to survive. That takes a different kind of strength." She paused, her eyes holding Jazzy's. "Lena's working on the fallout. It's going to be messy. A lot of powerful people are going to fall. But they'll want to bury it. And they'll want to find anyone connected to Malik who might still have something to say."

The implication was clear. Jazzy was a potential threat, a loose end. "So, I'm still in danger?"

"Always," Tasha replied, her tone devoid of melodrama, merely stating a fact. "But now you have options. You can disappear. Start fresh. Or,,," She let the word hang, an unspoken invitation. "Or you can use what you learned. What you saw. You have a unique perspective, Jazzy. You understand how these networks operate from the inside."

Jazzy's mind reeled. Disappear? The thought held a certain appeal, a yearning for a life free from the constant threat, the lingering guilt. But Tasha's words resonated deeper. She had seen the machinery of corruption firsthand, had navigated its treacherous currents. Was it enough to simply retreat, to let the darkness continue to fester? Or did she owe it to herself, to Jazzy, to do more?

She picked up the burner phone, its smooth plastic cool against her fingertips. It felt like a key, a potential bridge to a different future. She thought of Jazzy, the woman she had pretended to be, the sacrifices that woman had made. Had that Jazzy truly been lost, or had she merely been buried?

"What happened to Malik?" she asked, her voice barely a whisper.

"Lena and Tasha are handling it," Tasha said. "He's in custody. But the real work is just beginning. Cleaning up the mess. Making sure his network doesn't simply reform under new leadership." She studied Jazzy's face, the tension in her jaw, the flicker of something akin to resolve in her eyes. "You've got a choice to make, Jazzy. The life you had is over. What do you want the next one to be?"

The next few weeks were a period of intense introspection. Jazzy moved between safe houses, a phantom herself, always looking over her shoulder, always aware of the invisible net that could still ensnare her. She listened to the news, the carefully curated reports that hinted at the massive upheaval caused by Malik's downfall, but revealed little of the true extent of his operations or the shadowy figures who had profited from them. Lena and Tasha were a ghost presence, ensuring her safety, feeding her information sparingly, allowing her the space to decide her own fate.

She practiced with the burner phone, sending coded messages, testing its capabilities. It was a lifeline, a way to connect without leaving a trace. She started to research, using encrypted networks, delving into the publicly available information about the companies and individuals implicated in Malik's web. She saw the patterns, the familiar maneuvers, the carefully constructed facades designed to hide illicit activities. It was a world she knew intimately, a landscape of deception and exploitation that she had once been a part of.

One rainy afternoon, while holed up in a quiet, anonymous apartment overlooking a bustling city street, Jazzy made her decision. She looked at her reflection in the rain-streaked window. The face that stared back was thinner, harder, the eyes holding a wariness that hadn't been there before. But beneath the surface, something else was stirring. A quiet defiance, a nascent purpose. She was no longer just a victim, or a pawn. She had survived. And survival, she was beginning to understand, was not about hiding, but about fighting back.

She activated the burner phone, her fingers moving with a practiced, almost instinctive grace. She typed a short, simple message, a string of code that Tasha would understand. *'I'm ready. I want in.'*

The response came back almost immediately. *'Meet me at the usual coordinates. 0300.'*

The coordinates led her to a discreet industrial district on the outskirts of the city. A nondescript warehouse, its corrugated iron walls bearing the scars of time and weather, stood silent and imposing. As Jazzy approached, a single light flickered on in an upper window, a subtle signal. She entered, her senses on high alert, the familiar hum of anticipation thrumming through her.

Inside, Tasha was waiting. The space was functional, sparsely furnished, but Tasha had clearly made it her own. A map of the city, dotted with numerous markers, covered one wall. Files and dossiers were neatly stacked on a long table.

"Took you long enough," Tasha said, a hint of amusement in her voice. She gestured to a chair. "You seem to have made up your mind."

Jazzy sat down, her gaze sweeping over the workspace. "I've seen enough. I can't go back to pretending none of it happened. And I can't just... disappear."

Tasha nodded, picking up a file. "Malik's empire was built on more than just his personal network. He had enablers. Investors. People who kept him insulated, who profited from his activities. Lena's team is working on dismantling the core operations, but these periphery players, they're harder to track. They operate in the shadows, protected by layers of plausible deniability."

She slid the file across the table. Jazzy opened it. It contained information about a prominent financial institution, its executives seemingly untouchable, their reputations impeccable. But within the file were details – encrypted communications, offshore accounts, shell corporations – all pointing to a direct link with Malik's illicit enterprises.

"This is just the tip of the iceberg," Tasha continued. "People like this exist in every major city. They're the unseen architects of corruption. Lena can't get them all. Her focus has to be on the immediate fallout from Malik's arrest, on securing the evidence, on managing the public narrative. But there are others who need to be brought to light."

Jazzy absorbed the information, her mind already working, piecing together the connections. This was the language she understood, the intricate dance of deception and manipulation. She had been a participant, a dancer in this very same ballet. Now, she could be something else.

"What do you need me to do?" Jazzy asked, her voice steady, devoid of the fear that had plagued her in the initial days.

Tasha met her gaze, a flicker of something akin to pride in her eyes. "I need you to be my eyes and ears, Jazzy. You know how they think. You know where to look. You can move through those circles without raising suspicion, gather the intel that Lena's team can't get to. It's dangerous, of course. And there's no guarantee of complete safety. But you'd be helping to finish what Jazzy started. For real this time."

The mention of her adopted name, of the original Jazzy, sent a shiver down her spine. It was a responsibility, a legacy. She looked at the file, at the faces of the powerful men who had fueled Malik's reign of terror. They were the shadows she had once inhabited, the darkness she had survived. Now, she had a chance to bring them into the light.

"I can do it," Jazzy said, her voice firm. "I know this world. I can navigate it. And I'm not afraid anymore." It wasn't entirely true, the fear was still a low hum beneath the surface, but the resolve was stronger. She had seen the cost of corruption, the devastation it wrought. She had been a pawn, a victim, but she would not remain one. Her new horizon was not one of escape, but of engagement, of actively shaping a future where those who thrived on illicit gains would no longer be able to hide.

Tasha offered a genuine smile this time, a rare flash of warmth that illuminated her typically stoic features. "Good. Because we've got a lot of work to do." She gestured back to the map. "Let's start with this guy. He's been quietly moving Malik's assets to an offshore account in Cyprus. We need to intercept that transfer before it disappears for good."

Jazzy leaned closer to the map, her fingers tracing the lines of interconnected networks, the intricate pathways of illicit finance. The sterile, quiet room faded into the background. The shadows still lingered, but they no longer felt like an inescapable prison. They felt like territory waiting to be explored, understood, and ultimately, dismantled. Her new horizon was taking shape, not in a place of safety and anonymity, but in the heart of the storm, armed with knowledge, driven by a purpose that had been forged in the fires of betrayal and tempered by the quiet strength of survival. The path ahead was uncertain, fraught with peril, but for the first time in a long time, Jazzy felt like she was finally in control of her own destiny, no longer a mere player in someone else's game, but an architect of her own future, a future where the shadows would no longer hold dominion. She was ready to start building.

The quietude of the interrogation room was a suffocating blanket, far heavier than the oppressive heat of the city outside. Detective Lena Cross sat rigidly, her uniform crisp, her posture betraying none of the internal tempest that raged within. The events of the past week had coalesced into this single, stark moment. The raid, the intel gathered by Jazzy, the apprehension of Viktor Morozov – it was a culmination that had played out like a meticulously orchestrated symphony, each note leading to this crescendo of judgment. The air hummed with an unspoken question: hero or villain?

She remembered the frantic urgency of the last communication from Jazzy, the raw fear laced with defiance that had emanated from the young woman's voice. Lena had felt a flicker of recognition, a kinship born of shared peril, even as she orchestrated Jazzy's extraction. There was a raw, untamed spirit in Jazzy, a resilience that mirrored Lena's own, though forged in vastly different fires. Lena had promised safety, a clean slate, a future unburdened by the suffocating tendrils of Morozov's empire. But even as she'd assured Jazzy, a cold certainty had settled in her gut: such promises were fragile things in their line of work.

The files spread before her on the polished table were a stark testament to her transgressions. Not the official police reports, those were sanitized, stripped of the morally ambiguous choices that had paved the way to Morozov's downfall. These were her personal notes, scrawled in hurried shorthand, annotated with red ink that bled into the pages like fresh wounds. The unauthorized access to Morozov's private servers, the bending of procedural rules to accommodate Jazzy's unique situation, the calculated risk of using an operative outside established protocols – each decision had been a tightrope walk over a chasm of consequence.

Her captain, Miller, a man whose cynicism was as ingrained as the lines on his face, had been conspicuously absent from the debriefing. He'd simply nodded curtly when the operation's success was announced, his eyes holding a complexity that Lena couldn't decipher. Was it relief? Or a veiled warning? Miller was a veteran of the force, a man who understood the shades of gray that bled into the black and white of law enforcement. He knew the sacrifices, the compromises, the moments when the line between right and wrong blurred into an indistinguishable haze.

She traced the edge of a photograph – Morozov, his eyes like chips of glacial ice, his smile a predatory baring of teeth. This was the man who had orchestrated so much suffering, so much destruction, all from the gilded cage of his power. And Lena had, in a way, become his reflection, a mirror of his ruthlessness, albeit wielded for a different purpose. She'd leveraged fear, exploited vulnerabilities, and manipulated information, not for personal gain, but for a justice that felt increasingly elusive.

The internal affairs investigators, their faces impassive, their questions polite yet probing, had laid out her transgressions with chilling precision. They spoke of chain of command, of evidence integrity, of the sanctity of the rulebook. Lena listened, her jaw tight, a silent battle playing out in her mind. She could fight them, deny the extent of her deviations, couch her actions in the language of necessity and strategic advantage. Or she could own them, accept the responsibility, and face whatever consequences followed.

She thought of Jazzy, of the young woman's quiet strength, her nascent resolve to dismantle the very networks that had almost consumed her. Jazzy was a survivor, a phoenix rising from the ashes of her own destruction. And Lena, in her own way, had also survived. But had she done so with her integrity intact? The question gnawed at her, a persistent ache that no amount of success could fully assuage.

The lead investigator, a woman named Davies, leaned forward, her voice low and steady. "Detective Cross, your actions, while ultimately leading to the apprehension of Viktor Morozov, represent a significant departure from established departmental procedures. The unauthorized access to proprietary data, the utilization of an unregistered informant under circumstances that bypassed standard vetting processes – these are serious matters."

Lena met her gaze, her own eyes unflinching. "I understand the protocols, Detective Davies. And I acknowledge that my actions deviated from them. However, the threat posed by Morozov was unique. His operations were clandestine, deeply entrenched, and resistant to conventional investigative methods. Standard procedures would have taken months, perhaps years, to yield the same results, if they yielded them at all. In that time, countless lives would have continued to be affected by his influence. I made a judgment call, a calculated risk, based on the information available and the urgency of the situation."

Davies steepled her fingers. "A judgment call that could have compromised the entire investigation. Had Jazzy's intel been faulty, or her motives been other than what you perceived, the evidence you've presented might have been inadmissible. We could have lost Morozov entirely."

"But her intel wasn't faulty," Lena countered, her voice rising slightly. "And her motives, as you can see from the subsequent developments, were aligned with justice. She was instrumental in uncovering the full scope of his network, the extent of his reach. Without her, we would have only scratched the surface. We would have secured Morozov, but his empire, his enablers, would have remained largely intact, free to continue their destructive work."

She paused, gathering her thoughts, the weight of her choices pressing down on her. "I understand the need for procedure. It's the bedrock of our profession. But there are times when procedure itself becomes an obstacle to justice. When the system, in its rigidity, fails to adapt to the complexities of the world it's meant to protect. I chose to prioritize the outcome, the ultimate goal of bringing a dangerous criminal to justice, over the strict adherence to a process that, in this instance, was insufficient."

Davies remained impassive. "And what about your involvement with Jazzy after the initial extraction? The continued communication, the facilitation of her new identity, the intel she's now gathering on Morozov's associates – that goes beyond the scope of your initial intervention."

Lena felt a prickle of defensiveness. Jazzy was more than an informant; she was a key to dismantling the entire corrupt edifice. "Jazzy possesses a unique understanding of Morozov's operations, a perspective from the inside that no one else has. She's not just a witness; she's a vital asset in bringing down the remaining elements of his network. My continued involvement ensures that this critical work can continue, that Morozov's influence doesn't simply resurface under a new banner. It's about finishing the job, Detective. About ensuring that his downfall has a lasting impact."

She looked directly at Davies. "I understand the implications of my actions. I'm prepared to accept the consequences. But I want to be clear: I do not regret my choices. I believe I acted in the best interest of public safety and justice. If that makes me a criminal, then so be it."

The silence that followed was thick with unspoken judgment. Lena held her breath, waiting for the gavel to fall, for the pronouncement that would define her career, perhaps her life. She had walked a razor's edge, and now she was standing at the precipice, the outcome hanging in the balance.

The door to the interrogation room creaked open, and Captain Miller entered, his expression unreadable. He carried a single, thin file, placing it on the table between Lena and Davies. "Detective Davies," he began, his voice calm but carrying an undeniable authority, "Detective Cross has provided us with irrefutable evidence that led to the successful apprehension of Viktor Morozov, a man whose criminal enterprise has caused untold damage. The intelligence gathered, the operational planning, the execution – it was a masterclass in unconventional, yet effective, law enforcement."

He looked at Lena, a hint of something that might have been grudging admiration in his eyes. "Yes, Detective Cross deviated from protocol. She took risks. She operated in a gray area. But she did so with purpose, with a clear objective, and with a dedication to justice that is rarely seen. The information she obtained from her informant, Jazzy, has not only led to Morozov's arrest but has also opened up new avenues of investigation into his international network, avenues that standard procedures would have taken years to uncover."

Miller picked up the file he had brought in. "This, Detective Davies, is a preliminary report from the financial crimes unit. It details the initial findings from the seized assets. The scale of Morozov's money laundering operation, the depth of his corruption, it's staggering. And much of this would have remained hidden without Detective Cross's initiative." He gestured to the file Lena had brought. "Her methods may have been unorthodox, but her results are undeniable."

Davies remained silent, her gaze shifting between Miller and Lena. The captain's intervention had clearly shifted the tide, but the ingrained skepticism in her demeanor lingered.

Miller continued, his voice softening slightly. "Lena, you know the rules. And you know the potential ramifications. This department thrives on order, on process. Your actions, however successful, have created a precedent that could be... problematic. But I also recognize the dedication and the courage it took." He paused, letting his words sink in. "For now, we'll consider this matter closed. However, I want you to understand that this is a one-time occurrence. Any future deviations will be met with the full force of departmental inquiry. You will submit a detailed report, outlining every step you took, every justification. And then, we move forward. Together."

Lena let out a slow, almost imperceptible breath. It wasn't a complete absolution, not a clean slate in the way Jazzy had been promised. It was a reprieve, a conditional acceptance. The moral ambiguity remained, a shadow that clung to her, a constant reminder of the price of her choices. She had achieved justice, but she had also compromised the very system she served.

As Davies gathered her files, her expression still unreadable, Lena's thoughts drifted to Jazzy. She had helped a young woman escape a life of darkness. She had brought down a formidable enemy. But in doing so, she had walked a path that tested the very foundations of her own moral compass. Was this redemption? Or simply the consequence of a necessary compromise?

She left the interrogation room, the sterile air of the precinct feeling both familiar and alien. The city outside, with its cacophony of sounds and its endless stream of faces, felt like a vast, uncharted territory. She had navigated the treacherous waters of Morozov's empire, and now she had to navigate the equally complex currents of her own conscience. The victory felt hollow, tainted by the knowledge of the lines she had crossed.

Her phone buzzed in her pocket. A single, encrypted message. Jazzy. '*Meeting Lena. Usual coordinates. 0300.*' Lena's lips curved into a faint, almost imperceptible smile. Her own path was far from over. The reckoning, perhaps, was just beginning. But for now, she had chosen her side. She had chosen to fight, not with blind adherence to rules, but with a fierce, uncompromising commitment to the pursuit of justice, even when it meant walking in the shadows. The echoes of Morozov's fall would reverberate, and Lena Cross would be there, ensuring that the light of justice, however imperfectly illuminated, would continue to shine. The path ahead was uncertain, fraught with the consequences of her choices, but it was a path she would walk with her eyes wide open, a detective who had learned that sometimes, to catch the wolves, you had to become a little bit of one yourself. The question of redemption would remain, a constant companion, but for now, survival, and the relentless pursuit of justice, was enough. She had made her choices, and she would live with them, even as she continued to fight the battles that lay ahead, armed with the knowledge that the line between hero and villain was often as thin as the decisions made in the quiet solitude of an interrogation room.

The quiet hum of the precinct seemed to mock Lena's internal turmoil. The Morozov operation, a triumph by any objective measure, had left her adrift in a sea of ethical compromise. Her conversation with Captain Miller, though offering a temporary reprieve, had underscored the precariousness of her position. The question of Jazzy's safety, of her future, remained a knot in Lena's stomach. But the most haunting question, the one that gnawed at her during the long, sleepless nights, was the fate of Tasha Reed. Tasha, the architect of Morozov's downfall, the ghost in the machine, the woman whose machinations had, in a twisted way, paralleled Lena's own journey through the moral murk.

The official reports, the sanitized narratives that would eventually make their way into the archives, offered no solace regarding Tasha. She was an enigma, a cipher who had operated from the shadows, her existence confirmed only by the devastating effectiveness of her actions. Lena had followed the breadcrumbs, piecing together fragments of Tasha's life, her rise to power, her meticulous dismantling of Morozov's empire. But the final act, Tasha's ultimate fate, remained shrouded in the same mystery that had defined her entire operation. Had Tasha, the puppet master, been pulled too far into the spotlight, her carefully constructed world collapsing around her? Or had she, like a master illusionist, simply vanished, leaving behind only the spectacle of her triumph and the void of her absence?

Lena found herself drawn to Tasha's story, a morbid fascination that bordered on obsession. She had pored over every scrap of information, every whispered rumor, every intercepted communication that hinted at Tasha's presence. Tasha had built an empire not on brute force, but on information, on leveraging weaknesses, on a chillingly precise understanding of human avarice and fear. Her methods, while criminal, possessed a certain brutal elegance, a cold logic that Lena, in her own way, had come to understand. Tasha was not merely a criminal; she was a force of nature, a disruptor who had exposed the rot at the heart of Morozov's seemingly impenetrable organization.

The implications of Tasha's involvement were profound. She had acted as an anonymous benefactor, a silent saboteur, feeding Lena the crucial intelligence that had tipped the scales. But the source of this intelligence, the identity of the woman orchestrating this elaborate scheme of retribution, remained elusive. Lena's intuition screamed that Tasha was more than just a victim seeking revenge; she was a strategist, a survivor who had meticulously planned her escape from the very inferno she had ignited.

The official narrative, the one that would be presented to the public and likely disseminated through the controlled channels of information, would undoubtedly paint Morozov as the sole architect of his downfall, with the police acting as the instruments of justice. But Lena knew, with an unsettling certainty, that Tasha Reed was the true catalyst. Her actions, though operating outside the law, had been the linchpin of the entire operation. The question of whether she was a victim of the circumstances she found herself in, a woman pushed to the brink and forced to fight back with the only weapons she possessed, or a cold, calculating criminal who had used the system to her advantage, was a complex one with no easy answers.

Lena revisited her private notes, the annotated files that documented her own descent into the moral ambiguity of her work. The details of Tasha's operations, as far as they could be extrapolated, mirrored Lena's own difficult choices. Both had operated in the gray areas, bending rules, taking calculated risks, and pushing the boundaries of what was considered acceptable. Tasha had used information as her weapon, manipulating it, weaponizing it, and ultimately wielding it to dismantle an empire. Lena, in her own way, had done the same, using her detective skills and her network to achieve a similar outcome.

The idea that Tasha might have been a victim resonated deeply with Lena. The intelligence she had gathered suggested that Tasha had been deeply enmeshed in Morozov's operations, perhaps unwillingly at first, before forging her own path of retribution. The scars of her involvement were likely deep, her life irrevocably altered by the choices she had been forced to make. Had Tasha orchestrated Morozov's downfall as a means of escape, a desperate bid for freedom from the very world she had helped build?

Lena's mind replayed the fragmented communications she had intercepted, the coded messages that hinted at Tasha's strategic brilliance. There was a chilling precision to Tasha's planning, a foresight that suggested she had anticipated the consequences of her actions. It was this very foresight that fueled Lena's suspicion that Tasha had a contingency, a plan for her own disappearance. To have orchestrated such a massive takedown without a meticulous exit strategy would have been entirely out of character.

The thematic conclusion of Tasha's story, Lena mused, was likely to be one of calculated liberation. Tasha had been bound by the very empire she had helped cultivate. Her actions were not simply about revenge, but about severing those ties, about reclaiming her autonomy. The dismantling of Morozov's network was, in essence, the dismantling of her own prison. And her disappearance, if that was indeed her fate, would be the final act of her liberation, a symbolic shedding of the past and a step into an unknown future.

Lena imagined Tasha, after the dust had settled, meticulously erasing her digital footprint, creating a new identity, and vanishing into the anonymity of the global populace. She would be a ghost, a legend whispered in hushed tones, the woman who had brought down a king from the shadows. Her legacy would be complex: a criminal to some, a phantom avenger to others, and to Lena, a cautionary tale, a testament to the lengths one would go to for justice, or perhaps, for survival.

The question of whether Tasha was a victim or a villain was a false dichotomy, Lena realized. Tasha was a product of her environment, a woman who had been forced to play a dangerous game with devastating consequences. She had made choices, undeniably criminal ones, but those choices had been born from a desperate need to survive and to reclaim her life. Her legacy was not solely defined by the destruction she wrought, but by the intricate tapestry of motivations and circumstances that had shaped her actions.

Lena's gaze fell on a photograph of Morozov, his eyes cold and calculating. He had been the architect of so much suffering, a titan of industry who had built his empire on a foundation of exploitation and fear. Tasha had been a pawn in his game, a skilled operative who had been ensnared by his machinations. But Tasha had refused to remain a pawn. She had learned the rules of the game and had used them to her advantage, turning the tables on her captor.

The finality of Tasha's story was not about her capture or her demise, but about her ultimate escape. She had played her hand with absolute precision, ensuring her own survival while simultaneously delivering a decisive blow to Morozov's reign of terror. Her legacy was not one of a fallen criminal, but of a phantom who had orchestrated her own liberation, leaving behind a trail of shattered power structures and a lingering sense of awe.

Lena felt a pang of something akin to respect for Tasha. In their own vastly different ways, they were both survivors, women who had navigated the treacherous landscape of their world with a tenacity that defied convention. Tasha's final act, her disappearance, was a bold statement, a declaration of her ultimate control over her own destiny. She had refused to be defined by her past, choosing instead to forge a new future, unburdened by the weight of her former life.

The absence of any concrete information about Tasha's whereabouts only solidified Lena's belief in her meticulous planning. Tasha had not been apprehended, nor had she met a violent end. She had, Lena suspected, orchestrated her own vanishing act, a final, masterful stroke that left the authorities searching for a ghost. Her legacy was, therefore, one of an elusive victor, a legend forged in the shadows.

Lena closed the files, the weight of her own choices settling upon her. She had brought down Morozov, but in doing so, she had danced with the devil, blurring the lines between right and wrong. Tasha Reed, in her own way, had done the same. Their stories, though distinct in their details, shared a common thread: the complex reality of justice in a world that was rarely black and white. Tasha's legacy was a testament to the power of information, the resilience of the human spirit, and the enduring allure of a perfectly executed escape. Lena knew that the world might never know the full truth of Tasha's story, but she would carry the knowledge, the understanding that some victories were achieved not through adherence to the law, but through a defiant pursuit of a higher, albeit more dangerous, form of justice. Tasha had been a victim, yes, but she had also been a conqueror, a woman who had seized control of her narrative and written her own ending, an ending that was as enigmatic and as powerful as she had been. The echoes of her actions would continue to resonate, a silent testament to the woman who had dared to challenge an empire and, in the process, had become a legend.

The city of Las Vegas, a glittering mirage built on dreams and deceit, was already beginning to shed the ashes of the Morozov implosion. The official narrative, meticulously crafted by those eager to restore a semblance of order, declared victory. Morozov was gone, his empire in ruins, his network of corruption exposed. Yet, for those who had navigated the labyrinthine depths of his operation, the victory felt hollow, a fragile peace bought at a steep price. Lena, back in her own world, the precinct buzzing with a frantic energy that felt both familiar and alien, couldn't shake the feeling that this was not an ending, but a transition. The 'Swipe Right' empire, a colossal edifice built on the insidious marriage of technology and vice, was too vast, too deeply entrenched, to simply cease to exist. Its components, like fractured pieces of a shattered mirror, would inevitably reassemble, perhaps in a new, even more dangerous configuration.

The immediate aftermath saw a flurry of activity. Task forces were assembled, their mandates to dissect Morozov's vast network, to trace the flow of illicit funds, to identify and apprehend the remaining cogs in his infernal machine. But Lena knew that the true power of Morozov hadn't resided in the physical infrastructure, the gleaming casinos and opulent penthouses, but in the intangible web of information he had woven, the exploitation of human desire and vulnerability that technology had amplified. 'Swipe Right', the app that had been the genesis of so much, the innocuous portal to a world of forbidden pleasures, was now a symbol of the city's darkest secrets. What would become of it? Would it be scrubbed from existence, its code purged like a digital virus? Or would it, as Lena suspected, be salvaged, its potent algorithms repurposed by new, equally ambitious, and undoubtedly less scrupulous, players? The thought sent a shiver down her spine. The technology itself was amoral; it was the hands that wielded it that determined its purpose.

The ripple effects of Morozov's downfall spread beyond the immediate police investigations. The economic landscape of Las Vegas, so intricately tied to the shadow economy, began to shift. Certain establishments, once humming with activity fueled by Morozov's influence, now stood eerily quiet. The influx of cash, the easy money that had lubricated the city's underbelly, had suddenly dried up, leaving a void that was palpable. The high-stakes games played out in the hushed, exclusive rooms of private clubs were no longer about mere fortunes; they were about survival, about re-establishing dominance in a suddenly fluid power structure. Lena imagined the whispered conversations in those smoky rooms, the clandestine meetings, the forging of new alliances as old ones crumbled. The players remained, their hunger for power and profit undiminished, simply seeking new avenues to sate their insatiable appetites.

Captain Miller, ever the pragmatist, had cautioned Lena against dwelling on the "what ifs" and the "maybes." His focus, and by extension, the precinct's focus, was on the tangible victories, the arrests made, the assets seized. But Lena's mind, already attuned to the subtle shifts and hidden currents of the city, couldn't help but trace the deeper implications. Morozov had been more than just a criminal mastermind; he had been a symptom, a manifestation of the city's inherent duality. Las Vegas, in its very essence, was a testament to humanity's capacity for both extraordinary creation and profound corruption. The glitz and glamour were merely a veneer, a carefully constructed illusion to mask the raw, often brutal, reality beneath.

The investigation into Tasha Reed, though officially closed with her presumed disappearance, continued to occupy a significant portion of Lena's thoughts. Tasha had been the ghost in the machine, the unseen hand that had guided the operation, the architect of Morozov's undoing. Her motivations, her ultimate fate, remained an enigma, a tantalizing puzzle that Lena felt compelled to solve, not just for professional closure, but for a deeper understanding of the forces at play. Tasha's methods, though clandestine and ultimately illegal, had exposed the rot, forcing a reckoning that had been long overdue. Had Tasha, in her pursuit of justice or perhaps simply survival, become a new kind of player in the city's perpetual game of power? Lena couldn't discount the possibility that Tasha, having dismantled Morozov's empire, might now seek to build her own, operating from an even deeper, more impenetrable shadow. The very technology that had been instrumental in Morozov's rise could, in Tasha's hands, become a tool of unprecedented influence.

The narrative that would be presented to the public would undoubtedly be one of law and order prevailing, of a dangerous criminal element being brought to heel. But Lena knew that the truth was far more nuanced. The lines between victim and perpetrator, between justice and vengeance, had been irrevocably blurred. Tasha, in her own complex way, had navigated these murky waters, emerging from the wreckage of Morozov's empire not necessarily unscathed, but undeniably triumphant. Her story was a potent reminder that in a city built on illusion, the most dangerous truths were often hidden in plain sight, obscured by the dazzling spectacle.

Lena found herself staring out of her office window, the neon glow of the Las Vegas Strip painting shifting patterns across her desk. The city was already rebuilding, its resilience as undeniable as its capacity for self-destruction. New ventures would emerge, new technologies would be adopted, and new individuals, driven by the same relentless ambition that had fueled Morozov, would seek to carve out their own empires. The 'Swipe Right' empire, in its original form, might be gone, but the spirit of it, the exploitation of human connection for profit and power, would undoubtedly endure. It was a cautionary tale, a stark reminder that the allure of easy money and unchecked power could corrupt even the most sophisticated systems, leaving a trail of broken lives and shattered dreams in its wake.

The question of Jazzy, of her future, hung heavy in the air. Lena had done what she could, navigating the treacherous currents of the legal system and the labyrinthine bureaucracy of child protective services. But the long-term implications, the shadow of her father's legacy, would undoubtedly cast a long pall. The city, so adept at forgetting its own sins, could easily cast Jazzy aside, another casualty of the perpetual cycle of vice and redemption. Lena felt a profound sense of responsibility, a lingering unease that the battle had been won, but the war for Jazzy's soul was far from over.

The whispers about Tasha continued to circulate, morphing into legend. Some said she had vanished into the digital ether, her identity erased, her existence rendered untraceable. Others claimed she had resurfaced in a different guise, a phantom orchestrating events from the shadows, her influence subtly reshaping the city's power dynamics. Lena couldn't dismiss these whispers entirely. Tasha's ability to operate with such precision, to manipulate information and orchestrate events from behind a veil of anonymity, suggested a level of skill and foresight that transcended conventional criminal enterprise. She was a ghost in the machine, a digital specter whose actions had sent seismic tremors through the foundations of Las Vegas.

The dismantling of Morozov's empire had been a monumental task, a testament to the dedication of those who had pursued justice against overwhelming odds. But Lena knew that justice in Las Vegas was a fluid, ever-shifting concept. The city was a living, breathing entity, constantly adapting, constantly evolving. The corrupting influences of power, greed, and the relentless march of technology were not easily vanquished. They were deeply embedded in the city's DNA, a constant undercurrent that threatened to resurface at any moment.

The chapter's closing thoughts would inevitably circle back to the lingering question: what now? The immediate crisis had passed, the storm had broken, but the aftermath was a landscape littered with the debris of shattered fortunes and exposed secrets. The 'Swipe Right' empire might be a relic of the past, but the technology and the mindset that had fueled its rise were very much alive. Lena felt a sense of weary resignation, a dawning realization that her role was not to eradicate these forces, but to understand them, to anticipate their next move, and to continue the fight, one carefully calculated step at a time. The echoes of Tasha Reed's actions, the phantom whispers of her triumph, would continue to resonate in the city's underbelly, a constant reminder of the complex, often brutal, nature of power and the enduring allure of a perfectly executed escape. Las Vegas, in its eternal dance between light and shadow, would always find new ways to betray its promises, and new architects of its own downfall. The city was a testament to the fact that while individual battles might be won, the war against the darkness was a perpetual one, a constant struggle waged in the unseen corners, in the digital shadows, and in the hearts of those who dared to chase the impossible. The legacy of 'Swipe Right' was not just a story of a fallen empire, but a chilling premonition of what was to come, a testament to the enduring power of technology to both connect and corrupt, to build empires and to sow the seeds of their inevitable destruction. Lena knew, with a certainty that chilled her to the bone, that the story was far from over. The city of dreams was also a city of endless nightmares, and the players, though perhaps new, would always remain the same, driven by the insatiable hunger that defined the very soul of Las Vegas. The pursuit of justice, she understood, was not a destination, but a relentless, often lonely, journey through the city's ever-shifting moral landscape. The echoes of the past, the specter of Tasha's brilliance, would continue to guide her, a silent promise to never stop seeking the truth, no matter how deeply it was buried.

Back Matter

Morozov Implosion: The dramatic downfall and dismantling of Viktor Morozov's vast criminal empire in Las Vegas.

Swipe Right Empire: The network of illicit activities and technological exploitation built by Morozov, centered around the fictional "Swipe Right" application.

Digital Ether: A metaphorical term referring to the vast, interconnected space of digital information and networks.

Veneer: A superficial or misleading outward appearance.

Underbelly: The hidden, often illicit, aspects of a city or society.

Made in the USA
Coppell, TX
19 February 2026

72015130R00098